"Serve the light and seek the truth resting in darkness. Aid those in need, to the utmost of your power. Learn the avenues of magic and protect the secrets of the Association whenever possible. Risk your own life before putting the life of another in danger."

– *The Oath of the Association of Magical Arts and Sorcery*

Also by T. Thorn Coyle

Novels

Like Water

The Panther Chronicles

To Raise a Clenched Fist to the Sky
To Wrest Our Bodies From the Fire
To Drown This Fury in the Sea
To Stand With Power on This Ground

Collections

Alighting on His Shoulders
Break Apart the Stone

To Raise a Clenched Fist to the Sky

Book 1 of
The Panther Chronicles

T. Thorn Coyle

PF

TO RAISE A CLENCHED FIST TO THE SKY
Panther Chronicles, Book One

Editing:
Dayle Dermatis

ISBN-13: 978-1-946476-01-2 (trade paperback)
ISBN-10: 1-946476-01-3 (trade paperback)

To Raise a Clenched Fist to the Sky

"When Black people really unite and rise up in all their splendid millions, they will have the strength to smash injustice."

– Huey P. Newton

"...the Black Panther Party, without question, represents the greatest threat to internal security of the country."

– J. Edgar Hoover

Chapter Zero
Jasmine

July 15th, 1968. Oakland.

I stepped off the Greyhound from Los Angeles, stinking of body odor, barbecue chips, and the beer the old man spilled all over my green corduroy bell bottoms.

I was a long way from the quiet streets of Crenshaw.

My mouth was foul. Fuzzy teeth and a tongue coated with nasty. Chips and Coke didn't taste so good once they were three hours gone.

I badly needed a bath. And to wash my clothes. Some things you just couldn't magic away. Dirty clothes and stinky armpits were on that list.

If I could've magicked myself up here without getting on that bus, I would've done that too. Believe me.

The bus depot was dingy, the gray walls smeared with layers of grime. There was a bloodstain on the wall that I didn't want to know anything about. The place smelled like old coffee and piss. I wanted the hell out of there, but had to admit that I felt a little nervous being on the street in a strange city by myself.

No time like now. After folding the brocade coat that had served as my blanket into my heavily stuffed khaki duffel, I hoisted the bag's straps over my shoulders. I had no idea how I was even going to walk five blocks with the thing on my back, let alone figure out how to walk to my aunt's house on the edge of Chinatown.

I had no idea where Chinatown even was. Just had a vague idea that it was walkable from where I was. In nice weather without a fifty-pound duffel on my back.

I was starting to regret packing books in with my clothes. Then I remembered: I could adjust the physics just a small amount. I magicked the bag a little bit lighter. There was nothing I could do about the long-sleeved navy T-shirt tied on the handle, smelling like old beer.

The bus trip had been a dance of staving off boredom and keeping grabbing hands off my breasts and thighs.

I'd started with a seat to myself, curled against the scratched-up window, reading Langston Hughes. When we stopped in Fresno, this old white dude got on and made straight for the skinny black girl traveling alone.

Of course.

You'd think after the first time I sent a jolt of magic to bite his pink sausage fingers, the old dude would've given up. But no. He had to try again, just to make sure.

The second time, the blue spark burned his hands and I sent a jolt to his balls at the same time.

That's when his brown-paper-wrapped beer spilled all over me.

But at least it got him to change his seat, as I mopped myself up as best I could with the old navy T-shirt from my bag. I tied it around one of the duffle handles in an effort to keep the stink of cheap beer off the rest of my clothes.

My dad—who doesn't have a magical bone in his body, bless him, and doesn't understand protection spells—hadn't wanted to put me on that bus, but how else was I supposed to get up to Berkeley for school?

I talked him out of Amtrak because the cost was almost double and the bus was faster, and had begun to regret it almost immediately. But I was here now, and that's what mattered, with the rest of the summer to settle in before the semester began.

My Aunt Doreen had moved up here when I was just a girl, and had a little house between Old Oakland and Chinatown with an extra room off the kitchen. I could stay there in exchange for some housekeeping.

While my parents could pay my tuition just fine, they just couldn't really afford a dorm, not without more juggling than I felt okay with. I wasn't sure I wanted to live surrounded by strange white folks like that anyway. School was going to be adventure enough, I thought, without having to figure out if I could trust the people across the hallway when I fell asleep at night.

Sure, I could magic the doorknobs every day. And my mother taught me several protections for situations involving rape or assault. But no one has enough magic for the daily little jabs and comments, the coffee spilled on class notes, or the toothpaste tube squeezed out in your toiletries bag. I'd heard the stories.

I was sure to figure all that stuff out, too, eventually, but it'd be nice to acclimate to it all bit by bit, instead of all at once, by force.

It was a long-ass ride through the Central Valley and on up the state, and here I was, about to step outside the big Deco doors banded with metal.

Nothing to do but move on through.

The breeze hit me, frizzing out my afro, carrying some of the bus stink away. The breeze smelled like ocean, just around the edges. Different than Bay Street Beach in Santa Monica. The beach of my childhood smelled like ocean, sunny sand, and barbecue, this smelled a little more earthy. Brackish.

Then I remembered the water would be coming off the bay, and not the ocean, accounting for the difference in the smell. Just the same, it was a little slice of home. Some of the tightness in my belly eased up and I felt my magic boost.

Exiting at 20th and Taylor, I looked around. A lot of parking lots and warehouses. Not much right here. The driver had told me to walk down Taylor, heading to Uptown. A right on Broadway would take me near where I needed to go.

Waiting to cross the street, I saw the rained-on white paper, wheat-pasted to the crumbling bricks of an industrial-looking building. "The Ten-Point Program of the Black Panther Party for Self Defense."

The name alone electrified me.

The country was still reeling from the assassination of Dr. King and the Panthers were stepping up their game. Black Power was fueled by Black Rage.

My parents had tried to steer me as far away from the Panther materials as possible, though I'd heard their murmured, worried conversations about the Panthers showing up on the State Capitol steps, rifles slung across their shoulders. And the fact that there was only one beach in Southern California we could enjoy during the summer? My parents tried to protect me from that news as well.

My parents, and the rest of the Association—The Association of Magical Arts and Sorcery, or AMAS—had no truck with revolution. Magic was the only important thing to my mother, and our family was the main thing that concerned my dad.

Though I knew they'd started organizing in LA, the Panthers had seemed so far away from the neat houses and small, trimmed lawns of Crenshaw. Less than five minutes after my pulling up in Oakland, here they were.

Standing on that dirty sidewalk stained with grease and garbage, I was frozen in place by the first point: "We Want Freedom. We Want Power To Determine The Destiny Of Our Black Community."

The points went on, each one more radical than the next. An end to capitalist exploitation. An end to incarceration. Trial by a jury of our peers… And then, point number ten: "We Want Land, Bread, Housing, Education, Clothing, Justice and Peace."

The boom of voices came toward me, echoing between the canyons of buildings. I couldn't make out what they were saying at first, but they were coming from the direction I needed to walk, so I headed that way.

Maybe not a smart move, but here I was. The rumbling and shouting finally resolved into words.

"Free Huey! Free Huey!" The words were punctuated by claps and stomps. I magicked the duffel slightly lighter and hurried toward the shouting, ducking down what I thought was a street but what was really an alley.

Shit. My parents were going to kill me. Sweat was running down my sides by now, but I didn't want to let the voices get past me without figuring out what they were shouting for.

I reached the spot right where the alley hit the street. Broadway.

And there they were. The voices that had sounded so loud to me. Around thirty people, mostly black, with some Latino faces in the mix. A couple of white folks brought up the rear.

I ran up to one of the women, marching head high, brass earrings almost touching her shoulders.

"What's happening?"

She glanced at me, taking in my afro and green cords.

"Huey Newton's trial is starting at the courthouse. We're going to support."

Welcome to Oakland, Jasmine.

My parents were so not going to dig this. They liked their revolution at a distance. And their daughter even further from the center of it all.

I joined the group. When we hit 11th street, we marched toward what I would come to know was Lake Merritt. I could see the white, Art Deco rise of what must be the courthouse ahead of us.

The closer we got, the more people I saw, all heading toward that white stacked building with the flagpole spire. The blue waters of the lake shimmered just beyond.

There were thousands of people. *Thousands.* All shouting and holding signs. Children rode on shoulders, raising chubby arms into the air.

And then...hundreds and hundreds of Black Panthers, marching in formation. Berets and leather jackets on, despite the warm July air.

Fists raised.

They were the most beautiful thing I'd ever seen in my life.

Clutching the duffle bag straps on my shoulders, I wept.

Chapter One
Jasmine

I hauled a giant sack of oatmeal in from Leroy's gold El Camino, knees bending at the weight of it, eyes squinting at the low winter sun bouncing off the spotless back window.

Just another afternoon, done with classes, and working for the revolution.

Leroy kept that truck in cherry condition, that was for sure. Reminded me of my Uncle Hector. Didn't matter how old the car was, it was always going to look almost new.

"Let me get that, sister!" Leroy shut his door and hurried toward the back of the low-slung truck. He was a big man, with a raggedy natural and impressive sideburns. A gold chain winked from under the paisley shirt that strained a little at the push of his muscles and stomach. I swear, this cat could've played football or something if he wanted to.

He liked me, I could tell. But unlike some of the brothers I'd met, Leroy was always polite.

"I got it, brother. Thanks, though." It felt good to finally have some muscles to offer the work. Not like when I started out with the Panthers, and could barely lift a thing without a boost of magic.

I'd been in Oakland a little over a year, and was already turning into something little middle-class Crenshaw Jasmine only dreamed about. Working with the Panthers. In college. Living, not quite on my own, but not under my parent's gaze.

Practically free.

Walking through the propped open metal kitchen door, I saw Tanya plopping biscuit dough onto big metal sheets, getting ready for tomorrow's breakfast. In a silky blue blouse, sleeves rolled up, tan A-line skirt, and brown knee-high boots, Tanya was overdressed for the kitchen, but dressed just right for her teller's job at the bank downtown. "Working for the Man pays for the revolution," she told me once. It had taken Tanya and I a while to warm up to one another, but we liked each other just fine now.

Tanya was one of the few Panther women who pressed her hair. The Man insisted, and she had kids to feed.

"Making biscuits?" I asked her, just by way of saying hello.

I bent toward the big steel counter and flipped the sack of oatmeal off my shoulder. It thunked onto the metal and started to slide. I shoved it more firmly into place, looking around the industrial kitchen, shabby from years of hard use. Brick-red tile squares covered the floors and on up the walls, forming a backsplash behind the deep, stainless steel sinks. Metal counters with cabinets underneath them lined the walls, and there was a large pantry to the left of the outside door.

One of the fluorescent bulbs was buzzing. Needed to be changed, I guessed.

"You know it! The kids love them," Tanya replied, opening the creaking oven door to slide the first sheet in.

When I was a girl, my mother, Cecelia, and I would bake together. I sifted flour, turning the crank on the metal canister and watching the powder float from the sieve into the bowl. The ratcheting sound was the counterpoint to my mother's voice, talking about what it was like to do magic. About why we did magic. About what life would be like when I became a woman.

It made me feel like making magic would be just like making those cookies, or Tanya's biscuits. I would gather flour, sugar, eggs. I would measure in the water, add in some shakes of cinnamon. Stir.

Magic isn't like that. It isn't exactly the way I imagined it would be. At all. My mother left out the confusion. She left out the parts about sex. She left out…so much.

Like, mostly it seemed the Association was about doing magic to stop *other* people from doing magic. Bad sorcerers. Rogues. Sure, some charms for the people on occasion. And we were charged to keep our neighborhoods as safe as we could.

Leaving Tanya to her biscuits, I headed back to the truck for more supplies.

Mother left out the fact that, while we did and could do spells—and putting them together is a bit like making cookies, it is true—sorcery, our main power, is nothing like that at all.

Doing sorcery is like harnessing a lightning strike in the middle of a storm. Or making something out of nothing.

Sorcery is grabbing the æthers and shaping them on your skin, forming magic in the palms of your hands, or on the tip of your tongue, and then spitting that magic back outward, toward your goal.

I was barely on the edges of all that. Could barely touch the æthers, seemed like. There was so much more to learn inside my blood. I needed to open up the crevices of my mind and let the magic flow through like ocean water. But frankly, I was scared of that, too. Even though the magic was bumping up inside me, longing to connect with the waters of the bay, I wasn't quite sure how to answer its call. More importantly, I no longer knew why.

Back at the truck, I bent my knees again to grab a case of powdered milk that Leroy had slid to the dropped tailgate. Cases were harder to carry, with my slender wrists, but I was determined to get my body used to it.

I kept thinking back on those afternoons with my mother, sneaking bites of dough out from the yellow ceramic bowl, forming lumps on the battered cookie sheets, and smelling the sweetness as it filled the kitchen.

Talking about magic with Mother was one of my favorite things to do. I liked it even better than the stories about African princesses. Better than reading about Mrs. Whatsit, Mrs. Which, and Mrs. Who.

Better than jumping rope on the playground after school, or running in the streets until dusk fell.

Then there I was, bumping my way through high school, and hanging with Carol, a blond transplant from Minnesota, who lived at the Association's Mansion. The other teachers set me up to be like a mentor to her. She ended up my friend.

We couldn't have been more different—Carol with her pale skin and straightforward manner. She wasn't quite poor, but she had less than me. And she couldn't see how gorgeous she was, or how much magic she actually had.

Not like me. I'd always known it.

Sorcery was my destiny. I liked having a destiny. It gave me a sense of power in my body that nothing else ever did.

But I didn't feel *satisfied* with that power anymore. Since joining up with the Panthers, I couldn't help but wonder what the hell it was all for. If I had a destiny, it should be for something important. Something true.

Thunking the case of milk on the counter next to the oatmeal, I paused to catch my breath.

"Tanya, can I ask you a question?"

"It don't bother me," she said. "Go ahead." One of the oven doors screeched open, and she slid a second sheet of biscuits in, then leaned against the long, twelve-burner stove.

"How do you fit it all in?" I gestured around the big church kitchen. "You raise two kids, work for that bank downtown, and come here most mornings and a lot of afternoons."

Tanya frowned a bit, wiped a hand across her forehead.

"You know," she began, "I used to think I didn't have the time. And then Clarence—a boy down the street from my pad, couldn'ta been more than fourteen—got offed by the pigs."

She opened the second oven under the stove and grabbed the tray laden with golden-brown biscuits, sending their steaming, doughy smell into the air.

"That changed me, you know. I figured if my kids were gonna grow up...if they were gonna see a different world, I better *make* time."

She slammed the oven door and looked me in the eye.

"If you ain't working for the revolution, what're you doing?"

We stood there, eyes locked for a moment, like she'd just issued me a challenge I'd better accept.

I nodded, and went back out to the truck for more supplies.

Tanya's answer reflected something back at me, even though I couldn't tell her that. It made me question pretty much everything about my life. About school. About my middle-class life in Crenshaw.

And that "what're you doing?" questioned the sorcery still flowing through my veins.

Feeding kids before they went to school was righteous. I was down with that. But I had all this other stuff I could be doing, if only I knew how. Cecilia—my mother—hadn't taught me how to direct the magic toward something other than basic self-protection and a few minor spells. She hadn't started actually teaching me the sorcery yet. The sorcery that kept me from falling asleep every night. The sorcery that was knocking on my head and in my heart. Every. Single. Day.

Even though I wasn't doing shit about it.

It was starting to piss me off.

And the Association? Seemed like a bunch of people stuck in a fantasy world to me. Scared of their shadows. Scared to actually *do* something other than fight each other over protocol, or fight other sorcerers over territory or some imagined sense of evil and good.

Evil walked the streets of Oakland. And I was beginning to suspect it wore a white man's face. There was a sickness that seemed to infect everything around us. A state of disquiet masked by numbness. Every time someone rose, they were smothered again.

I hoisted another sack of oats onto my shoulder and went back into the kitchen.

Leroy was spouting out some quotes as he stacked supplies on pantry shelves. I recognized the words as Frantz Fanon. *The Wretched of the Earth.*

"'Come, then, comrades,'" Leroy rumbled, "'it would be as well to decide at once to change our ways. We must shake off the heavy darkness in which we were plunged, and leave it behind. The new day which is already at hand must find us firm, prudent and resolute.'"

Firm. Prudent. Resolute. The only times I felt that were certain moments at Party headquarters. Usually when Tarika or Leroy were rapping about something. Mostly though, when I was reading the purple mimeo'd sheets filled with Chairman Fred's words.

The oats smacked on top of the other sack. Rolling my shoulders, I massaged my neck and leaned against the counter, listening to Leroy and taking in the smell of baking biscuits.

I didn't feel resolute about the Association. Or my family. Not Cecelia, not Doreen. Not even my sweetheart of a dad, going to work selling insurance during the day and coming home to tinker in the yard. Laughing with Mother and me.

Dad worried, I'm sure. He had his experiences of being a black man in America. The scorn. The sense of danger or defeat. He had to. But he never spoke of it much, though I would hear my parents talking late at night sometimes, especially after Watts erupted. Dad never wanted me to be afraid. Never taught me how to hate. Or deal with anger. Never taught me how to handle the rage that bubbled up inside because of the sheer desire the white man had to control us all.

Chairman Fred would say it wasn't the white man who was the problem. It was the ruling classes that oppressed us all. I knew he was likely right. But the ruling classes are made up of white folks. So it's hard to not just hate them all.

Dad would say this is just my youthful idealism rising up, and that when I'm grown I'll see the world is made up of all different sorts of people. But I wasn't quite seeing that yet.

Sighing, I loped back out to the truck, ready to carry in another crate of powdered milk.

Some days I did see it. There's white folks, and Asians, and Chicanos that come to help out with the clothing drives, or the People's Clinic, or to bag food for the pantry. They're down with the revolution, too.

Maybe I was just having a bad day. Maybe I didn't know which way was up all the time. Thing is, I was taught to believe that my destiny would guide me. But in that moment, I felt at sea with no compass. And I didn't know what my magic wanted, either. But it surely wanted something.

When I came back into the church kitchen, Leroy took the case of milk from my arms. He was still quoting Fanon.

"'We must leave our dreams and abandon our old beliefs and friendships of the time before life began. Let us waste no time in sterile litanies and nauseating mimicry.'"

That's what the Association felt like to me these days. Sterile. Litanies and mimicry.

Somehow I needed to figure out who I was and how to act like Jasmine.

I needed to learn how to be me. Whether I end up a sorcerer or a revolutionary, I had to take my destiny back.

Chapter Two
Carol

Carol wasn't sure she'd ever get used to living and working in the Mansion. It was always capitalized, by everyone who entered its intricately carved double wooden front doors. The capitalization was felt by Carol's whole being.

The Association of Magical Arts and Sciences headquarters was a Spanish Revival–style hacienda, three stories high, with round turrets and balconies set under arching windows and topped by rust-colored Roman tiles. Palm trees flanked the driveway that curved in front of the sprawling building.

Carol's room was tucked away on the second floor in the back, and she stared out the single window overlooking the rear lawn and gardens. It had been a long four years, but she still hadn't found her place.

Mr. Sterling thought she should feel grateful for it all, and she was. But Carol also felt dissatisfaction gnawing at her spine, right at the spot where all her energy centers converged.

As if her sorcery was telling her there was something she was missing. As if the earth itself was trying to tell her bones that something was wrong. Something basic.

Carol was starting to wonder what Mr. Terrance Sterling was hiding.

She knew that sorcerers who could command several elements, like Mr. Sterling, thought Earth sorcerers were the least useful of them all.

Lowest rung on the ladder. Carol snorted, then turned to the makeshift altar on the three-shelf bookcase tucked near her closet door.

She picked up the hunk of malachite that was her focus. Different shades of green in layers like the rings of a tree, the smooth chunk of rock soothed her. But it also reminded her that she knew things deep in her bones, just like this rock knew minerals and soil.

They both answered to the earth.

And the earth under the Mansion was trying to tell Carol's bones that something was seriously wrong.

Little Carol Johansson had been so cowed by it all when she arrived from Minnesota.

Not only was Los Angeles a different planet, with its palm trees and the brown air that sat trapped in the basin of the huge valley, she could swear people spoke a different language. But the main problem? Carol was way behind on her magical training, and she hadn't been born rich. Well, that was two problems, but they felt rolled up into one another.

Carol was adopted as a baby and her parents only discovered she had magic when she started an earthquake in her crib the year she turned three.

They had no idea what was going on, just felt a rumbling in their bedroom one night and rushed into the small nursery in the converted walk-in closet. They'd never felt an earthquake before and had no idea how Carol could be causing the floor underneath the blue-painted crib to shake.

She was standing up in her sherbet-green footie pajamas, gripping the bars of the crib and laughing, little blond waves of hair standing out all over her head.

The mobile above the crib was spun and shook, the red and yellow fish looking like they were trying to swim in a storm, her mom told her later.

They were so afraid. Carol was laughing and they were terrified. What sort of child had they brought into their home?

It took them two more years to find someone who knew what was happening. In the meantime, they spent a lot of time and energy just trying to keep their little Caroline safe. Finally, when she was thirteen, the Association stepped in, offering a full scholarship plus room and board, and brought Carol out to LA. Her parents were both grateful and distressed.

They had wanted a child so badly, and it had taken time, effort, and money to get her. Plus, good parents that they were, they'd fallen in love with Caroline. Her dad cried when they put her, all awkward knees and straight hair, onto a brand new DC-9 with the Association member deputized as her temporary guardian.

Working-class people, her parents couldn't just up and move out to Los Angeles, even though the Association offered to pay for moving expenses and help them find a house.

"Where will we find work?" they asked. "How will we afford the property taxes?"

There were a lot of things wealthy people just didn't have to think of. So in Minnesota her parents stayed.

It ripped Carol's heart apart, too. But she was also pretty excited to be really learning not just magic, but actual elemental sorcery. "In the big leagues" was how she thought about it. She just hadn't reckoned on how alienating it would all feel.

Thank the Powers for Jasmine. She'd been in a magical family since birth and kindly showed Carol the ropes, both of Los Angeles and the Mansion.

Jasmine showed Carol where to catch the bus downtown. She dragged her to shops that had clothes that were cool, but that Carol could still afford on the small stipend the Association set in place once they finally figured out what exactly a working-class Minnesota salary was.

The two girls listened to music in Carol's small upstairs room at the Mansion. And since they had the same tutor, they practiced their homework together. And sat through Saturday morning magic class.

One day, when they were about fifteen, they were working with their tutor in the room sometimes called The Lab. It looked nothing like a science lab at all, with the exception of some strange potions locked away, and Bunsen burners on benches along the walls to cook up spells.

"Try it again." Their tutor, Mr. Ernesto Alvarez, leaned against the white window sill of the goldenrod-painted, high ceilinged workroom.

If they didn't call it The Lab, people called it The Workroom, but to Carol's eye, it looked like some fancy study, with two long wooden tables in the middle, and narrow standing tables—the lab benches—under the windows, and shelves of strange supplies on the other walls.

There were jars of buttons. Glass retorts. Bunsen burners. Dried herbs. Porcupine quills. Seagull and raven feathers. Bottles of liquids she didn't even know the names of yet. Incense. Wooden wands and sharp, sharp knives. Carol knew that last because of a slip with one two months earlier. She wasn't allowed to touch a blade again for three months.

The remaining wall, the one closest to the door, was lined with books specific to applied, not theoretical, magic.

The room should have smelled musty and weird, but the combinations of vegetation, brewed-up liquids, books, and old incense managed to work together somehow. Likely the magical cleansing just before the dark and full moons helped, too.

Unlike the rest of the Mansion, this room had light oak floors. Wouldn't want the children to spill things on the cushy carpet. Jasmine never had that problem. She had a hot temper and was impatient with her spells, but Carol was a clumsy one.

They were instructed to float feathers. Dumbest thing ever for ocean and earth sorcerers. as if they were ever going to need the skill.

Carol screwed up her mouth and furrowed her brow. Jasmine was always telling her that if she wanted to rebel, Carol was going to need a better poker face.

"I don't care what color or essence the fire you carry inside you is." Mr. Alvarez started pacing. "I don't give un bledo if your energy is blue, green, orange, yellow, or purple." He stopped at that and stared first at Jasmine, then at Carol, who froze like a doe in the sights of a pointer dog.

"You will learn the rudiments of all the elemental magics. It is your job. Without learning the basics, you won't be able to help another sorcerer. It is too hard to link if you don't comprehend the energy signatures. Claro?"

Alvarez clapped his hands together like rifle crack.

Carol was so freaked out, her energy surged and the feather shot up in the air.

"Control it!" he shouted.

Carol waved her hands out, trying to get the feather to do what she wanted it to do. The energy from her hands spewed out her fingertips, green as summer grass, ricocheting off an alembic cooking on a Bunsen burner on the far work bench, shattering the glass and spreading a small fire in its wake.

"Shit!" Jasmine called out, jumping up with her hands out, ready to cast.

"Hold!" Mr. Alvarez shouted, throwing a small wool blanket over the whole mess, smothering the licking flames.

The smell of wet wool and singed fibers filled the air, along with the scent of whatever the hell ignitable liquid had been slowly brewing for the last three hours. Carol had ruined *that* spell.

A burst of laughter filled the room. Jasmine. Of course she would think this was funny. Meanwhile, Carol was fighting back tears. And her feather was still stuck up near the ceiling.

The funniest look crossed Mr. Alvarez's face then. It looked like he needed to sneeze. His eyes and mouth were all tight and squinched up. Raising one brown hand, he wiped it across his face, silver coyote ring staring at Carol with onyx eyes.

Then he started laughing too, a big, booming, delighted laugh that took up the whole room.

"What?" Carol was seriously confused and could feel a red stain spreading across her white skin.

She'd felt so sure she was going to be demoted or something. Told to go back to Minnesota after all, now that she was finally growing used to LA.

"That. Was. Unbelievable," he said.

Jasmine fanned her face with her hands. "Hoo, sister. That was awesome."

Mr. Alvarez grinned at them. "You are going to have the clean up this mess. Both of you. I guess it's time you learned to deal with exploded spells and potentially harmful waste. We shall go through all of that step by step."

He raked his hands through the thick shock of black hair on his head. "But first, get that feather down from the ceiling. Slowly."

***

Snapping out of her reverie, Carol looked up from the malachite and frowned.

That wasn't Carol's last disaster, though she'd gotten a lot better.

She missed Jasmine's laugh. She missed her sorcery.

Carol missed the way Jasmine always knew just what to do.

And she wondered why holding her focus stone had brought up those particular memories, right now.

"What are you trying to tell me?" she whispered to the polished green rock.

Breathing across the green whorls, and tracing them with her thumb, Carol tried to strengthen her link with the stone.

A small voice whispered, deep inside her head.

All it said was "Run."

Chapter Three
Doreen

Hector and Doreen had lived a quiet life. He tinkered with the old Edsel and went to work down at the port. They liked him there because he was so strong. No need to tell them why. Hector came home dirty, but with a smile on his face. He would shower and wrap Doreen in an Ivory-soap-smelling hug as she washed lettuce in the sink.

That kitchen had blue curtains, just like her Oakland one had red. Hector had built their old kitchen table with his own capable hands.

Doreen left that table with Cecelia and William. She barely took anything from that little LA bungalow and half regretted it.

In those years, Hector made good enough money that Doreen only worked half-time in a pharmacy downtown. Mostly stocking shelves. Sometimes helping customers. The pharmacist was a skinny old black man named Dr. Petty. Funny, that name; he was generous to a fault.

Doreen liked to recall that she and Hector always knew one another, because that was how it felt. They were warm together. They danced around that tiny house, as in love as you please. Happy. Even after they discovered we couldn't have a baby.

"That's okay, sweetheart. You're the one I need," Hector would croon in Doreen's ears as he swung her away from the sink.

And then Jasmine had come along. At first, that stabbed at Doreen, seeing the look on Cecelia's face when she held that perfect brown baby to her breast. But by the time Jasmine's first birthday came around, Doreen loved her almost as much as if she were her own.

Doreen would take Jasmine for ice cream on Wednesday afternoons, and join the family for Saturday matinees in the balcony at the Rialto. They would bring in little bags of peanuts and hard black licorice buttons, shoes shined and hair all perfect. Jasmine loved those movies.

Doreen did too. Even if sometimes she wondered what the film looked like from the seats down below.

Doreen never thought until now how much it must have hurt Jasmine when she just up and left. There was no room in her life for anything except the pain of Hector's death. The move to Oakland kept her distracted enough for awhile.

Getting there. Finding a house in a neighborhood that could feel like home and that she could afford on Hector's pension and the bit of life insurance he had paid into every month without ever telling her about it.

Doreen just wasn't sure when she would be able to work again.

That took a few years, for the grief to ease enough for her to put her head up long enough to start to feel bored. She got a job with the florist then. Working with the plants and flowers eased her back toward life.

Despite her slow re-entry into the world, memory still held more power than the present. For a long, long while.

The day she met that broad-shouldered man with the slight crook in his nose, and the thick thighs dotted with small whorls of black hair…

He was just there, in the backyard of her friend Sunny's parents' home, when Doreen walked in carrying a big yellow bowl of potato salad for the barbecue.

Doreen had just turned twenty and was taking classes at a local community college. Hector was twenty-five and already working in the shipyards.

When she laid eyes on him, the potato salad bowl almost slipped from her fingers and onto the concrete walk way that skirted a small patch of grass. She barely even saw the white-and-red-checked covered table, already laden with food. Or the barbecue beyond it, though she could smell the meat and savory sauce floating toward them on the air.

She couldn't tell you who was turning the meat, or who was gathered around the table.

All she could see was this tawny-colored man in his tan slacks and white-and-brown-striped short sleeved shirt. His forehead was lit up by the sun. His eyes were gold.

That was it. Doreen had met her man.

Hector set his beer on a small table and walked toward her, hands out. Doreen tried to hold her hands out to grip his, forgetting they were already full. She almost dropped the bowl again. Hector took the bowl, their fingers brushing a little as the weight transferred from her small fingers to his broad, warm hands.

Hector smelled like sunshine and musk, with a slight hint of a pale beer snaking from his lips.

"Hello," he said, his voice a low rumble, as if it was coming from his chest. And something in her own chest opened wide. She either wanted to lean closer to him or run. Instead, Doreen stood stock still, just staring. She reached a hand up to smooth her already perfectly set and rolled hair.

He started to laugh and spoke again. "My name's Hector. Who are you?"

"Doreen," she said. Then she eased her way around him, making sure to not touch his arms with her own, though the slight bell of her purple-and-blue-flowered dress brushed up against his slacks. Sandals clacking on the concrete slabs, Doreen led the way to the table, as though she were a sophisticated woman who knew just how to handle a man. As though him following behind, carrying her potato salad, had been the plan all along.

One year later, they were married, the sorcerer and the mountain lion. The woman and the man. Mixing their families in a way that was more common than a person might think.

Magic calls to magic. It doesn't really matter exactly what form the magic takes.

Doreen went to their mother in tears after the doctor told her he couldn't find anything wrong and wasn't sure why she and Hector—despite trying several nights out of every week—weren't going to conceive.

Momma looked at Doreen with sorrow in her eyes that day, as she set out the lemon cake she'd baked the day before. Doreen allowed her to cut out a slice, and to place it on a white plate rimmed with daisies. Cutting off a forkful out of politeness, Doreen put the cake into her mouth. It was like eating sand.

"You were so in love..." Momma said. "I knew that I should tell you, but I also knew that if you walked away from a love like that, you might die. Sometimes love is the most important thing."

Momma—known as Momma Beatrice to everyone in the community—was making crumbs out of her own cake, on the plate. She didn't even put one bite into her mouth.

"You and Hector, you're meant to *be.* Can't you see that, girl? The way you are together? The magic you can do? Without him, your magic changes. A love like you have, the sort of power the magic taps into when you're with a man like him? It has the power to change the world."

Her eyes were pleading. Asking Doreen to forgive her the omission.

"You should have *told* me!"

"And what would you have done then?" Momma replied. Doreen would have married him anyway. But she couldn't say that. The pain was too keen.

She just shook her head that day. Doreen wasn't ready for it then. By the time Hector was killed by sheriffs in their khaki shirts and with their rifles and machetes, she had grown to understand just what Momma meant. At least partially.

To marry her magic with his was to make a magic stronger than the rest. A magic stronger, from being mixed, than any pure spark or flow. And what Doreen was coming to understand, more and more each year, was that Hector seeded her with his magic and she fed hers back to him.

They were changing one another, the way all couples do, but with this addition: they saw and felt and moved things no one else could see or feel or move. Together, their magic was like a sword forged from Spanish steel: two metals heated, and melted, and cooled, and pounded, until over time, it brought forth the strongest and most beautiful sword ever made.

That was what they were doing with the magic, once they got over the infatuated rush of ripping up the bed and waking curled into one another the next morning. Once they got through the pain of adjusting to one another's habits and to not enough money, and when there was enough money, not quite enough time. They were reaching an equilibrium and entering a time of deepening.

Hector and Doreen had started testing their two magics together, at the full moons and the dark. The glimmerings of what were possible emerged more strongly every week.

And then Hector was taken from her. And she flung the rest away, repudiating magic in all its forms. Running from the heat of it.

Collapsing into grief.

Doreen was ordinary now. She had her quiet life with her job, her tidy home, a few good friends to go to the movies or share Christmas dinner with. She would have told you she liked it that way.

But then Jasmine came, and slowly, so slowly, Doreen's neat little life was changing, whether she liked it or not.

Jasmine carried the stink of ocean magic into the blue bungalow every time she strode through the front door. Even though Doreen could tell the girl wasn't practicing like she should, the magic was there all the same.

And the embers deep in Doreen's belly were kindling again. Whether she liked it or not.

Chapter Four
Jasmine

Usually, I enjoyed walking across the Berkeley campus. It was so different from the streets of LA.

The old Beaux Arts buildings blended with a more classical minimalist style, and they both warred with the newer construction going up around the edges. My favorite thing was the trees. There were trees everywhere.

And no brown haze of smog marred the sky.

In the morning, I normally went out of my way to cross the short footbridge over Strawberry Creek that gurgled past the box elders and in between the pines.

Not today though. The quiet there was the opposite of what I wanted: that route hadn't felt quite populated enough. So my feet veered me toward the quad.

Someone was following me.

I'd felt them tracking me from the bus to campus this morning, which is why I shifted my route. The feeling disappeared during my statistics class. Maybe they didn't follow me inside, or maybe stats bored them as much as it bored me.

But I felt whoever it was now, reaching out toward me as I hurried from the math building, crossing campus to my next class. It felt like a small target was painted between my shoulder blades and someone's sights had locked on the base of my skull.

The freaked-out child in me wanted to run, but I remembered my magical training and tamped that child back down. Unless I was under active threat, and knew my target, moving quickly was not necessarily the best option.

Magical training told me: I needed to pay attention. Focus my mind.

It also wouldn't be a bad idea to unbutton the bottom of my brocade coat though, just in case I needed to run.

Hitching my fringed purse higher on my shoulder, I slowed my steps way down as I approached the quad and the small green hills rolling gently toward the walkways. The gray stone clock tower rose above it all. The pinnacle. The pointy-topped structure that symbolized the university even more than its mascot, the California Grizzly.

We'd all gotten the orientation lecture about keeping safe and alert on campus, about not walking alone at night. The "rape talk," some of the students called it. It was all good, common sense, but wasn't helping me now. Not in the middle of the day.

There was no way to be alone walking across the UC Berkeley quad in the middle of the afternoon. But when magic was involved, numbers didn't always help. Sometimes they were a hindrance. The only part of the anti-rape advice that applied was the *stay alert* part. I needed that.

Glancing up at the tower, I saw that it was five minutes until two, meaning I was going to be late for my 2:10 class if this foolishness kept up.

Despite the chill in the air, a group of hippies were playing guitars and bongos under the big box elders. To my right was the copse of plane trees, their pollarded limbs stretching out scraggly fingers from stumpy, arthritic looking arms. The copse was nice during spring and summer, but in fall and winter, I just felt sad for the brutally pruned trees.

"They're trying to tame you, comrades," I muttered.

The usual crush of students was hurrying to and from the libraries and the various class buildings. Math. Music. Paleontology.

So why, in the middle of all this activity, was I so sure I was being followed?

Call it a hunch.

"Or call it what it is, Jasmine," I said under my breath. "It's magic."

I could smell it on the crisp air, like something papery and dusty had crawled out from the shadows, dragging a patch of darkness with it. Or like a shed snake skin, desiccated, dried and crackling into nothing.

Carol had called me, her usually calm voice frantic across the sputtering phone lines. I had to tell her to slow down and to be careful what she said. While the Mansion could afford a private line, Doreen couldn't. Or just didn't see the need to pay extra. Whatever the reason, we had a party line, so talking about magic was tricky business.

Of course, since I'd started hanging with the Panthers, I'd discovered there were a lot of things people didn't like to discuss over the phone at all, party line or no.

As I slowed my steps, I decided that more investigation was in order, so I slung my heavy purse onto one of the wooden benches spaced out across campus and sat down. Rummaging past the textbooks and tissues, my fingers alighted on the pencil and pen case that also held a slim wand. I wasn't actually looking for anything, but I wanted them to think I was.

And the wand might come in handy if I needed backup.

Okay. I cast my attention outward. First to my own edges, then beyond, three-hundred-sixty degrees.

I felt the variety of trees, talking to each other as usual, though I had no idea what they were saying. The waters of the bay beckoned to me, way off campus to the west. I didn't visit it enough.

All the different brainwaves, scents, and energy signatures of the students. There was a reason I didn't usually cast attention out like this. There was always too much going on.

Here was something. There was one mind that stood out…a girl who seemed to also be casting around. I gave her a little push and felt her surprise. Ah. There she was. The white chick reading a paperback book two benches down.

She swung her dark hair off her face, looking around. I ducked my head back down to my purse.

Damn. It wasn't her. She was just some wannabe witch, practicing her psychic skills. Nothing wrong with that. It'd be good if more folks did the same.

But her energy was too light. Floaty. She wasn't any papery snake.

I opened my senses further, trying to taste the scent on the back of my tongue.

Shit. Snake all right. And not the good kind. Or not the kind that was doing Association magic, anyway. This magic was strictly off the books. And it never would be brought into the fold.

It wasn't wild magic, though. And no sort of indigenous magic I'd ever come across.

It's funny that it had that dried-out snaky feel, though, because layered on top of that was a magic that had more structure than the deepest Ceremonial cats I'd met even rolled with.

It wasn't Hermetic. It wasn't Egyptian. It wasn't Mayan or Ethiopian. This was some serious Solomonic shit.

But not Association Solomonic, which tended to blend in Hermetic and Egyptian when it felt like it. This was crazy, unadulterated, First Temple shit.

Whoever snake guy was, he knew his magic.

"Gotcha," I muttered.

The snakey stuff was his personal signature. Ceremonial magic mixed with animal totem magic was rare, but not unheard of. I just didn't realize anyone was practicing that way these days.

The Campanile clock now read 2:05. Time to get to class.

I slipped the little wand out from among the pens and pencils and palmed it into the pocket of my coat.

Couldn't hurt. Up against a snake like that? I'd do well with a little extra preparation and a tool pre-charged with oomph.

I swung my heavy fringed bag back over my shoulder and hurried on to class. Off to Moses Hall and philosophy. Utilitarianism.

John Stuart Mill wouldn't have believed in my magic, but that didn't make it any less useful, or any less real.

Did I need any of these classes? I had no damn idea.

What I needed was to know who this dude was. I had his scent now, which was good.

Only trouble was, he also had mine and I had no idea why. But I wasn't gonna sweat it.

Not yet.

CHAPTER FIVE
JASMINE

That afternoon, I put magic and revolution out of my mind and went for a walk with Jimmy. I'd have to mention the snake to Doreen at some point. I knew that. But frankly, she wasn't even doing magic and I just wasn't sure how helpful she would be.

Jimmy had met me on campus and we'd hopped the bus down to Old Oakland. Walking through the fragrant streets of Chinatown, we were winding our way toward DeFremary Park.

Jimmy, whom I'd met the first day I showed up at the Free Breakfast Program. That day, I walked through the church hall door, and saw two black men around my age—maybe a couple years older—conferring as they set up the long tables that would soon fill with children on their way to school.

Jimmy looked up at me and smiled, teeth big in his narrow face. One front tooth slightly overlapped the other and I could see faint acne scars on his cheeks. Jimmy was thin bordering on skinny, with lean, muscled arms sticking out from a tight T-shirt printed with a big sunflower.

That sunflower made me grin, that some tough-ass Panther would be wearing a shirt like that. Turned out he was a tough-ass Panther all the same.

Jimmy reached out now and grabbed my hand as we strolled past red and gold paper lanterns, guardian ceramic Foo Dogs, and piles of fruits and vegetables. Aunt Doreen's favorite places to shop.

It was a sunny Oakland day, with a few white clouds streaking across blue sky, warm enough that Jimmy had slung his leather jacket over one arm. I kept my brocade coat on over the white peasant blouse that was my current favorite.

The smells of spices mixed with the smell that was just Jimmy, a combination of mushrooms moist from the earth and some quiet, musky smell that reminded me a little of my uncle.

"What you thinking about?" Jimmy asked. I could feel his gaze on me, but pretended not to notice, looking at the flat-soled black cotton shoes piled in bins, and the porcelain cats and Buddhas in the windows.

I sighed. "My uncle. I miss him sometimes."

We walked another block in silence. Jimmy wanted to eat lunch before heading to the park, and was looking for a place he'd been before, that he was sure was on this street, though he couldn't remember exactly where.

"What happened?"

Furrowing my brow, I picked up a toy from the display in front of another shop. A drum you played by twisting the red painted handle between your palms, causing two little balls on strings to strike the skin. I would have loved that sort of thing when I was a child.

Rubbing my palms together, with the stick held in between them, the balls kept missing the drum, hitting my hands. After a few seconds, I got the hang of it, and soon the balls were tocking out a beat on the tiny drumhead. I could feel Jimmy waiting for an answer.

Putting the toy back amongst its friends, I continued walking.

"He was killed in the Los Angeles hills one night when Aunt Doreen was waiting for him to come home. Sheriffs. A rifle hit to the chest and head." That part was true. I just left out the machete that had severed his head from his spine. The thing I wasn't supposed to know about.

The thing I couldn't figure out still. Why had those men done that to my uncle?

Jimmy drew a hissing breath in between his teeth. "Damn."

"Yeah. Doreen went a little crazy, I guess. That's why she moved up here. She had to get away."

Jimmy tugged gently at my fingers. An offer of comfort if I wanted it. I looked up at him. His brown eyes had a golden glint about them, and the musky smell was stronger, drawing me in. I shook my head a little, not dropping his hand, but pulling back a little. Distance.

"I don't think I'm gonna find that place," he said, stopping again. "Why don't we just eat here?" I saw that we had stopped in front of a tiny storefront with red-skinned ducks hanging in the window and a fish tank just inside the door. There were tables in the back.

I wasn't very hungry anymore, but realized I needed to sit down.

"Yeah," I said. "Let's go in."

The tables were mostly filled with Chinese people intent on bowls of noodles and rice, sometimes gesturing to their friends with chopsticks. We found an empty two-top halfway down the room. A woman stopped, mid-reach, holding a tea pot across the table to refill her friend's tiny cup with tea. She stared at us as we pulled out our wooden chairs and sat at the white, plastic-covered table. Jimmy stared right back and she looked away.

I put a hand on his arm. "It's okay. They just don't see many non-Chinese in here. That's why Doreen always goes back to the same place, so they know her."

Jimmy grimaced slightly, but sat down. He was pretty touchy at what he thought were signs of disrespect. It's funny; it made me realize how different our childhoods must have been. We were both raised in black neighborhoods, but clearly mine was...different. I never much thought about my parents having white friends. They just did.

Looking back, I could read the signs I'd missed as a kid, before coming into my power. My parents' friends all did magic. They were all Association members. They owned restaurants. They ran businesses. And we patronized them all. The miracle was this: how in the world had my non-magical father wooed my mother and become accepted into the fold?

"Love is its own magic," my mother, Cecelia, said. I supposed it must be, but wondered if there wasn't something more going on.

A waitress in a red smock set down menus and a pot of tea and two white cups inlaid with pale pearls of rice. Closing my eyes, I inhaled the jasmine steam emerging from the spout. Jimmy went to reach for the raffia-wrapped handle, but I stopped him, fingers gently covering his. We sure were touching a lot today. I wasn't sure how I felt about it yet, but I couldn't stop myself, either.

"It needs to steep another minute." We drew our hands apart and studied the cream-colored menus, red ink spelling out food items in Chinese characters and their English translations.

"Wonton soup," I said. "It's good."

Jimmy nodded, still bent over the paper. "Pork with pok choy? Whatever that is. And almonds. I like almonds," he said. "Think the tea is ready yet?"

When I gave my assent, he lifted up the pot and poured. Once our hands were wrapped around the hot porcelain, he looked at me with those gold-tinged brown eyes again. Like he was thinking something hard.

"Does your family know why he was killed?"

The waitress was coming toward us and I lifted my hand to let her know we were ready. She wrote the order down and disappeared again.

Jimmy was waiting. Again. I sighed.

"We aren't sure. He must have pissed off some white men, somehow. And when the white men are the sheriffs"—I shrugged—"what are you gonna do?"

Jimmy swirled his tea inside the cup, brow furrowed. "That's always how I'm afraid I'm gonna die. Some white men decide I done something and decide to take the law in their own hands."

He drank some more tea. "Like Little Bobby."

"Like Little Bobby." Little Bobby Hutton, the youngest member of the Black Panthers, gunned down by cops at age sixteen, just a few months before I stepped off that bus from Los Angeles. He died not too far from where Jimmy and I sipped at our tea.

We fell silent for awhile, drinking the pale, yellowy-green tea. What do you say after that? The waitress was back with a huge bowl of wonton, the little stuffed dough triangles floating in fragrant chicken broth. She ladled some of the soup out into two smaller porcelain bowls in front of us both. I picked up the curved porcelain boat of a spoon and dipped it in, closing my eyes at the smell before blowing across the soup. I wasn't trying a wonton yet. They'd be too hot to eat for awhile, but the broth was heaven.

Jimmy was a little tentative with the soup at first, but soon had his bowl emptied and was ladling out some more.

"My best friend in high school got killed like that," he finally said.

The breath stopped in my chest and the spoon paused half way to my mouth.

"Killed by cops, you mean?"

"Yeah. Said he stole some shit. I don't think that's true. Clarence was mister straight an' narrow. Never even stole his daddy's skin magazines."

He looked at me again, eyes serious. Calm. "You know that's why the Panthers got the guns, yeah?"

"Of course." Of course. Though they still made me feel uncomfortable, I was starting to accept them as a fact of life.

But I don't think a gun would have helped Uncle Hector.

If sorcery couldn't save him, how could metal bullets?

Chapter Six
Carol

The books weren't enough anymore. Carol couldn't concentrate, and really, she couldn't even figure out what she was supposed to be learning anymore.

Sequestered in the Mansion's library, November rain pattering on the windows, all Carol knew was, she was angry.

Damn all the Powers, Christian and otherwise.

Or maybe she was the one who was damned.

Maybe she was lost.

Against proper magical and psychic protocols, Carol's legs were crossed, right foot swinging out from under the purple maxi skirt she'd put on that morning. The tip of her granny boot tapped, seemingly of its own volition, repeatedly striking at the big knob of hard wood that supported the long table she was working at.

"Crossed limbs impede the flow of energy, making it harder to give or receive information, even when that information is only coming from a book." Her earliest magic teacher, Miss Carmody, told her that during Carol's first week in L.A.

Yeah, well. There wasn't any information that would help her today. Nothing had been helping lately.

She smacked the wood table support harder, causing a sharp pain in her big toe.

The extra pain pissed her off even more.

Usually, this was one of Carol's favorite rooms, with its arched windows set into plastered walls. The same deep blue carpet as most of the building, the tall dark cases of books, and two rows of wooden tables.

The library had seemed like a wonderland and refuge her first year in LA.

Not today.

Today, despite the carefully controlled temperature in the Mansion, the room just felt cold instead of welcoming, and the book pages felt as if they were going to crumble into dust under her dry fingers.

The words and sigils had stopped making sense an hour ago. And her back ached from hunching over the walnut table.

She looked out the rain-streaked window. Green blobs and gray, and some white and ochre from the wing of the Mansion that jutted out past this one, forming a large U shape on the grounds. All of it seen through a tracery of water continuously spidering down the square panes.

Her head throbbed. When did that start? The headaches had been coming on more and more frequently. She'd never gotten them before. None of the usual herbs helped, either, not even her beloved Mary Jane.

The dull ache started at the base of her skull, some days, increasing slowly until, at its worst, its stabbing claws gripped her temples.

It wasn't that bad today. Not yet. But if it kept up, she'd soon be puking in the small toilet down the hall.

Mr. Alvarez—Ernesto—told Carol that as an Earth worker, she should be able to help herself better. He was frustrated, trying to figure out why the headaches were happening, and why nothing was helping.

She'd begun to suspect it was being in the Mansion that was doing it. The tension had been growing for months, despite the wards on the building. Despite the cushy blue carpeting laid down special to "dampen both sound and vibration," she'd been told early on, when she asked what a Spanish-style mansion was doing with such incongruous carpeting.

Now, Earth sorcerers weren't supposed to be so susceptible to outside energies in the first place, but there was no getting around it.

Carol was.

Plus, she'd started having disturbing dreams. The kind of dreams that woke her in a shivering panic, completely frozen in her bed. Sheets like ice. Arms and legs too heavy, almost on the verge of dead.

Those nights, she fought to get her breathing under control, then tried to slowly shift her arms and legs. Take inventory of the room. Alarm clock ticking on the nightstand. Light from the grounds filtering around the edges of the curtains. Water running through the pipes somewhere in the building, telling her that someone else was having a disturbed night.

Then she would try to recall the dreams.

In some of them, she was drowning. In others, masses of people were washing up on shore, also drowned, having fought the currents and waves that had tossed them from whatever pitiful boats they had taken to the sea.

Carol's sense of the dreams was never about the water, though, which was strange. Her sense was always that something was happening deeper in the earth, fathoms down, below the ocean floor.

Geologists had only recently discovered proof of tectonic plate theory. A big quake in Chile had sent tsunamis rolling across the Pacific, drowning coastal cities and causing devastation all the way up to Alaska.

Something was trying to tell Carol to pay attention to the seismic shifts on a psychic level. Something big was rolling across the country, but she couldn't parse exactly what it was during waking hours—hence the headaches and the dreams, she guessed.

She knew it had to do with all the racial unrest, with what Jasmine was calling "uprisings" now, and what people in the Mansion called riots, when they spoke of them at all. But it also had something to do with magic. Ernesto just kept telling her to listen to her dreams, and to keep a journal.

The journal wasn't helping. The dreams weren't getting any more clear. And the headaches were growing worse.

Far worse.

And all these damn glyphs and sigils and ancient alphabets weren't telling Carol a damn thing. All the herbs in the world weren't taking away the headaches. And she didn't know what the hell Jasmine was getting herself into. Carol was worried more about Jasmine than any of this other stuff.

A snatch of song squeezed through the headache pain. That one by Traffic. Something about not feeling so good.

That song was always on the radio and must have embedded itself in Carol's head. Funny. The song started with a dream, too. Guess there was a lot of that going around.

Jasmine kept encouraging Carol to go to Cecelia for herbs, but something kept her away. It was as if going to see Jasmine's mother was a last resort.

Part of it was that Cecelia was going to grill Carol about Jasmine and she didn't want to lie. About the Panthers or anything else.

Mostly, though? She knew Cecelia was going to see more into her that she wanted anyone to see. Ever.

She flipped the heavy covers of the ancient tome closed, bracing the weight of the pages with her fingers so it didn't slam shut. Then she stood to stretch her back.

To the people at the Mansion, Carol was pretty invisible. She was their Jane Eyre, taken in for charity and not worth much more than being someone's governess.

The only two people who knew better were Ernesto and Jasmine. And two people putting pressure on her to be more than that was more than enough.

A voice started screaming from the west annex of the Mansion and Carol's headache spiked, the pain almost knocking her to the floor.

"Shit!" She grabbed her temples and staggered back up, across the thick blue carpet, past the tables and stacks of books, finally making it to the heavy wooden door.

Stumbling through, she ran toward the noise. Doors were slamming everywhere. Voices raised in agitation. The quiet Mansion wasn't quiet anymore.

The weird thing though? The pressure that had been building like a storm suddenly broke.

And her headache started to recede.

What the hell was going on?

Chapter Seven
Doreen

Doreen still hadn't had that conversation with Jasmine. About magic. And training.

Because, well, Doreen still hadn't really started practicing again. Every day, she woke up, determined to get to it, just as soon as she put the coffee on to perk.

And then she needed to wait for Jasmine to leave for school.

Or then Doreen had to get ready for work.

But the magic she was avoiding kept burning inside the soles of her feet. It was making it hard to wear anything but her crocheted slippers. Doreen started shaking talcum powder into her work shoes to soak up the sweat in the morning. Then a second time on her lunch break.

At first, it had been easy to ignore the magic rising in her, scenting her pillow with cinnamon. Doreen had work, Jasmine had school.

They'd been busy getting Jasmine settled in, showing her how to use the buses, and which streets to avoid in the neighborhood.

But it had been a year, now, of living with another magical person. And the pressure was rising.

And that pressure reminded Doreen of promises she'd made, a long, long time before....

Cecilia and Doreen were talking. It was a hot Los Angeles early July Saturday. Around 1955.

They sipped lemonade under the jacaranda tree with its ferny leaves. There was still a tinge of blue above, but most of the violet blossoms were weeping out their color on the patchy grass underfoot.

Hector grunted under the Edsel parked in the driveway out front. Doreen couldn't see him from where they were sitting in the backyard, but hoped he was able to fix whatever had caused the old girl to start limping and leaking oil.

She remembered feeling sweaty even in her pale yellow seersucker dress and bare feet. Cecilia tsked at those, always a proper lady in her sandals and blue checked shirtwaist. Doreen noticed, though, about half hour into their visit, Cecelia had slipped out of her shoes and tucked them beneath her chair.

Those chairs were the best. White curved metal that rocked just a little when you leaned back. They had dragged cushions out from the house, because it was going to be one of those looong talks.

"I think the magic has always been inside us, in our family. I don't know that it came from anywhere, unless it was wherever we come from in Africa," Cecelia said.

"Angola," Doreen replied.

Cecilia got the little creases between her brows that signaled she was annoyed.

"I don't know where you get that idea," she said. "Who told you our people were from Angola? It's just as likely we come from Nigeria or Guinea."

Doreen knew it because she talked with the ancestors every day, and they told her. If Cecilia had been talking with the ancestors like every magic person should, she would know it, too, Doreen thought.

But if they got started in on what Cecilia should or shouldn't be doing, the conversation was going to take a very different turn.

Doreen flapped a hand at Cecelia to stop her and picked up the sweating glass of lemonade again. The ice was melting fast, even in the shade, but it tasted good—just the right amount of tart under the sweet—and kept her throat from drying out with the topic at hand.

Magic. And family. There was something about the conversation that felt a little dangerous and she wasn't quite sure why.

Sorcery was dangerous, to be sure. They'd both had their hands burned, literally and figuratively, at some point since that time in puberty when the first surges started.

"Look," said Cecilia, softly.

A soft whiffling sound was coming from the bushes.

A group of quail emerged, little topknots shaking on their heads. Pausing a moment, they ran across a patch of sun to the next set of bushes bordering the neighbor's yard. They came through from the foothills, though how they survived the coyotes, Doreen was never sure. Maybe they had a magic of their own.

Most things do. That's what momma always said.

Cecilia spoke again. "What are you thinking about, sis?"

"Momma. She said everything had magic if we listened right. That feels like the key I'm still missing somehow. I'm used to the sparks moving through me. And I'm used to the taste of your spells. I can feel the moon tugging at the ocean, and feel the moment before the sun rises…I get all that's magic. But what about everything else?"

Cecilia pulled up the third chair and propped her naked feet up. Her heels were smooth, as if she rubbed them with cocoa butter every night. Unlike Doreen, whose heels would be cracking half the time if Cecelia didn't get on her about it.

Hector didn't care. "I didn't marry your for your heels," he would say with a grin at Doreen. "I married you for your legs."

Hector always got a swat for that. Right before she kissed him. Damn, that man could kiss. Softest lips in LA county.

Cecilia's voice brought Doreen back. "You know me: that mystical stuff is interesting enough, but I never took to it much. I want the practical applications of our gifts. What can we do? How does it work? What results do we get over time?"

The sun was moving, throwing shadows and bright spots on Doreen's lap. Her scalp began to prickle with small beads of sweat.

"But Cecilia, that's my point. What if that magic Momma was talking about is part of what makes everything else tick? What if the quail passing through the yard *mean* something?"

Doreen finished off the lemonade in her glass and rattled the ice cubes in the bottom. Thinking.

"You got more in the kitchen?" Cecelia asked.

"Yes. In the icebox. Top shelf."

Cecelia swung her legs off the chair and slipped her sandals back on before swaying toward the back door.

A muffled curse came from the driveway along with the bright sound of metal hitting concrete. It sounded like Hector was having trouble.

Hector's magic was completely different than Doreen and Cecelia's. He had the old magic. Animal magic. And Cecelia married William who didn't have a *lick* of magic.

"We make a magic of our own," Cecelia would say with a smile. The lack of magic would have driven Doreen crazy. As it was, it had taken a while to adjust William to the family, and the family to William. He was a good father and provider, Doreen gave him that. He'd even become a good friend.

The screen door banged and Cecelia sashayed back across the patchy lawn carrying the rest of the pitcher and an extra glass for Hector.

She set them all on a little metal side table under the tree.

"I figured Hector could use a break about now."

"You're likely right, but I want another few minutes. I want to ask you something."

Cecelia carefully poured the pale yellow liquid into the tall glass and topped up Doreen's before sitting back down. She kept her sandals on this time, and crossed her legs.

"Do you ever wonder how Jasmine is going to do, when she comes into her sorcery? I mean…"

"I know what you mean. Because of William." Cecelia frowned, setting her glass back on the table. Two scrub jays came screaming through the yard.

"Jesus! Those birds think they own this place."

"Maybe they do," she said. "Maybe you and Momma are right about how things work." Cecelia started worrying at the edges of her fingernails, something she only did when she was feeling upset about something.

She continued: "I never thought about it much before, but since Jasmine… I think I've started hoping that it's true. That the basic magics, the energy in the world, will carry her enough that having William for a father won't undermine her power."

Doreen leaned forward in her chair. Waiting for her to say more. Wanting for her to say more.

"I think I need you to help me, Doreen. When it's Jasmine's time, I mean." She looked up at that, peering into Doreen's eyes with her own, so dark under their curling lashes. Her ruby lipstick was fading at the center, where it had transferred its color to the edges of her lemonade glass.

The smell of Aqua Net hairspray diffusing in the heat blended with the sweet decay of jacaranda and the summer smells of dirt, grass, and dirty Los Angeles air.

"Of course I'll help you, Cecelia. You didn't even need to ask."

But by the time she needed that help, Doreen had burned her books of magic and headed up the coast.

Chapter Eight
Spiders and Snakes

The ornately carved gold clock squatted on an oak wood bookcase, chiming midnight in twelve low bongs that barely penetrated the dim room. The clock did its job, but barely, for no one in the room paid much attention to the changing of the time. The clock's best work was done during the day.

Time in the darkness was a fluid, mutable thing. Time in the darkness was not a thing to be measured by clocks. It was measured in the snick of a match against a thumbnail. In the slip of a knife between sleeping ribs. Or the flurry of gunfire sparking yellow from around a hidden corner.

Time was conjured in the darkness, by the ones who had the will to do so. Those who couldn't? They borrowed time when they could, or stole it for scant moments of pleasure, or forfeited it to those who ruled the night. Only those who trained themselves to kiss the dark—for good or ill—could call it mistress, call it friend, or name it queen.

The only light in this place of darkness came from the candelabra set on the edge of the heavy, oak desk, and one small lamp on a side table near the low couches near the door. The air in the room was heavy with smoke from burning dragon's blood, brought all the way from Australia, here, to the seat of power of the greatest nation on earth.

The nation he controlled with the pulse that echoed from his fingertips, or from a few words from his moist and meaty lips.

Two men stood, bookending the thick wood door, feet shoulder width apart, black shoes steady on plush carpeting, right hand gripping left wrist. Ready for anything that came through the door, or through the windows bowed out behind dense curtains, set at the far edge of the long couches and the two wingback leather chairs.

The men's eyes were trained to see through night. They lived for months in darkness, getting used to knowing the world through the edges of their well-honed bodies and their sensitive fingers. The dark glasses they used to shelter their pupils from brightness were tucked away, slight bulges in the breast pockets of the otherwise clean lines of their suits.

One more small shape bulged in the back waistband of their trousers, barely marring the hang of their black suit jackets with their narrow lapels, only evident for those trained to notice such things. A person so trained might also notice that their left arm canted slightly outward from their body, to make way for the small bulge under that armpit. One more shape disrupted—oh so slightly—the hang of their trousers inside the right ankle. Almost no one ever saw these subtle breaks in symmetry. Unless the men wanted them to.

"Always use fear to your advantage," the Master had taught them. "Never give it away for free."

The men kept to that teaching. Those who noticed them were not afraid. Those who needed to be afraid? There was always a reason for it. And that reason was control.

The Master's desk was near neither the windows nor the door. They made sure of that. It hulked, four feet out, from the back, internal wall. The wall that had been reinforced with layers of wood and steel, and one layer of sound-baffling lead.

The hush in the room was almost palpable, highlighting the soft whooshing of rain that would never reach the sheltered bulletproof panes of window. The sound of the men's breath barely registered past their faces. The Master liked his quiet when he was thinking.

The Master was intent, fountain pen scritching black ink onto a ream of foolscap. There was no sense using his good paper. Or the bloodred ink he would use later, when things were just right. When the spell was set.

Things weren't right yet. But they would be. The Master could feel it in his tremulous belly, and in every bag under the dark eyes set on his doughy, squared-off face.

No need for robes tonight; he was in his usual black suit, jacket thrown carelessly over the arm of the cordovan leather desk chair.

The holy prayer ran through his head as he worked. It was almost there. The structure was set, but the words needed to rearrange themselves into the proper order and resonance, so when they were uttered properly, the power would heed itself, and work through his will.

Once the prayer was set, he would begin work on the sigil. The magical symbol was already worming its way into his head, and longing to seep out of the ink onto the paper. Steadying his breath, he picked up the small silver spoon and extracted another precious lump of dark red resin from the bowl next to the battered silver thurible.

A fresh spire of smoke spiraled upward. He breathed it in, and let it wreathe his head.

Then he reached with his mind to the dark jewel in his center, his lodestone, the compass that steered him through the dark night of righteousness. The jewel that would build a new day.

Boom! Boom! Boom!

A knock boomed through the thickness of the door from the carved pewter knocker he'd had set outside. A frown creased his doughy forehead, but he nodded to the man standing to the left of the door.

The two men stepped away from the wall, one coming to stand in front of the desk, 9 millimeter suddenly in his right hand. The other unholstered the snub-nosed black gun from the small of his back, then placed his left hand on the doorknob and swung open the door.

"Yes?" the Master said.

"It's Samuels, Mr. Hoover, reporting in."

"Come."

The man at the door let Samuels through. A slightly built man, Samuels wore the same dark suit as the other men, but instead of a black tie, his tie was stripes of gold and green. A coiled snake picked out in silver circled the thumb of his left hand. His feet seemed to glide over the carpet until he stood in front of the Master's desk.

"What is it, Samuels?"

The candle flames fluttered in the disturbance of the air in the room, casting shifting shadows across the bags and folds of the Master's square face. His broken nose pointed slightly to the left, smashed down like a pug dog's. The thought flickered briefly across Samuels' face.

"You'd best control your mind," the Master said. He knew what the men thought of him, and it served him well to remind them on occasion. That said, he didn't care what they thought of him, as long as a slight undercurrent of fear and respect was always present.

It was, in Samuels. Less than in some of the others, which made him both a valuable operative, and one who needed watching.

Samuels grimaced slightly, then became all cool slickness once again. Good man.

"Report."

"Things have been set in motion, sir, just as you asked. Your orders are being taken care of."

"When?"

"Our person in Chicago is well in place and assures us things will be ready within the month."

The Master growled a little at that, staring down at the black symbols spidering across the white pages.

"I've just returned from San Francisco." Samuels cleared his throat. "You were right. There's some magic building there. I put a tag on the person who seems to be the source. I should be able to reach them easily now, even from this distance."

The men had returned to their sentinel positions. Everyone waited in silence as the Master considered. The clock ticked and the rain shushed on outside.

He started muttering. "When is the right time? When? Show me. Show me."

"May I?" Samuels began to move closer, stopping suddenly, silenced by a wave of the Master's hand. Samuels froze in place.

The silent pressure in the room grew thicker. So dense it was almost choking. The Master's voice growled out into the dim room.

"Bring me the scrying bowl."

Chapter Nine
Jasmine

Breakfast with the Panthers had grown to be the core of my week. I was still hiding it from Doreen and her neat, conservative clothing, neat Shirley Chisholm hair, and neat life.

The Panthers felt too messy, too radical, in need of too much explanation still. I didn't want to explain. I just wanted to be around them.

I figured Doreen was hiding things from me, too. Mostly, I didn't want it getting back to my parents yet. They'd throw a fit that anything was distracting me from "my studies." The holy grail of middle-class achievement. Or a stepping stone, at least.

I couldn't blame them for that. Not really.

The kitchen off the side of the big, Craftsman-style church was just big enough to serve the hundred or so children who were just starting to arrive. Their voices bounced through the swinging kitchen door from the parish hall, greeted by Carlos's light tenor saying, "Good morning, brothers! Good morning, sisters!"

The kids chimed back, "Good morning!" Chairs squeaked on the floor, books thumped onto long pressboard tables, and someone laughed, loud, setting off peals from another group of kids.

Though I couldn't see them, just the sound of the kids made me smile, and I grabbed the red box of raisins from the counter. How they could be so noisy this early in the morning, I had no idea.

The kitchen was painted the same utilitarian cream as the hall. Buzzing fluorescent tubes whitened out any early morning winter sun leaking into the two windows, barely warming the rust kitchen tiles. Church tidiness met Panther discipline and kept the place clean.

I turned to the scratched-up iron six-burner stove, shook the raisins into the twenty-gallon pot of oatmeal, and began to stir. The scent of warm cinnamon rose up from the steam, reminding me of Aunt Doreen. She'd been acting a little different lately, but I frankly didn't have the time to figure it out. I just hoped…I'm not sure what I hoped. Part of me was bursting to talk to her about the Panthers, but I wasn't ready yet for my parents to find out. And I didn't trust her not to tell them.

"Never trust anyone over thirty," some of the white hippies said. I wasn't so sure about that, but it always seemed like the older folks wanted us to just calm down. At least my middle-class people did. That was part of my education from the Panthers: the poor folks were more down with revolution. They just had less to lose.

"Tanya, this oatmeal will be ready for bowls in about thirty seconds."

Tanya looked up from the long industrial steel table in the center of the room where she was setting slices of pale wheat bread onto paper plates, a stack of cardboard bowls at her elbow. She was wearing navy slacks today, and had a white apron tied on over her blue ribbed jersey sweater. Always ready for work, Tanya was, no matter what day it was.

That woman worked more than anyone I knew.

"Okay," she said. "Thomas, can you grab Leticia and Carlos from the dining room and get 'em in here?"

Thomas, a chunky Laney College student in bell-bottom jeans and a black turtleneck, black bandana tied over his hair, nodded and stopped mixing up gallons of powdered milk into the clear plastic pitchers arrayed on the metal sink counter. Wiping his hands on a red dish towel, he pushed through the swinging wooden door to the parish hall. Thomas never said much, but seemed like a good enough cat.

I began portioning oatmeal into the bowls, one giant ladle each, as tall, broad, Leticia and short, wiry Carlos slammed through the door.

They were a study in contrasts, from size to skin tone. Leticia was dark and gorgeous, Carlos was much lighter and, while he was handsome in his own way, mostly he somehow managed to pull off looking bookish and badass. I smiled. That was a combination I wouldn't mind cultivating myself.

Tanya was already shouldering through the swinging door, carrying a metal tray filled with food.

We were a little short-handed, and working as fast as we could. It was all hands in the kitchen today. Education and recitation wouldn't start until every child in that room had a bowl.

Working fast, we filled bowls and shuttled them out the door until we'd gone through one hundred and twenty plates. Tanya and I hoisted up the final two trays and made our way through to the parish hall.

This was one of my favorite parts of the day, seeing the kids in long rows down those tables, eating oatmeal or eggs, chattering, and drinking milk. I'd have to see if we could get some bags of oranges for tomorrow.

Working for the people was liberating my soul. I knew my parents wouldn't understand that. We helped people with magic when we could—folks in the neighborhood who needed extra attention and care to mend a broken heart, or heal a gash when they had no money for a doctor—but mostly it was working with the Association, who decided how we shaped larger events.

The Association of Magical Arts and Sorcery was most definitely not interested in revolution of any kind. They wanted sorcerers, witches, and other magic workers to assimilate, and help raise people up to live within the status quo. My middle-class family were firm believers in the status quo—whether it always worked for us or not, I was coming to realize—and so this all made sense to them.

It didn't make such good sense to me anymore. After I'd unloaded my tray of oatmeal, I grabbed a cup of orange juice and leaned against the cream-painted wall.

Carlos was going through the day's lesson as the children ate their breakfasts, and I felt something stirring in my belly. Just talking about

Black Power, and the importance of the people…even the simple lessons for children moved me.

There was excitement, yes. But also discomfort, like I was doing my family wrong. My maybe-beau Jimmy said a lot of middle-class people felt that way at first. We didn't want to look at the ways we had participated in our own oppression, and the oppression of our brothers and sisters.

I had so much to learn. And I was starting to wonder what all my magic was for. I had even thought about quitting school, but the Panthers said the revolution was needed everywhere, not just on the streets. And besides, they said we needed to know how the oppressors thought, so we could overthrow their thinking with our own. That was part of the insurgency: to replace what we were tearing down by building something solid. Otherwise, the world just turned to ash.

Chairman Fred said the struggle depended on education. Jimmy said I just needed to get the revolutionary education alongside education by the Man. That made a sort of sense to me, but I could feel myself getting itchy sitting in the classrooms at UC. Writing papers about things I wasn't sure mattered.

But I would stick it out for now. Everyone in Panther leadership said it would help to hone my brain. But I didn't have any clarity around that yet. I wanted to be *doing* something.

The best I could do for now was stir up oatmeal. Feeding children was part of the revolution. In the middle of the six-week educational program required to join the Party, I learned that the middle-class girl in me had been a little scared to join, even though the itchy part of me wished I could have joined the minute I first walked through the door.

I took a sip of juice and glanced at the big clock on the wall. 7:15. I should have time to help with cleanup before getting to school myself. The giant oatmeal pot was calling out to be scrubbed from the kitchen, but I wasn't ready to tear myself away.

Carlos was reading from a sheaf of papers. Snippets of Marxist thought, redesigned for children. Talking about working together and the importance of mutual support.

That was the thing. Panther leadership did call the shots, but they did it with the input from the people. The Association just decided what people needed, not the other way around. I hadn't thought about that much before, until I saw this other way in action, until I started serving coffee in leadership meetings. Or working at bagging up food at the pantry, or here, in the back of Father Neil's church.

"The proletarians have nothing to lose but their chains. They have a world to win."

Marx again.

Carlos's words washed over me as I stood propped against the wall, drinking juice. My throat grew tight with tears. The push and pull inside of me? I finally realized what the problem was: I was angry. For the first time in my life. I was deeply, truly, incandescently angry. I finally saw, as Marvin Gaye sang, "what's goin' on."

And as a middle-class young black woman, I wasn't sure exactly what to do about it. What to do about my parents. What to do about the Association. My chains were the chains of comfort, even though oppression forged the links. My parents couldn't keep that from me, not completely. So, how to win a *different* world?

And what was I supposed to do about the increasing feeling that something was watching me? Even though I tried to convince myself it was just paranoia from hanging with the Panthers, the feeling wouldn't go away.

Mostly though? I wondered where in this world my magic would fit in. Or whether it even could.

Chapter Ten
Jasmine

I walked through the black wrought iron gates at headquarters in West Oakland, past the painting of the panther creeping at me, and up the cracked concrete walkway. Armed men in leather coats, tan pants, and black berets canted on their naturals guarded the front stoop of the two-story white, ramshackle Victorian. A matched set of muscle, with ramrod-straight posture and big, easy hands that could strike in a moment.

Jimmy paced out front, his slender, muscled body tense, head bowed toward the grass tufts pushing up through the concrete cracks, his own beret crumpled in his hands. His usual smile was absent from that beautiful face.

The air felt thick around him, coming off in waves of heat and musk. My nose flared and the skin along my body tingled. I wanted to taste him, to bite the spot where the green turtleneck met his brown skin.

My fringed bag was heavy with books and notepaper, dragging my right shoulder down under the cushion of my brocade coat.

"What's up, Jimmy?"

"Jasmine," he said, his voice an exhalation of warmth moving toward me, just covering the slim edge of tension underneath.

He still didn't smile.

But he did hold out a hand. I slipped mine into his, just for a moment. It felt like my stomach would drop through my feet. If Jimmy hadn't been so distracted underneath it all, I might have fallen then and there. As it was, the parts he was holding back held me back, too.

This wasn't a time for love. This was clearly a time to stand alert. Things were heating up. I just wasn't sure who was holding the fire.

"Is something wrong?"

"No. No. Just needed some space. I get tired of all the smoke and talking sometimes."

I felt that. The conversations were both heady and heavy, and the air in that old house was always suffused with gray clouds layering fresh smoke over old. The old lath-and-plaster walls were turning yellow with it. I loved the words, though. Even the arguments. It was all so new, and so different.

My body wanted Jimmy, but my mind wanted…Huey. Fred. Kathleen. Tarika. Everyone.

There was magic past those leather-jacketed sentries, through that door. It was just magic I had never met before. A kind of magic I still couldn't quite put my fingers on, though it felt familiar to me. It wasn't sorcery. It wasn't witchcraft. But I was growing to respect it all the same.

I had never been taught that collective power could be as strong as the power of an individual sorcerer. All of our training was on getting our *own* shit together. Getting our power on point. Gathering our special flavor, our favorite tools. Finding the practices that complimented our powers, and forcing ourselves to do the practices that were more foreign, less natural. More difficult. I hadn't gotten to that part of my sorcery training yet, but I'd seen my mother, sheen of sweat on her forehead, doing what seemed like an impossible task to her, even if it looked easy to my eyes.

The magic of the Party was drawing me in closer. The power of the collective. All Power, to the People.

"You going in?" Jimmy asked me, dropping my hand. His distraction felt like a dismissal. I took a small step back. It bothered me how much I wanted him to see me.

"Yeah. Are you staying out here?"

"For a little while. I'll be back in soon."

I nodded and moved to step around him on the walkway. He paused me with a hand on my arm. Looked into my eyes.

"Jasmine, it's good to see you here."

Better. That made me feel better, though I felt like it shouldn't. What Jimmy thought and did was starting to matter too much to me. But I felt better all the same.

"Yeah. It's good to be here. See you soon."

His hand fell from my arm. As I passed him, the scent of musk and forest floor filled my nose. Man, I loved that smell.

My boots struck the wood of the front steps. I could see now that one sentry was bigger than the other, though they both still seemed huge to me. Raphael was on the left, clean shaven, and the one with the impressive ruddy sideburns was George.

"Evening, Raphael. George."

The sentries both nodded at me, and George opened the door.

Jimmy was right. The air was thick with smoke. The atmosphere felt…not heavy. But like your body feels when you're about to help friends roll a stalled-out Buick across the intersection. Ready. Prepared to push.

These people were getting ready to move on something.

The smell of cooking hamburger filled the air. The Panther houses always smelled like cooking meat. The cheapest possible. It was funny. We never served meat at the breakfast program. It was too expensive. And the food pantry bags were always filled with rice and beans. You'd think the Panther HQ would have been filled with the scent of red beans and rice. But it was always hamburger, cooked almost raw.

Disgusting.

I headed down the wood-paneled walls toward the kitchen. Tanya was cooking again. For the kids in the morning, and for leadership in the evening, after she got off work. A stained flowered apron covered the front of her blue skirt and emerald-green blouse.

I saw that she'd at least kicked off her shoes and was padding around the kitchen in stockings.

"Hey girl, you need some help?" I asked.

Tanya pushed her pressed hair off her face and continued stirring the meat in the giant pan on the electric burner. The kitchen was small, and it felt too crowded the minute I walked in.

Two men I didn't really know leaned against the counter. The one on the right was Mr. Slick in pale gray polyester pants. The one on the left was more of a hippie, jeans and a long fringed vest. Styling himself after Hendrix, but without the necessary swagger.

A third man—a little older, maybe thirty—sat at the scratched-up wooden table in the middle of the room, the day's paper spread out in front of him. He was deep into some article, pausing only to take another drag off the cigarette burning in a glass ashtray.

"No, girl," Tanya said. "Thanks, though. I'm almost done. You can help me serve it up though, if you want. And maybe help with the dishes later."

I glanced at the men. No way in hell they were going to do jack in the kitchen. Cecelia would be shocked I'd even say such a thing.

"If Chairman Fred was here, you'd be asking one of these fine brothers to do the dishes," I said.

The man at the table flicked his eyes up from the newspaper, face darkening.

"You'll get yours when the revolution gives Black people what's coming to us all," he said.

"But until then, I should know my place."

He exhaled. "You know we honor you sisters. But we got to take things one thing at a time. Right, men?"

"Right," said Mr. Slick. "I'll honor you, baby."

Tanya grew still at the stove. She wasn't stirring anymore. Her back was tense under her shirt. The meat was getting too brown. I could smell it.

"Tanya. The meat."

She startled at that, and dragged it off the burner. "Damn!" Tanya turned to the sink and turned the water onto cold, holding her hand underneath the flow.

I turned back to Mr. Slick. "You going to say that in front of Leadership?"

"I'll say whatever I want, sister. Whenever I want to."

Hippie tugged at his sleeve. "Let it go, man. We got to go anyway."

Mr. Slick grimaced, then shoved off the counter and pushed by me, through the door. He smelled of cheap cologne. Hippie followed, making sure to angle his body so he didn't touch me as he went by.

The man at the table just looked at me and shook his head. He opened his mouth like he was going to speak again, then shut it and went back to his cigarette and paper.

That was when I felt it, crawling up my skin, clinging to my magic, forcing its way up toward my throat.

Snake.

How the hell had it gotten in?

And what the hell did it want?

Dropping my bag to the floor, I pushed out with my power.

"Jasmine, you okay?" Tanya grabbed my arm.

"Don't touch me." I didn't want it to get at her, too. "Just open the back door."

She ran to the kitchen door and flung it wide. I could hear the guard on the back stoop bark something at her, but I didn't hear what he said.

I was too busy trying to get the twining energy off my body. But I wasn't sure what to do. How to get everyone safe.

"What's happening?" someone said.

I shoved past the guard and Tanya, out into the yard, pushing with my magic and pulling at the space around my skin with my hands.

"Jasmine's freaking out."

"Did she drop some acid?"

The air hit me then. I could hear Jimmy's voice in the kitchen, calling my name.

The snake was gone.

Just gone.

My fingers clutched my throat, but there was nothing there. Aching with the effort, eyes pricking and head pounding, I saw Jimmy, standing in the doorway.

Then coming down the steps.

He looked at me as though he was afraid.

Chapter Eleven
Carol

By the time Carol reached the scene, it felt like half the people in the Mansion were crowded into Mr. Sterling's massive office.

He was laid out on the blue carpet beneath the floor-to-ceiling sapphire drapes, completely still, as though he'd been knocked out.

"Calm down, Terrance." Mrs. Price, Helen, was bent over him, crouching down, the skirt of her red dress shoved above her knees.

He was fighting Mrs. Price. Carol could finally see that. Struggling against her pale, long fingers as Helen gently probed his head. The rest of his body seemed inert, immobile. That's what had fooled Carol at first.

"Something has gotten through the defenses," Mr. Sterling ground out through clenched teeth. "I don't have time for your ministrations!"

"We're working on it," Helen said. "You are in no shape to help right now."

He said something else, but it was too garbled for Carol to make it out.

She scanned the room, which had seemed so crowded upon her arrival, but now she saw that besides Helen and Terrance, there were only six others there.

And no Ernesto.

Carol turned and sprinted up the marble stairs, one hand clutching her long purple skirt to keep from tripping, the other smacking the black wrought iron to help drag herself up faster. He was in the temple space, she just knew it.

She also knew she wasn't allowed there.

Right now was not a time to care.

Damn, Carol needed to take up jogging. Two flights and she was already winded, breath heaving in her chest with a hideous crackling noise. Or maybe she needed to cut down on the Mary Jane.

One more flight of stairs to go.

Muffled chanting drifted in snatches down the stairs. How many voices? Throttling down to a walk, Carol paused to slow her breathing and calm her mind. She needed to not make a racket. The hallways upstairs were old, dark hardwood. Walnut, or stained to look that way. She made her way down the hallway lit by electric wall sconces converted from the original gas.

Seven voices, maybe eight. All of them chanting in unison, with Ernesto's voice in a rising descant above them. Carol still couldn't make out the words.

There were too many protections on the room, plus the thickest layers of lath, plaster, and the same old walnut she was walking on.

A small, leaded-glass window at the end of the hall, set into one of the little turrets that edged the east side of the Mansion complex, threw blurred shards of westering light onto the dark wood floor. Something pricked at Carol from that window. She passed the heavy double doors to the temple and crept further down the hall.

But not before she stopped once more and reinforced her shields.

Seriously. Something was up with that window and the people inside the temple didn't know it.

Breathing out, Carol sent a boost to the wards at the edges of her aura. She made sure the inner protections, closest to her skull, were strongly in place. Given her recent headache troubles, she couldn't skimp on the basic lessons.

Carol took her granny boots off and peeled away her thin cotton socks. Couldn't really say why; she just knew she needed to. She set them carefully, side by side, facing down the hallway away from the window, like they were ready to walk away at any second.

A psychic getaway car.

As fortified as she was going to get, Carol stepped carefully past the temple doors and on down the hallway, toward the square panes of light.

The chanting boomed at the edges of her wards, the combined magics of eight sorcerers battering at the protections, unable to get through.

If they'd actually been trying, it would have been a different story. Carol just wasn't that strong. Not yet. And not in that moment.

But the wards held, which reassured her in any case.

The wood was cool and smooth beneath her bare feet. Carol drew strength from the wood. She could almost feel it whispering, a deep, slow, dry voice, rising under the currents of the chanting. The wood-voice moved its way up her legs, twining like a vine around a trunk, until a sense of green leaves brushed Carol's cheeks.

"Stay," it said.

Stay as in hold still? Or stay as in stay in the hallway? Or something else?

Carol had no idea, and just took in another breath and kept creeping along the plastered wall, following the balls of her feet and the feeling of her heels placing themselves on the wooden floor.

A few yards out, she saw something in the upper corner of the top left window pane. Movement.

Moving as carefully as she could, Carol caught the scent of strange magic. Powerful magic that wasn't part of what the Association was doing here. It wasn't the chanting. She knew all the signatures that made up whatever they were cooking in the temple.

Everything went still. Silent. The chanting faded. The whispering of the walnut planks receded. The stink of strange magic increased, almost palpable, pressing on her wards.

All she could hear was her own breath. Whistling into her lungs and out again.

Then a different chanting, tinny, like from a long, long way away, from some old-timey radio. "Come. Come. Come."

Carol rooted her feet into the walnut planks, recalling the injunction, "Stay."

The wooden "Stay" under her feet pulled against the power of the distant febrile chanting, "Come."

Stay and come were at war within her. Around her. Dawn and dusk. Night and day. Hot and cold. Age and youth. Death and birth. Everything and…Nothing.

Obliteration.

Then she saw it. She saw what the movement in the pane of glass was. It was two shapes. Two specks. Pale and dark.

They resolved themselves into two spiders, fighting over a paralyzed fly.

Carol broke the spell and ran back toward her shoes. No. No time.

Pounding the palms of her hands against the heavy doors, she screamed. "Ernesto!"

Nothing. Nothing. Nothing. Spinning out to capture her.

Carol clenched her fingers into fists and pounded, then started kicking at the door with the soles of her feet, putting all her Earth magic into the balls of her feet so it would transfer through the door.

The chanting crescendoed and then stopped.

She kept pounding at the doors, Earth ringing through her fists, amplifying the sound through the wood.

"Ernesto! Ernesto!" Carol's voice was hoarse with the effort of screaming, rasping in her throat.

The energy in the room dropped and stabilized. A humming started. A magical bass line. Then under that, a rustling, like someone standing up.

The lock on the door shot back and there he was, standing in floor-length, unbleached linen robes. His dark hair was disheveled.

"Ernesto. Come. Please."

Grabbing his cool hand with her sweating one—when had she started to sweat?—she dragged him toward the window until he tugged her to a stop.

"Jasmine," he said.

"It's Carol! Carol!"

He stopped as though she'd slapped him. "Caroline. Of course. But something is wrong with Jasmine. There's some danger."

"That's what I'm trying to tell you."

Carol tugged his hand again, and drew him one yard from the window. Pointed to the upper pane that was beginning to crack from the efforts of the tiny beings there. The spiders were still at war.

"Oh no," he sighed. "This is far worse than I even imagined."

Covering one hand with the skirt of his robe, he reached up and smashed the warring spiders.

"What are you doing!" Carol shouted.

The chanting rose and fell behind them, but the air changed again. Normalized. The pressure of the Void receded.

He looked at Carol and she realized his brown eyes were staring at her for the first time without the protection of their glasses. How could he have even seen what was going on?

"It was not the spider's fault, but it was the only way."

Carol shook her head.

"Carol. They were being used."

"What are you talking about?"

"Sit. Please." Ernesto slid down the wall to the floor. After a moment, Carol joined him. The solid plaster behind her back felt good. So did the wood under her thighs and feet. She gathered her skirts around her legs, resting her chin on her knees.

"Something has been trying to break through…" he started.

"It got to Mr. Sterling," Carol said.

Ernesto nodded. "Terrance. Yes. It is also getting here through you."

Hands clammy and ice cold under the sweat, Carol felt the stabbing pain in her temple again. Pressing her hands against her head, she tried to draw more power from the wood. Ernesto's hands covered her own, and she felt his breath ruffling her hair. Soothing the pain away. Shoring up her wards with his magic.

"But the spiders?" she said, still cradling her head. Her mouth tasted like plastic.

"They were just spiders. But whoever has been trying to affect our magic affects whatever creatures are closest to them."

"Creatures?"

Ernesto let out a big breath.

"Think back to your first year here, maga. When you were learning about how you were Earth, and Jasmine was Water. What else did we talk about?"

He was back to being Mr. Alvarez, her teacher, which was more comforting to Carol than this weird in-between relationship they had now. Mr. Alvarez made sense to her, mind and heart. Ernesto just confused her.

She searched her memories. "Some people have affinity to The Powers through animals, or insects. I remember you saying that, but I don't get how it works."

"That's because it isn't our kind of magic. Sorcerers just use whatever is always around us, linking to the Elements we're born into. Witches channel power through specific combinations of herbs, or through their psychic skills, using cards, or crystal balls. Remember?"

Carol took her hands from her head and stared at the wall. Her head felt better, but the energy in the Mansion still roiled around them.

"Spiders?" she asked. She wasn't getting it yet.

"There are certain ceremonial types who mostly use structured rituals to train their souls. They learn to walk the ætheric planes in physical form. They don't need to go into trance. The most powerful ones can pick an object or an animal, and see through them. Hear through them. Sometimes fight through them. Or they can make a person think there is an animal or a man in the room, trying to kill them, when it is only a Sending."

Carol's guts churned at the thought.

"So…how are we safe? If they can just get through our wards? If they're strong enough to Send like that?"

Ernesto stood, robes falling back around his legs. The wolf's head ring stared at her from his hand.

"They shouldn't be able to do what they are doing. All I know is that they are very strong. And we're going to need more help."

Chapter Twelve
Doreen

The candles blew themselves out again.

Doreen muffled a curse and took two steps back from the makeshift work space on the old oak dresser. Three squat white candles sat in a triangle, with a pile of cinnamon on a small dish in the center.

Cecelia had been poking and prodding at her mind. Probably on purpose, the ways sisters did. But even if it was just her own guilty conscience speaking, Doreen figured she better listen.

Every day after Jasmine left, Doreen would either get ready to go to work at the florist's shop—blasting Nina Simone from the hi-fi cabinet in the cream-painted living room, dancing in her stockings until it was time to slip into shoes—or she would gather what she needed to start practicing magic again.

She dreaded the magic days. As if she were going to some punishment. Or had gotten a note to go to the principal's office.

The sorcery was starting to keep her up at night, clamoring to *move*. To *do something*. Fire crept into dreams. And everywhere she turned, there was Hector, staring at her with those golden eyes.

The magic was starting to hurt. Not just the dull ache in her solar plexus, but like needles pricking all over, burning her up from the inside out. She hated it. And she wanted it.

It was real.

And Doreen had to face it. All the signs she could barely read anymore from lack of practice—because she hadn't want to *see*—pointed to the fact that change was rising fast.

Her mouth felt dry.

The candle smoke made coiling patterns in the air, slowly beginning to dissipate with time. She watched the ripples and whorls, the way the smoke from one candle drifted toward the next…there must be a draft coming from underneath the door.

Doreen used to know how to read the smoke. She didn't even used to need to refocus her eyes. Everything in her used to just know, that this swirl meant that, and the thinning at the top revealed this other thing. Doreen *was* fire, and therefore, Doreen was smoke. At least, that's how it used to be.

The patterns didn't seem to make much sense anymore, but Doreen's heart beat a little faster just looking at them, so something significant must have been trying to get through.

But she just didn't know what it was.

Doreen walked into the kitchen, crocheted slippers catching at something sticky on the floor. Jasmine must have spilled juice that morning before running out the door. She ran water into a tall, clear tumbler, drinking half of it down before taking a breath. The wet felt good after all that fire.

The practice was tedious, but she needed the formal work in order to get fit again. Even though Fire was her natural birthright, every Element took training for sorcery to be effective in this world. Otherwise, the energy didn't do much, just giving a Fire person some extra creative oomph, or a Water person a little more intuition than the average person had.

To be a sorcerer took training.

Which meant Doreen needed to get back to it. Back to raising up the fire along the edges of her body, learning how to let it move around her again, so she could direct it at things, or store it inside tools and spells.

Eventually, Doreen would be able to tap the fire at the heart of every living thing. Sparking synapses. Sunlight stored in leaves. But for now, she needed a more direct source, like the candles. The candles that had snuffed themselves because of a too-quick, inexpert draw. As if Doreen were a teenager fumbling in the æthers. Messing with primordial fires when she could barely light a match.

She set the tumbler in the sink and walked back into her tidy room.

Looking in the big wood-framed mirror above the chest of drawers, she sighed. Sixteen she wasn't. The lines on her face weren't so much from age as they were from years of grief. She was past forty now. Not so young anymore.

Not thin or fashionable by any stretch of imagination, Doreen was still young enough and trim enough to catch men's eyes on the street. She'd grown pretty used to ignoring them. But if the magic was coming back, that was going to grow more difficult.

The scent of cinnamon hadn't yet started to rise up off her skin, but it would. It always did. And then they would come flocking, wanting more than a firm smile.

Maybe, just maybe, that wouldn't be so bad. To have a man again. An ordinary man, someone who didn't turn into a mountain lion at will. One who didn't look at her with magic pouring out alongside the love from amber-colored eyes…

For the first time, Doreen understood Cecelia's attraction to William a little bit better. Lack of magic could be a restful thing. None of Doreen's friends up here had magic, and that was just fine. She liked her new friends, especially Patrice. Life with them was a far less complicated thing than life with sorcerers.

Picking up the matchbook, she looked at the white candles in their equilateral positions, and paused. What were they trying to tell her?

The candles were mute. Just candles, waiting for a match to bring their small flames back to life.

That was it. Until she regained some finesse, she needed a bigger source of fire.

She had thrown her sorcery on the fires of grief. It was time for Fire to bring it back.

Every type of magic had a feeling and a scent. Every type of magic had a base, a core, a root. Witchcraft was different than sorcery, and root work, sorcery, and temple magic were like morning, noon, and night. They all overlapped, of course, but the training and trappings were different. Energy signatures, too.

Parents and personality affected what came after, and training, intention, or whimsy shaped it to the magician's will. Doreen learned this from her parents, from the ages of fifteen-and-a-half to close on twenty-four.

Even after Doreen and Hector married and had moved into the tiny apartment twenty miles away, she was at her parent's house once a week, without fail, until Momma deemed Doreen's training "good enough for now."

Jasmine should have been learning all of this. Doreen had been failing at that, and knew it.

She'd been suspicious when Cecelia and William had sent Jasmine north, knowing that Jasmine's training needed more time. Wondering why they'd sent their daughter to a dried-up sorcerer. But they made the excuse that they wanted Jasmine out of Los Angeles, because of the unrest.

But things weren't calmer up here, not with helicopters spraying tear gas over Berkeley, and truncheons smashing students' heads.

There was no place in America that was safe for a young black woman in 1969. There was no place to keep a girl sheltered.

What Doreen knew now was what she suspected all along: Cecelia's plan included forcing Doreen's hand.

They had sent Jasmine to Doreen for Doreen's sake. They wanted to see what would happen when Doreen's Fire met Jasmine's Water. Would their strength increase, or would the two women cancel one another out? Damn.

It was all a test. Whether Terrance or Helen or the rest of the Association had a hand in it, Doreen hadn't figured out yet. If they were, she would need a fire as big as she could make it. And fast.

If Water had been sent to Oakland California to see if the Fire was all the way out…that Water was going to find out that she had a lot to learn from Fire.

Not that Doreen blamed Jasmine. She was a pawn in all these politics. She just needed to grow into herself. But Doreen? She knew better than all that. Sending Jasmine up to Oakland was either an opportunist move on the Association's part, or they were gathering forces because a storm was on its way.

And that wasn't good. It wasn't good at all.

She looked from the candles to her own reflection, and something in her decided. Right then. The Association wouldn't find they needed to replace Doreen for good. She would get it back together. She would train herself up, and start in training Jasmine.

Doreen would build that bigger fire. Jasmine was going to need help with whatever she was messing with, and Doreen was starting to have suspicions about that, too.

She lit the candles and started again.

Chapter Thirteen
Jasmine

"Jasmine, babe! You okay?"

The energy left in a rush, collapsing me to the ground, concrete slamming into my right hip.

Pain rocketed through my whole skeleton, forcing a gasp from my throat. The magic whooshed up from my fingers and then died.

I struggled to refocus my eyes. Right. The back of the house. I had landed on the cracked concrete pad that started life as a patio umpteen years before. A patch of weeds bordered the concrete, straggling toward a grayed-out redwood fence.

"It was a snake," I croaked, still trying to bring my eyes into focus.

Jimmy had called me "babe".

"What? What did you say?"

"I said I'm okay."

The guard—what was his name?—Jerrold. Skinny, flat-faced Jerrold. He was leaning over me, .22 in his right hand. He looked at me, dead in the eyes from beneath his beret.

"She said it was a snake," Jerrold said, "and I'd like to know just what she meant by that."

Damn it.

Jimmy offered me a hand and started to pull me up.

Pain spiked through my right hip again, and my back seized.

"Wait! Wait a minute. Please."

By this time, two more guards had stepped outside, and I could see Leroy looking out the kitchen window. Damn, damn, damn. Putting on a show for the top cats was not my intention.

I didn't need that kind of notice.

But I had it now.

I took a breath. "I think if you can get an arm under my shoulder. Left side…" Hissing through my teeth, I leaned into his chest, moved through the agony of my clenching back muscles, and stood, weight on my left leg.

"Sound like a snake yourself," Jerrold muttered. I ignored him.

"Can you walk on that leg?" Jimmy asked.

"I think so. If we take it slow. It's my knee and my back."

The kitchen curtains twitched back down.

After an agonizing five minutes, and a lot of maneuvering up the back steps, I was propped up on two of the orange-and-yellow–flowered kitchen chairs, one bag of frozen peas on my knee, and another tucked between my lower back and the padded chair.

The scent of burnt hamburger filled the air, along with the undercurrent of sweat, cigarettes, and musk.

I had upset the Panthers. This was so not good for me. But neither was the snake getting into HQ. How the hell had that happened?

I was just debating calling Doreen for backup when Tarika and some of the other folks in leadership entered the room. They must have been conferring in the back.

Leroy cleared his throat, crossing his arms, muscles outlining themselves across the white-T-shirt expanse of his chest. "Jasmine, what happened here tonight? You drop acid before showing up to the meeting?"

Damn again. Oh, Jasmine, you are so far away from Crenshaw now. The heat of fear moved up my spine. These people could seriously kill me if they wanted to. For the first time since moving up to Oakland, I wished I were behind a white picket fence in LA.

I tried to adjust myself into a position that hurt less, and only caused more pain. A headache from the smoke and kitchen smells throbbed at my temples. I throttled down the fear. No place for that right now.

It wasn't going to help.

"It's not that."

"Well, what is it then? We're waiting."

"She just needs some time," Jimmy started.

Leroy held up a hand. "I believe that Jasmine needs to speak for herself."

Hoo, man, there came that fear again. I looked from face to face, trying to read them. They were as inscrutable as stone. I took another breath. In for a damn penny.

"I do magic."

Shoulders straightened and spines snapped to attention. Hands moved toward guns. The musk grew thicker on the air.

"Magic?" Tanya blurted, before covering her mouth with her hands.

Jimmy put a hand on my shoulder and moved in closer. Backup. I fought the urge to shake it off. I didn't want to jeopardize him. But he'd clearly made his own decision here.

He'd chosen me, whatever his reasons were. A smile flickered at the edges of my mouth, but I contained it. Now was not the time.

Clearing a blob of phlegm from my throat, I nodded. "I was born a sorcerer. I'm still in training, but yeah, I have what you'd call magic."

Folks exchanged glances, but said nothing. A technique, I knew, to get me to talk more. I'd fall for it. It might as well come out now, anyway.

"Tonight, a thing that's been following me somehow got into HQ."

"The snake…" Jimmy said.

"The snake."

"This some sorcery grudge? You bring a battle to our pad?" one of the men said, glaring at me.

Leroy plopped his bulk into a kitchen chair across from me. Scratching at his sideburns for a moment, he looked at Jimmy, then Tanya. Jimmy held Leroy's gaze. Tanya darted her eyes down to the floor. I could tell she didn't want to look at *me*, either.

"Guards on both doors?" Leroy asked over his shoulder.

"Yes," someone said.

"Then open a goddamn window. It's stifling in here."

Leroy turned his deep brown eyes on me. I'd never noticed before, the way they slanted slightly upward at the outside corners.

"I'm interested in that answer, too. You bring a battle to our door?"

"No. I mean. I didn't mean to. I thought I'd warded myself well enough. Plus, I'd shaken them off hours ago."

"But they were here," he said.

"Not exactly. I mean…" I rubbed my hands over my sweating face. My pores burned with the cigarette smoke.

"Can people…can people stop smoking? I'm having trouble breathing here."

And I needed to buy myself some space. Some time. What the hell had happened and how the hell was I going to explain myself?

"You dangerous, Jasmine?" Leroy was asking.

I made a decision then. Grimacing with the pain, I straightened up, and put both feet on the floor. Looked straight at Leroy's face, not caring about the massive muscles under the tight white T-shirt he was wearing. Not caring that a word from him could have me expelled from the Panthers.

"I can be," I replied.

He nodded, some glimmer of respect flashing across those tipped-up eyes.

"Good. Now we just have to figure out if you're dangerous to us. And whether or not you're still useful."

Crossing his arms over his chest, he leaned back in the ugly chair. "Start talking."

Chapter Fourteen
Jasmine

The talk was not fun. I wasn't sure if leadership believed me. All I knew was that I was wrung out, needed a shower, and didn't want to talk to Doreen right now.

Jimmy had to stay for another meeting—about me, I supposed—and had gotten me a lift home from Jerrold, who was not happy about "babysitting no snake," as he put it.

Well, for some reason, taking care of me trumped Jerrold's feelings. I didn't know why—it had to be more than just Jimmy—but I was grateful to be home safe all the same. Grateful to be behind the freshly pumped-up wards Doreen had put up just a few days before. She hadn't said a word about them, but I felt the tingle of the edges as I approached the house.

After a quick, very hot, shower, I dragged the purple shower cap from my hair and ran a sea green towel across my body. Padding naked into my bedroom, I grabbed my pajamas and sent a thanks out to the Powers that Doreen was already asleep.

I just needed to be alone for awhile. To think. I was way too keyed up to sleep, and was almost tempted to root through Doreen's cupboards for some cooking sherry to dull the edges the shower hadn't taken care of. But if something really was after me—and there wasn't much doubt about that now—I needed to be alert. Even in my sleep.

Sighing, I sat down at the small desk under my one window, and pulled out some crackling mimeod pages. The words of Chairman Fred rose through the smeared purple ink.

They were what I needed now. To remind me what I was doing, and why. I might not understand the Association right now, but I needed to be clear about the Panthers. Whether they kicked me out or not.

The tensor lamp on my desk puddled light on the paper in front of me, casting shadows on the textbooks stacked at the edge of the desktop, braced against the wall.

The only sounds in the house were the slight hum of electricity and the kicking over of the old refrigerator in the kitchen, and the alarm clock on the little nightstand by my single bed.

I tried to put the snake out of my mind, and concentrate on Chairman Fred's words.

Passion crackled off the purple mimeographed pages, staining my fingertips with an inky, musty smell. The scent of it drove the smell of snake out from my nostrils.

Kids tried to get high off that smell. I was getting high off the words.

Jimmy drew on my body, that was for sure, but I had to admit that Fred Hampton drew on my mind the way the full moon drew my magic like the tide.

It didn't matter that the man who spoke the words on my stinky mimeo was all the way across the country in Chicago; Chairman Fred had made part of me his own.

Only a couple of years older than I, he felt infinitely wiser. More insightful. He talked about things it seemed I'd just forgotten to even notice, let alone think about.

Fred had been organizing, thinking, and speaking since he was a kid. When I was a kid, sheltered by my parents from the world as best they could, I was mostly concerned with my grades. Sure, LA was as filled with racists as anywhere else, and I heard my parent's talking sometimes at night, about things that happened on the street, or in the bank, or the grocery store. But sometimes months went by when I could pretend the racists just weren't there. Fred, it seemed, had always noticed everything.

I stretched my back. Should probably get to bed soon. Doreen woke up early and would be bustling about, putting coffee on to perk by 6:30. But I just wasn't ready to go to sleep yet.

"I don't care how much theory you got, if it don't have any practice applied to it, then that theory happens to be irrelevant. Right? Any theory you get, practice it. And when you practice it you make some mistakes. When you make a mistake, you correct that theory, and then it will be corrected theory that will be able to be applied and used in any situation."

Fred's words could apply to my sorcery, that was for sure. All types of magic were fine in theory, but could only be learned, and honed, through practice.

But Chairman Fred was talking about something else here. This revolutionary magic was more potent than anything my white-picket fence and Association-of-Magic-and-Sorcery-Crenshaw-upbringing had prepared me for.

I tapped a pen against my lips. Was I mostly engaged in theory, taking classes at UC? Was the theory worth it, if I couldn't put it into practice? Jimmy said we could practice anything, anywhere, and I should stay in school. Finish my degree. I wasn't sure yet.

And the white kids getting their heads bashed in People's Park? I wasn't sure exactly what they were up to. Wasn't sure yet if that was either theory or practice, or if they were just playacting some dream, putting themselves in front of the cops when they didn't have to.

"Our magic needs to be grounded in what's real," my mother always taught me. Chairman Fred, Huey, Bobby, and Kathleen, they all said the same thing about revolution.

Was I doing anything that was real, outside of feeding the kids breakfast three days a week before I went to school myself? *That* felt real. But those mornings also made me wonder what my life would have been like if I had stood up every morning and shouted out "Black is beautiful!" with my friends.

Blaming my parents was stupid. But I wanted something more than they had given me. I just wasn't sure exactly what that was, but it felt a lot like what Chairman Fred was preaching.

"We in the Black Panther Party, because of our dedication and understanding, went into the valley knowing that the people are in the valley, knowing that our plight is the same plight as the people in the valley, knowing that our enemies are on the mountain..."

How the hell had he *learned* this stuff? Who had awakened him, the way he was awakening me?

I could feel the waters of sorcery moving through my veins. Blue sparks were wanting out of my fingers. The hum of magic wanted to go somewhere. To do something. So did I. At this rate, I was never going to get to sleep.

Snapping off the desk lamp, I sat in the near darkness, with the pale light of the streetlamps filtering through the white curtains that covered the single window between my desk and bed. I could taste the ocean brine coming through the small space at the bottom of the casement, where I'd cracked the window open. It tasted a little salty on my tongue.

Allowing the magic to rise like a tide inside of me, I let the power build along the edges of my skin. It was like my skin was tight and needed to grow. A snake about to shed.

But not the snake I'd felt tonight. Not that dry and dusty thing. This was something else. This was me.

I relaxed my body, and imagined the edges of my skin expanding. The magic began to rise up from my fingertips. I was deliberately not focusing it anywhere, just allowing it to emerge.

Pale blue light rose up, sending waves into the air. My brain and heart let go of all their questions, giving over to the magic that was mine, and mine alone.

"Magic for the people," I said softly to the night. There had to be a way to be who I was, a sorcerer, a student, and a revolutionary, too.

I shaped the magic with my hands, formed glowing orbs the size of fishing floats. Pushing them toward the ceiling, they bobbed there together, casting the entire room in shades of blue. What good was this? Who knew. But it comforted me.

Hanging with the Panthers was galvanizing. But it also caused a tension in me that was sometimes hard to ease. I knew that tension was cultivated on purpose, to get people to act, but when I looked at leadership, I could see that their intensity didn't translate into this same tension.

One thing that set them all apart from the rest of us was that they were comfortable in their bodies, and only coiled when it became necessary to strike.

Leadership just lived. Those cats were ready all the time.

That was one thing working magic had taught me well: the more energy expended on unnecessary things, the less energy the sorcerer had for magic when she needed it.

Yet here I was, filled with tension from a need to *do* when I wasn't exactly sure what doing looked like. I wasn't the only one. Everyone else—from the soldiers with their rifles slung across their shoulders or 9mms strapped to their hips, to the women making endless pots of coffee or the men and women running the newspaper and keeping the medical clinic stocked—was filled with coiling tension. Like springs wound tight, we were all waiting for action.

And we knew that action could come knocking on the door any time. Any time at all.

Revolution, I was coming to understand, was ongoing. That's what leadership kept telling us: every interaction is a choice. Bow your head, or hold it high.

I started arranging the globes of blue, lighter shades toward the edges, darker in the center. I allowed the rising tide to keep moving out from my core, letting my breath come easy, just like my mother taught me.

I relaxed my vision, not trying too hard, instinct guiding my actions, guiding the magic into the shape it wanted to make in that moment. The shape that would be right. The magic that my heart and soul drew out from the æther would form into the pattern that was meant to be.

My mother's voice was my companion in the blue glowing night: "Sometimes the sorcerer sets the pattern in advance. That's good. But even then, things change according to what the tides and forces need for it to be. Other times, we step into the flow of fire or water, or let the earth or air shift our cells according to what our minds can't even know. Sometimes that magic is the most powerful magic we do. That is the magic that happens when we allow everything to work with us. Through us. Relax and let it come."

My hands traced the air, releasing balls of glowing light, pushing the patterns together and apart.

Finally, the tide receded. The glowing on my fingers stopped. The scent of ocean filled the air and there was moisture on my face and hands. I could hear waves, so gentle, lapping at the shores of my heart.

Looking up, I saw that the pale blue balls of light surrounded the darker, indigo blue orbs.

They had formed a glowing fist.

Chapter Fifteen
Doreen

With Jasmine in the house, all the things that Doreen had put on ice for so many years were melting her inside as if she were on fire.

She woke up sweating in her pale blue bedroom again, taste of a man's clean sweat in her mouth. Panting, desperate, her feet kicked at the white chenille bedspread and the lilac-patterned sheets, leaving them a spilled tangle, half off, half on the carved walnut bed.

Drawing a shuddering breath, Doreen blinked, and darted her eyes across the room. Sun was just beginning to filter through the white curtains. It glinted off the mirror whose frame matched the dark walnut dresser it hung above. The light caught a perfume bottle—L'heur Bleu—and a jar of Pond's cold cream. Ordinary. Simple.

Like her life for the last ten years. The way she'd gotten used to it.

Jasmine's low humming rose above the sound of water running in the bathroom sink down the hall. Doreen hoped she was getting ready for school. Jasmine had been up to some other things lately, though she was trying to hide it.

Doreen was keeping her counsel for the moment, but could feel a conversation brewing in the air every time they passed in front of the percolator, heading for coffee.

But Doreen didn't feel like dealing with any of that this morning. The black-faced alarm clock on her nightstand read 7:30. Doreen had overslept. Damn dreams.

She'd been dreaming of Hector again.

His golden eyes bored into her, trying to tell her something. She couldn't read what it was. His hands cupped her face and he looked more serious than he ever was while he was alive. Usually, Doreen's memories of Hector included his smile.

And she hadn't dreamt of him in two years.

Two years of peace and quiet. Two years of crocheting while watching the evening news, and reading a library book in its crinkling plastic cover until sleep came. Two years of working part time in the florist's shop, eating Chinese food or a pork chop and green beans she picked up on her way home.

Two years of dinner with friends, who kept trying to convince her to join the YWCA. Like that was going to happen. Walking was all the exercise Doreen wanted or needed.

She thought she was finally over Hector. Over his big strong body. Over his rumbling laugh. Over him smacking her bottom. Over his gold-tinged eyes, and the smooth, delicious way he tasted, like some honey powder underneath the clean salt of his sweat.

His sweat which came from working in the sun, or running in the hills. Not like the sour sweat sticking Doreen's nightgown to her thighs.

It was that sorcery Jasmine had brought into Doreen's tidy, blue-painted home in her wake. That potent, elemental magic Doreen had left behind a decade ago.

Damn.

The girl was shining with it. The æthers glowed from her eyes and left shadowy trails across her arms. Jasmine was luminous like the moon on a dark ocean. She brought the breeze off the bay water with her every time she came into the house. The old one-story worker's bungalow wasn't used to being this awake anymore. Doreen wasn't used to it, this energy of a young woman reaching for her life.

Exactly how Doreen was when Hector met her, except she was a bit more sassy than Jasmine was. Jasmine had a serious bent Doreen didn't take on until after Hector's murder.

Doreen sniffed at her skin, wondering if she'd catch a hint of cinnamon, the smell of her own elemental Fire magic, rising up beneath the sour sweat. But no, it wasn't there. Just the memory of Hector. And the memory that Doreen had power too, once upon a time. Groaning, she hoped Jasmine would finish up soon. Doreen really needed a wash. The dreams had troubled her, and she wanted to rinse them down the drain.

It was good to see Hector again, though. Doreen had to admit it. Even through the pain the dreams brought. She missed him. Wanted him. She wanted his big arms and his quiet rumble of a laugh. She wanted him cooking up steak on the stove, splattering grease all over the kitchen, cigarette crushed into a glass ashtray on the counter.

Mostly, she wanted his perspective on things.

Hector always knew the right angle to steer toward, and would do it without condescension. He knew Doreen had to make up her own mind, and that if she asked for his opinion, it was because she had painted herself into a corner again.

She missed his golden tawny fur, too, those dark moon nights before he took off for the hills. The way he bumped his shoulder against her hip by way of saying "Be back later, gorgeous," as though he had the man's voice that wouldn't return until the morning.

"Hector."

The hand she wiped across her face to scrub the sleep off, came away wet with tears. How had she been crying in her sleep without knowing? Grabbing a corner of the sheet, she dabbed at her face to soak up the sweat and tears.

Her soul missed Hector that bad. What had she been pushing away for all these years?

Doreen groaned her way up and swung her heavy legs over the edge of the bed, feet feeling for soft slippers on the flowered rug that covered the hardwood floor. She hoped she wasn't in for another year like the year he died.

That year was unbearable.

After pulling on the crocheted slippers, she opened the door and paused. It was way too hot for a robe. Jasmine would have to just deal with her aunt in a sweaty nightdress.

"Jasmine girl? You getting ready for school?"

Jasmine came out into the hallway from the bathroom, sunlight from the bathroom window casting a square onto the photos that lined the hall. Her hair was already styled into a carefully sculpted short natural, picked out even all around. Blue bell-bottoms rode lower on her hips than Doreen liked, but that was the way with girls, wasn't it? The white peasant top had long, belled sleeves, and some satiny ribbon tied the front closed.

Jasmine looked beautiful. Just like her mother. Dark-skinned, thin, just slightly lush at hip and breast. Not like Doreen, who grew a little rounder every year.

That was all right. And Hector had always loved to sink into Doreen's curves.

She wiped a hand across her face again and sighed.

"Are you okay, Aunt Doreen?"

Jasmine was looking at her like…she didn't know what. Like she was nervous. Like Jasmine was hiding something. And Doreen knew she was. She just wasn't sure exactly what it was yet.

"Just had some bad dreams. I'll be all right once I get some coffee in me."

Jasmine nodded at that, and turned to go back through the kitchen to her room. Doreen was just too worn out that morning to figure out the right words to say. The words that would open up the doors her niece was locking up tighter than her curls.

Tighter than Doreen's heart had been these past years.

Maybe that was what the dream was about. Hector was asking her to open up again. Something was brewing, that was for sure. She could taste it on the wind and feel it in the sweat between her breasts. When she was cooking lately, every time she wanted something a little more than onion, salt, and pepper, she opened up the cabinet looking for ground red pepper, or oregano, and ended up with a jar of cinnamon in her hands.

That was a message from the elements for sure.

In the green-and-white bathroom, she ran cool water in the sink. Splashing at her face, she held the water over swollen eyes. She'd want a shower later, but decided that coffee would come first.

The face looking back in the mirror, water dripping down onto her chest, looked older than it had for awhile. Middle-aged and tired. And she needed to do something about her hair. Her Shirley Chisholm 'do was looking raggedy.

Maybe she'd stop going to the hairdresser and grow out a natural. She grinned wryly at that. Doreen with an afro? That was a funny thought. But she did need to change the style a bit, update it. A little less Shirley maybe, and bit more Diahann Carroll.

She'd make time to go to the beauty parlor soon. Perhaps.

Taking in a deep breath, she grabbed a green towel from the rod and patted her skin dry. Her chest still felt a little tight, but the cool water had eased the aching in her eyes, at least.

Shuffling to the red-and-white kitchen, she saw the warm orange light at the percolator's base. Jasmine had made the coffee already. What time had she gotten up?

Jasmine was a good girl, but she was sneaking around. Sniffing around those Panthers.

Some things were in the blood.

Chapter Sixteen
Carol

Things around the Mansion only pretended to be quiet. A current of unrest hummed gently underneath, making Carol's breakfast sit not quite right. The orange juice still tasted sour on her tongue, even after she'd brushed her teeth twice.

Carol hadn't been sleeping well since Mr. Sterling had his incident. She still wasn't sure what to think of it all.

The carpet was so thick her feet barely even made a sound as she walked down the dark, wood-paneled hallway toward Mr. Sterling's office. She supposed she should start calling him Terrance, but it still felt too awkward. She'd had a hard enough time calling Mr. Alvarez, Ernesto. Of course, Ernesto had insisted. Mr. Sterling never would.

Rapping on the door, she could smell the frankincense Terrance burned each morning. It permeated his office, clinging to the thick, sapphire-blue drapes that hung straight all the way to the carpet with their patterns of blue, burgundy, and gold.

"Come!" His voice was strong today. That was good. It meant at least he was sleeping more.

Carol pushed at the heavy brass knob and entered the room. The drapes were opened and Los Angeles sun was streaming in. Even in early December, there was sun. Some years more than others. This year, not so much as last.

Carol loved it; coming from Minnesota, she still reveled in it, even after six years.

"I brought the papers you requested." She crossed to the big slab of a dark wood desk backed by shelves filled with leather-bound books and curios. He reached out, and she set the files directly into his outstretched hands.

Mr. Terrance Sterling matched the room. He matched the whole building, really, as if he were a creature of the place. The dark wainscoting topped by pale blue wallpaper was hung with small oil paintings and magical artifacts from around the world. Old money meets the occult.

Terrance always wore a sharp, well-cut suit. Today's was deep gray, though the jacket hung neatly from a wooden coat butler. Crisp white shirt. Blond hair tastefully going silver, cut by a barber who came to this very office once a month. Perfectly knotted burgundy silk tie.

Mr. Sterling looked like any wealthy, successful businessman, except the silver tie bar had the Kabbalistic tree of life on it, and the heavy silver ring on his right hand held a scarab done in blue faience.

Carol always felt underdressed in this office, even though she'd dressed well today, and her clothing was a huge upgrade from what she arrived with. Thanks to Jasmine's taste, Carol was finally acquiring some of her own.

"Caroline. Thank you. Would you pour us both some tea, please?"

Huh. That was a surprise.

Crossing to the dark walnut sideboard, she poured from a thermos into two blue-patterned china cups on matching saucers. The amber liquid was fragrant. Darjeeling.

"Lemon?"

"Nothing, thank you."

Squeezing a wedge of lemon in her own, Carol picked up the saucers, fingers stiff, trying not to rattle the china as she crossed back to his desk.

"Please. Sit."

She sat in the burgundy armchair across from the desk. Her stockings swished as she crossed them under the tasteful black A-line skirt that came to just above her knees.

Inside, she was not a patient or quiet person, but she had learned to act like she was. That was part of the magical training.

She had learned to control her natural impulses and quiet her mind and emotions, regulate breathing, and simply sit or stand still. The tutors said Carol still had a ways to go before she presented the strong, solid front they all affected so well.

Her magic would be stronger once she learned what they clearly thought was a basic skill. Basic if you'd been practicing since you were five.

Like she hadn't.

She kept her right foot still, feeling the pressure of the need for it to bounce up and down. Training allowed her to do that much.

Mr. Sterling trained his blue eyes on her face. Carol could feel him assessing her energy fields, too. Testing her edges. Making sure her shields were strong.

And trying to extract information if they weren't. Terrance stooped to just about any energy violation if he deemed it for the greater good. Despite strictures against that sort of probing.

Sending a breath into her core, Carol boosted her edges. Terrance smiled, all shining teeth.

Sipping at the tea, she winced, puckering. Should have followed his lead. Darjeeling didn't need lemon. Who the hell drank tea in Southern California anyway? But this was yet another stupid social nicety she had to keep trying to drill into her head.

The whole world order was crumbling and Carol was trying to remember what the small fork at the top of the plate was for. Jasmine rolled her eyes at that, and simply rejected it all. Carol still just didn't have Jasmine's spine.

Finally, Terrance spoke again, after taking one or two ceremonial sips from his cup.

"What did you see the other day?"

Carol inhaled sharply, aspirating her tea. She coughed into her hand, almost spilling the rest of the cup in the process. Smooth, Carol. Really slick. She set her cup and saucer on the big desk. That earned her a slight frown.

I saw you practically foaming at the mouth, rolling around babbling on the floor. And then I saw two spiders in an epic battle.

Right. Couldn't exactly say that. So what the heck was she supposed to say?

Terrance just waited, teacup held delicately in his hands. Carol swore the blue scarab moved, about to stretch its wings.

"Um…" She picked up her tea again.

"Yes?"

Okay. May as well go all in.

"I saw you, surrounded by a bunch of people. It looked like you'd fallen. You were saying a bunch of things about the Powers weaving around us. That we needed to be ready."

He waved his hand at that. "I want to know what you saw upstairs."

Of course he knew about that. No one kept anything from him in this place. Well, except Ernesto's radical newspapers. Carol kept meaning to bring that up with Ernesto, but hadn't yet.

"I went up to the Temple. Don't ask me why; I can't exactly tell you. I just knew I needed to."

She looked down at the orange-brown tea in the blue-patterned cup.

"I saw two spiders in the window. Brown and white. Fighting. They were fighting so hard, they started to crack the panes of glass. I got Mr. Alvarez."

"Then what happened?"

"He killed them. Said they were being used."

Carol cast her mind back to the hallway, the feeling. The spiders.

She turned to Mr. Sterling. Everything clear inside her. Those spiders were just stand-ins for the real thing. The one tugging at the strings.

"You were right. We need to pay attention. A web is building. Threads strung out across the nation. The white spider grows large with prey. It spins out old magic. Ancient magic. Ceremonial. Magic from the shadows of the Temple long gone. There are symbols…I can't see them. But I can feel them on my skin."

Her voice changed timbre. "There's a storm coming. A big storm."

The room dropped away, and Carol's eyes rolled back in her head, hands shaking at her sides. "The clouds are gathering fast and strong. The earth is trembling under my feet at what is coming. The animals are burrowing deeper in their holes."

Carol rose up from her seat, swaying forward and back, forward and back. Rocking faster and faster. "The birds are shaken from the tops of trees. People are dying. There is blood in the streets. Smoke and fire. The wind is shrieking. The spider spins a web across the earth. A new Temple will rise."

She couldn't speak anymore. The images were coming too fast. Symbols poured through her mind, black glyphs on stark white paper.

Charged with blood.

Chapter Seventeen
Jasmine

Jimmy relayed the message that leadership had met for two more hours after I'd been sent home.

No decisions had been made, but I was assured they would be, once Leroy and the others had met with me again.

Just great. Not what I wanted or needed. But it was just the way things were. I dug that.

They needed to decide if I was a security risk or an asset to the cause.

So here I was, heading back to HQ.

The streets were busy with evening traffic, folks streaming on and off of buses, cars honking at the stoplights. Folks stepping into the corner store en route to home, or picking up some food to go.

I still didn't have a clue what the snake was, and hadn't even figured out what, if anything, I should tell Aunt Doreen. Messages from my parents kept piling up, little slips of paper in the hallway nook next to the phone.

Did Cecelia feel something, or were they just checking in? No way to tell without calling. And I wasn't ready for that.

It was twilight, my favorite time of day, when ocean grays and blues warred with salmon and gold as the sun was swallowed by the bay.

I was finally adjusting to living up here, to walking and busing everyplace, like a real city person. In Los Angeles, the only bus I was allowed on was the one to and from my school, and the occasional bus downtown for shopping with Carol. Other than that, Cecelia drove me everywhere.

My time at the library had run later than I'd thought. I'd become buried in a stack of books and papers on the Restoration and had to rush to make my meeting.

I was hurrying up the sidewalk when a kid ran up to me, blood streaming down his face. He was huffing and panting, and smelled like copper and sweaty fear. I recognized his little round nose and tight 'fro, and the brown jacket he habitually wore, which was looking a little more scuffed than usual.

Drake. That was his name.

"Drake! What happened?"

I leaned toward him as he panted, bent practically in half on the sidewalk in front of me. I could see now that the blood came from a slash high on his forehead, where a bump was raising under his skin.

"Got jumped, Jasmine. We gotta get outta here."

Straightening again, I looked down the sidewalk. Two white kids with snarls on their faces loped toward us. Squaring my shoulders, I headed toward them.

"Jasmine!" Drake tugged at my heavy, fringed bag. Right. I dropped it to the sidewalk.

"Take this and stay behind me. Better yet, head to HQ. Meet me there."

I was several steps from him by this time, though I could still feel his quaking body, rooted to the sidewalk, unsure whether he should run, or stay and protect me.

"I ain't leaving you," I heard him say, voice growing a little steel. Good. While I'd rather Drake was gone, it wasn't a bad thing to have him learn to stand his ground when help was around.

The boys and I were closing distance, as my boot heels clicked on the uneven ground. People slunk toward doorways or the edges of the sidewalks, like they could feel what was going down.

Or like I was packing.

Which I was. But their conscious minds had no way of knowing that, as I never did carry a gun.

Never thought to, before I hooked up with the Panthers, and once that was done, I realized I most likely wouldn't need one, not with the arsenal I already had.

The power built in my blood. I drew on the light of the setting sun, letting it connect me directly to the waters of the bay. That water was my backup, every last drop of it, down to the sandy, silty floor.

I could feel the strength of that water moving toward me. Could feel the cormorants. The mussels. The tuna. All of the creatures who lived on and in the water lent their power to me.

But mostly, it was the salty brine itself. The sheen of it was making me sparkle, with the tingling on my skin that always let me know something in me had changed.

That something must have been visible in the moment, because, just as I'd felt Drake hesitating behind me, I could now feel the two white boys hesitate in front.

I was scaring them.

That was just groovy.

One thing I had learned was that if we couldn't get respect, we could get fear. In other words, Black was Beautiful, and if we couldn't get them to work with us, we'd get them to leave us the hell alone.

My hands itched with the power by now. But the other thing I'd learned from the Panthers that went along with my magical training was that I needed to bide my time. To wait until the right moment. I also needed to always assess what level of force was needed, if at all. The Association called it control, while the Panthers named it discipline.

Discipline was the only thing that kept us from always acting on the impulses to fuck or fight. Which were the same, with this kind of power. Always the same.

Life. It was all life.

I was close enough to the boys now that I could speak without shouting. Their eyes widened, one pair of blue and one of brown. Sandy blond, stringy hair, and dark brown hair that fell just above the collars of their denim jackets.

They were trying to look tough, but I could feel that what they really wanted at this moment was to run the other way.

Flexing my fingers, I spoke.

"You boys messing with my friend?"

Blondie looked down at his shitty white sneakers and his friend glanced sideways at him, hoping for direction.

I moved my hands upward. Just a few inches.

The acrid scent of piss hit me then. Brown-haired boy had peed his jeans.

"You mess with a black boy again, I'll hunt you down."

Sniffing the air between us, I said, "Got your scent now, boys. It won't take me long to find you if I need to."

They took off running, slamming into an old lady dragging a red, two-wheeled shopping trolley behind her down the sidewalk.

"You help her!" I shouted.

"Sorry, ma'am," Blondie shouted over his shoulder without slowing down.

Drake ran to help me right the small metal cart and put her bread and tuna cans, a few oranges, and one sorry head of iceberg lettuce back inside.

"Are you all right?" I asked her.

She slid her black, cat eye glasses back up her nose and patted the navy felt hat straight on her hair.

"I'm fine, young lady. Those boys didn't hurt me. I just got startled some."

"Can we walk you anywhere? Or do you need to sit down?"

Drake was looking from her to me, confusion on his face.

"No, no. I told you I'm fine. I only live a few blocks from here, and can walk myself just fine. Thank you both kindly."

We stood on the sidewalk as she pulled the red trolley, one wheel squeaking, toward the intersection, and then pressed the button, waiting for the green walk light.

"You changed so fast. How'd you do that?" Drake asked.

"I didn't want to scare her." I looked down at Drake. "But I did need to scare those boys. It's good to be able to act differently when we need to, Drake. It'd be a good thing for you to learn."

I shoved his shoulder gently. "You wear too much up front all the time. That can be all right, but sometimes it's okay to act like you're hard."

"*Act* like I'm hard? I wanna *be* hard."

Shaking my head, I turned him toward HQ and started walking.

"No one should have to be hard, Drake. That's no way to go through life."

He just shook his head again. Maybe he'd understand someday, or maybe he would raise an impenetrable steel wall inside him by the time he turned fourteen.

Regardless of what happened to Drake, I just hoped he stayed alive.

"Let's get that forehead looked at, okay?"

Chapter Eighteen
Jasmine

I dropped Drake off at HQ, handing him off to Tanya to look at that swelling forehead of his, and left.

"You not staying for the meeting?" Tanya asked me.

No. All of a sudden, for the first time since I'd started hanging around the Panthers, there was something more important than a meeting with leadership, even though missing it was going to piss them right off.

After dealing with the snake and this new incident with the boys, I finally realized talking with Doreen had to happen before I talked with anyone else.

"Tell them I'm sorry, but there's an emergency I need to take care of." Tanya nodded, a worried look on her face, then, putting an arm on Drake's shoulder, she steered him into the house.

Trying to remember how late Doreen worked, I decided to take the chance and head to the shop in uptown Oakland before going home.

After tapping my booted toes at the bus stop for five minutes, I realized I was way too impatient to wait for a bus that was likely stuck in traffic. Luckily, I'd chosen Army surplus boots to go under my green cords that day. Walking wouldn't hurt me much.

Might even do me good.

Walking would certainly help disperse some of the magical energy that was starting to bubble under my skin. It was like the whole damn ocean all of a sudden decided to crash onto my shore.

The sidewalks were too crowded. Kids with book bags. Parents laden with sacks of groceries. People just starting to get off work.

I was like to give Doreen a heart attack, walking toward uptown from West Oakland on my own. But with the magic as strong as it was, I seriously doubted anyone would bother messing with me.

Hurrying toward the nexus of Telegraph and Broadway, I avoided a clump of papers blowing down the streets. The papers smacked my legs anyway, wrapping around my shins before I kicked them off.

Some old men sat on the ground, legs splayed out, passing a bottle back and forth.

"Hey girl," one of them slurred out. His friend smacked at his hand that held the bottle.

"Leave 'er 'lone. She's one a them."

Huh. I didn't have time to figure out what that meant and sure as hell wasn't going to stop, either.

A few blocks later, I was in front of Doreen's shop. I could see her, neat hat pinned onto her curling hair, navy coat over a flowered dress. Sensible shoes, as always.

She was locking up. Perfect. But her friend Patrice was with her. Not so perfect. A good-looking, dark-skinned woman with a rounded figure poured into the tight orange knit dress that flashed under her open swing coat, Patrice was a study in contrast with Doreen.

I liked Patrice, and she was good for Doreen, but I really wished she wasn't around today.

I was still too far to call out to Doreen, and wanted to get her attention before Patrice saw me anyway, so I sent a small wave of magic to tap her shoulder.

Doreen looked around at that, didn't see anything, and kept fumbling with her keys, trying to keep her navy pocketbook from falling off her shoulder. Patrice was laughing at something. Doreen shook her head, a big grin on her face.

I curled up my fingers, putting a little extra oomph in this time, and sent another wave her way.

Doreen dropped the keys this time, head whipping my way at the same time as she crouched toward the sidewalk, using the keys as an excuse for her defensive stance. Patrice looked around, confused. I could see her mouth working, asking Doreen what was going on.

Shit. Too much.

I waved. Picking up her keys, Doreen shook her head again and stood, locking the grates across the door and turning to wait for me, frown on her face.

"Sorry," I called out as I got closer.

"What in heaven's name are you about, girl? What are you doing here anyway?"

"Hi Patrice!"

"Hello, lovely girl."

Doreen just stared.

"I'm sorry to interrupt you two; were you heading out somewhere?"

Patrice laughed. "That was my hope. I needed to order some flowers for Thanksgiving and was trying to convince old stick-in-the-mud here to go get a cocktail."

"Jasmine, what do you need? Is something wrong?" Doreen had stopped looking angry and had gotten that worried crease of hers in the center of her eyebrows.

"Yeah, actually. A few things have come up and I really needed to talk to you."

Patrice put a dark hand on Doreen's shoulder. "You go on with Jasmine, Doreen. But I insist on dragging you out with me. Maybe Friday evening?"

Doreen dropped her keys into her bag, snapping the clasp shut.

"Yes. Soon, Patrice. Thanks for coming by."

Patrice kissed Doreen's cheek, then clacked her way to the black Impala spread out at the curb, unlocked the heavy door, and waved.

I waved back, and Doreen and I fell into step, my boots and her low, lace-up shoes, heading toward Chinatown and then home.

Doreen rubbed the smear of orange lipstick off her cheek with a crisp white handkerchief. She ironed the things, which I never could understand.

"I'm sorry, Doreen, but I really need to talk with you. I realized something today, which has to do with the Association. And something happened last night, too."

She shook her head again, to head me off. Right. Too loud. Too public.

Much as I wanted to start babbling about magic, I knew better. I'd wait until we were home.

"Talk quietly. I can hear you just fine. It's clear you're upset and don't want to wait."

Okay.

"I'm not sure how to talk about this…"

Doreen tucked her pocketbook more firmly under her arm, adjusting the strap on her shoulder again.

We walked passed some boarded-up windows, toward the candy cane stripes of a barber pole. I glanced inside. Two men were laughing, one smacked the other with his newspaper. The barber in his white smock was running a little whisk brush across the neck of another man in the big barber chair.

"You want Chinese for dinner? Or you want to eat at home?"

Startled, I stopped in the middle of the sidewalk and someone slammed into me, hard.

"Hey nigger bitch!" A white face contorted itself into a snarl as I whirled.

"Don't. You. Dare." Doreen said, at my side. Two men ran out of the barbershop, broadening their shoulders and flexing their arm muscles under tight, ribbed sweaters.

They weren't Panthers, but they would do.

"You sisters need some help?"

The white man spat on the sidewalk and ran.

What the hell was up with the white folks today?

"Thank you, gentlemen," Doreen said. "I think we're fine now."

The men nodded and walked back into the barbershop.

"What do you need to talk with me about?"

"Chinese. I want Chinese food for dinner." I was suddenly ravenous; the magic I'd used was making me hungry. It hadn't been much, but I clearly needed to up my training.

A pile of rice and meat would do me good.

Doreen looked at me funny, nodded again, and led the way.

I lagged a little, my gaze caught on a swirl of orange and purple. A new shop selling dashikis and head wraps.

"Talk," she said. "But keep your voice down, and no more stopping on the street."

Right. I huffed out a sigh. Where to begin?

"I stopped some kids from beating someone up today."

"Are you all right?" Doreen was the one who slowed this time. I kept walking, head down.

"I'm fine. And that isn't exactly what happened." The concrete was cracked under my boots and I could feel the left one starting to pinch under my pinkie toe from too much walking. Huh. You were supposed to be able to walk for miles in these things, but I guess they'd already done their duty in a jungle somewhere.

"Well, tell me what happened, girl!" She dropped her voice again. "I know you used magic. I can smell the brine all over you. Plus you shoved me with it. And what was that about?"

Okay. She was pissed off and trying to keep it in. Just like she could smell the magic on me, I could feel it coming off of her in waves. Made me wonder what it was like back in the days when she'd used it all the time.

"I'm sorry. I'm just feeling…I don't know. Weird. Strange. Fired up. These white kids jumped a black boy on the street. I caught them chasing after him and threatened them. You know."

"With magic." Doreen said, voice flat.

We were almost at Chinatown. The sidewalks grew more crowded and the black faces were mixed more and more with Asian ones. Most of them Chinese, I guessed.

My stomach growled.

"Doreen, we've got to do this. These people need our help. We can do something to protect them."

"These people. Protect them from what, exactly?"

I stopped dead in my tracks again, tucking myself into a brick wall and dragging my aunt away from the crowds.

She ripped her elbow from my hand.

"Don't you..."

"I'm sorry, Doreen. But I need you to listen to me. I need someone to listen to me. The Association doesn't know shit about what's happening and you, frankly, have to wake up, too."

She was pissed off, I could tell. The scent of cinnamon cracked the air between us. I didn't care. I had her attention and that was all that mattered.

"A snake showed up last night, Doreen. I had to fight it. And then those kids today... It's time, Doreen. You have to stop hiding from yourself. The Association has to wake the hell up and help these people."

She sighed at that, deflating a little. The scent of cinnamon dissipated.

"Let's get some food, girl. You've got a lot more to tell me about all this."

Chapter Nineteen
Doreen

It was after midnight and Doreen just couldn't sleep.

The attic was a dim and dusty mess. Piles of boxes, some mementos, a chair or two, one long table that didn't really fit in the house... She'd had the movers hump it all up the outside stairs and leave it in the wood-raftered room with its single dormer window and bare bulb. Ten years ago.

That was when Doreen had arrived in Oakland. She'd meant to get to them after...after she'd had a little space and time to grieve.

Pulling her navy cardigan tighter with one hand, she dabbed at her nose with the handkerchief in the other. It was cold enough in the space that she could've practically worn a coat.

Stupid to be up here. But it couldn't wait another minute, let alone another day.

Doreen had never even set foot on the stairs leading up from the tidy garden in all the years in the house. Oh, she'd had plans at first, to fix the attic up. Maybe turn it into a studio apartment to rent out.

Or use it for a temple space.

It was strange, that thought even being in the back of her mind when she'd moved here. She was so sure she'd renounced it all, the sorcery. Some instinct must have still held the training that magic would be done. No matter what.

That was the way the world was. That was the way *she* was. And surely as Momma taught Cecelia and Doreen to keep a clean kitchen, she'd taught them sorcery.

The dust floated through the air, agitated by the current moving through the open door, swirling into the shadows on the edges of the pool of light in the center of the room.

The place smelled of old paper and despair. It dragged at her. Doreen fought simultaneous impulses to crumple to the floor in a boneless heap, or slam and lock the door to run back down the stairs.

Funny, she would have thought one of those impulses would have been to snap her fingers and set the whole of it on fire.

But she'd done that once before, and it hadn't done much good.

So Doreen held her ground, feet sinking a little deeper into the wide-planked Douglas fir, and straightened her spine. Then she took in a long, careful breath, dust tickling the small hairs in her nostrils. She willed herself not to sneeze.

Looking around the dimly lighted room with its angled ceilings, Doreen saw two things. She saw what the space could be. And she saw the carcasses of all her shattered dreams.

To get to one, she damn well had to clean up the mess of the other. No way around the piles of boxes and dirt.

Those dreams, though.

But a woman had to keep on with her life, no matter what. Momma taught her girls that, too, even lying in bed, emphysema taking over her lungs. She'd birthed fire and earth, and died without sorcery being able to help her. An air magician tortured to death by the slow betrayal of her lungs.

It was time. Past time. The magic was zinging through the house, between Jasmine and Doreen, despite the wards, drawing itself out.

One thing Doreen hadn't told Jasmine during dinner, when it all spilled out about the Panthers and her magic coming out on the sidewalk. And that snake insinuating itself into what should have been a safe place. Doreen was plenty mad about all that.

Just like Jasmine would be mad if she knew the secret Doreen was keeping.

Terrance had started calling at odd hours, when he knew Doreen would be home. She avoided his questions as much as possible, but knew he could feel what she was doing, could sense it. It wouldn't be too long until the conversation he was wanting to have would happen.

Doreen hadn't said a damn thing to Cecelia yet, either, though she could feel *her*. The silence of Cecelia giving Doreen space was tangible. They knew each other far too well.

Jasmine. Doreen was going to need to talk to Cecelia about that soon, too. Jasmine was growing harder. Seemed like the thinner she got, the sharper her insides became as well. She was all angles, like an air or fire worker tended to be. Water and earth were more curves than planes. Not Jasmine. Not these days.

Jasmine needed training. The sorcery was eating her alive. Or maybe it was that "revolution" hollowing her out from the inside.

Doreen had enough oomph and practice back that it was time to take things in hand. Fulfill her promise to Cecelia. Uphold her oaths to the Association.

Even though she'd let all that lapse, they'd never suspended her vows.

It was time Doreen kept those vows. Including the criticism the Association had coming. Especially as it seemed things were moving fast. Heating up out in the streets.

And in Jasmine's life, with that snake. Whatever it was, it couldn't be good. When Doreen found out Jasmine had been followed magically, she'd been both angry and afraid.

"You didn't think this was worth mentioning to me?" Doreen had hissed out over the pot stickers.

Jasmine had shrugged a bit sheepishly. "I thought I could handle it myself."

Handle it herself. As if the girl knew what she was doing. As if she had any sense.

Doreen looked at the boxes piled under the eaves.

Jasmine needed structure. The training Doreen had promised Cecelia she'd take care of all those years before.

Besides, Doreen couldn't clean up this mess on her own. Along with working magic, it was high time she started asking for some help. Another lesson to learn.

Too much time alone hadn't been good. Jasmine had woken up the good and the bad, but at least Doreen was alive again. Which was going to make Patrice happy. Bless that woman for trying so hard over the past few years to get Doreen to "Act your age, girl! You aren't dead yet! You are a woman in her *prime*."

Getting Jasmine into the attic would help them both. Get them moving on building something. Get Jasmine's apprenticeship on track, and Doreen motivated to clear out the rest of her old fears.

She reached up to pull the switch on the bulb, turned back toward the open door framing the weathered landing and the bare branches of the apple tree in the backyard.

Doreen locked the door and turned to gaze down on the garden, lit only by the streetlights filtered through the trees. She'd worked the soil around the edges, and put in a small vegetable patch, but that night, for the first time, she realized something.

She'd disobeyed the cardinal rule of magic workers everywhere.

"There's no offering stone," she breathed.

Doreen had never set up a stone, or set aside a hollow. There was nowhere in the garden to thank the spirits of the place.

In her unhappiness, she'd forgotten how to give thanks.

Jasmine had cracked the placid shell of Doreen's life. Angry and frustrating as it was, Jasmine was making her remember.

Sometimes remembering was painful. Like physical therapy after an injury. Or the reawakening of a soul.

At one in the morning, the garden was quiet. The white blur of a possum lumbered by below, pausing at the garden beds to sniff for worms.

Doreen sat herself down on the steps to watch.

When Jasmine first moved in, Doreen thought it was all going to be all right. She'd have her lovely, intelligent niece staying, studying and doing chores around the house. They'd watch the news on occasion, or share meals together.

Doreen would make the coffee. Jasmine would do the dishes.

That lasted about a month. Then the whole world tilted, much as Doreen fought to right things once again.

But really? The cracking started as soon as Doreen felt that ocean magic walk up the well-swept steps and through the door. The ocean pushed and prodded. Testing edges. Seeking a way in.

Not that Jasmine knew any of this. She was just being herself: a young woman racing toward her power, sails aloft, moving full tilt toward the sun.

Doreen sighed, inhaling the scent of night blooming brugmansia spilling over her neighbor's fence. The yellow trumpets were vague shapes in a dark corner. But she knew they were there.

Like she should have known that magic was there. It was always there. And someone young, and brash, and filled with life was going to force the scent of it into Doreen's nose and wave it in her eyes. Wrap it around her shoulders so tightly Doreen couldn't escape.

The magic was in her dreams now. And in the house. And in this garden.

How had she missed it all?

She hadn't wanted to know.

Doreen stood up, brushing her hands over the seat of her dress. Despite Patrice's prodding, she hadn't made herself available to anything in so long, she'd learned to ignore that the patterns and the rumblings, all the signs she'd trained her whole life to read. She'd forgotten it had anything to do with her.

Her safe house had become a cloister of avoidance. She'd forgotten that to work magic meant she had to care.

Jasmine's sun she was sailing toward? It was the heat of change.

Doreen wasn't quite ready for that. No one could be ready for that. But "change gon' come."

"I'd best *get* ready," she said to the possum. Then she went into the house.

Chapter Twenty
Carol

Carol pitched forward and the palms of her hands smacked heavily onto the edge of the massive, polished desk.

Mr. Sterling was suddenly at her side, hands warm on her shoulders. "Sit. Sit."

Carol's breath heaved and it felt as if her bones were locked in place. Then the shaking started, her teeth clacking together in her mouth like spoons.

Terrance pushed her back into the chair, and held the cup of tea back to her mouth.

"Drink."

She tried, fighting to keep her teeth away from the delicate porcelain cup, wincing at the taste of lemon in the tea when she finally got some of the liquid into her mouth. It was cool enough by now that she gulped it down. So thirsty. Her head was pounding.

"Marjorie!" Mr. Sterling shouted for his secretary at the door before taking the cup away. He lay one hand across Carol's forehead and the other cupped the base of her skull.

The door shushed open. "Did you need something, Terrance?" Not Marjorie. That was Helen's voice. Mrs. Price.

"Helen. Would you ask Marjorie to please pour a glass of water for Miss Johansson? And then we may need you here."

The warm energy pouring from his hands soothed Carol's head as she fought to get her breathing under control.

"That's right. Breathe deep in the belly, letting the air rise to fill your chest. Open your feet to the earth, Carol. You need more support from your source right now."

She did as he asked, flushing with relief the moment her feet felt the earth beneath the floor. That was what she needed. He was right.

Carol had never been this closely linked to Terrance's energy before. It was funny; she'd never even thought about it.

Whenever Mr. Alvarez—Ernesto—shouted that he didn't care if Carol and Jasmine's energy was blah, blah, blah, or purple, she'd always thought that was just exaggeration for effect. But it wasn't.

Mr. Sterling's energy was purple. Violet, really. The energy of æther, of someone who was master of all the four elements plus the fifth that bound them all together. She had suspected that Ernesto came close to being a master of all four...but not the fifth.

A sound intruded on Carol's thoughts. The office door shushing open over the thick carpet.

"Here's the water you asked for, Mr. Sterling." Marjorie's voice.

Helen tapped Carol's shoulder and placed a heavy tumbler in her hand before stepping back, out of Terrance's way. Mrs. Price knew not to interfere with someone else's magic.

A Quintessence. Carol hadn't been sure such a thing actually existed. Or if it did, that it was commanded only by people a long time ago. If Mr. Sterling was a Quintessence, he could command every element together, plus something else. Something that Carol didn't even understand yet.

The thing she needed to understand.

Carol drank down the heavy tumbler of water, and set the glass down with a thunk. Marjorie whisked it off the walnut desk immediately, before it left a ring.

"Thanks," Carol said. Marjorie nodded, thick black hair swinging, stick-straight and shining, around her face. Marjorie never said much.

Working for Mr. Sterling, she likely got used to not being the one doing the talking.

"Thank you, Marjorie," Helen said. "I think that's all we need right now." The door shushed closed and clicked.

Carol reached her hands up to Terrance's, signaling for him to stop. "I'm okay now. Thank you."

Once he stepped away, and she could see his blue eyes behind the gold-rimmed glasses, framed by his silvery-blond hair, she took a breath.

Then cleared her throat and spoke.

"You can do all that? You can command every element and do things I can't even dream of, but you won't help the people outside our door?"

Mr. Sterling dropped his hands. "What are you talking about?"

"These prophecies…these visions. That something bad is coming. I've been having them, and I think that you have, too."

Mr. Sterling walked back around the desk, sitting down stiff-backed into his comfortable chair.

"But you know what?" Carol continued, "I think that something is already here. All *I* need to do is watch the news. Or take a phone call from Jasmine. All *I* need to do is walk out the door and down the hill. Outside this damn Mansion, away from the Association."

Damn. Carol's head was pounding again. But her mind was clear. Her whole *being* felt clear. Just like that moment when the fullness of her vision poured through.

"You don't know what you're talking about," Helen was saying, clutching her fingers, knuckles turning white, fear tightening the lines around her brown eyes. Everything about her looked brittle all of a sudden, from her taupe patent pumps to her ecru Chanel suit to the shellacked chestnut Jackie O bob of her hair.

"Magic is complex, Carol. And I would thank you not to start spouting rash accusations in this room." Mr. Sterling pulled his cuffs straight.

"Rash accusations?" Something inside Carol grew hard in that moment. Unyielding. The little girl from Minnesota shouted at her to shut up, but really? Carol didn't care anymore. She was done.

"I get it," she said. "You've tried to keep us safe. You've tried to keep things quiet..."

"That is *not* the point!" Terrance spat out, face reddening with the effort. "Our safety is important, yes, but more important still is the safety of those people *'down the hill.'*" His fingers made scare quotes in the air.

"What do you think would happen to the world if magicians started flinging power around willy-nilly? What would happen if people woke up one day and sorcerers were battling in their neighborhoods? What do you think would happen then?"

"It is happening now!" Carol said.

"Carol." Helen put a hand on her shoulder, pressing her back into the chair.

Carol shook it off and rose up from the soft burgundy chair, called on all the training she had—plus a bit of Jasmine-like anger and bravado—squared her shoulders, and planted her feet.

"No! I'm sorry, but I can't be quiet anymore. You all think I'm stupid. Just some barely-magical backwater chick from Minnesota. Someone only fit to mind the children. But I *see* things. Things that you don't want to admit."

"Stop this, Carol!"

"*You* stop this." Carol looked dead at Terrance, head throbbing, the taste of earth on her tongue.

Then she looked at Helen. "You stop this."

They stood mute in front of her. Carol felt the power of earth beneath her feet, and gathering in the palms of her hands. If she willed it, she could cause the ground to shake.

"You need to do something besides sit here in this mansion, brokering deals between magical factions who barely even matter anymore."

"We have given you everything," Terrance whispered.

"No. You haven't. You've given me a lot, and I'm grateful for it. But you've also taken a lot of things away." Stamping one foot on the floor, she caused his desk to tremble.

"I'm going to figure out what those things are, and I'm going to call them back. And if I have to go out into the streets myself, mark my words, I will."

Terrance ran a hand across his face. Helen was preternaturally silent, standing as though abandoned on the plush, diamond-patterned blue carpet.

"And what do you propose we do? Take up guns for revolution?" Terrance asked. "What do you think of that?"

"You should be ashamed of yourself, sir. That's what I think."

Then she turned and walked through the heavy door.

Chapter Twenty-One
Jasmine

Doreen and I had talked a long time. Everything came out. Her magic, and my work with the Panthers. Thought I still felt like there were things she wasn't telling me. Some important piece that would make all the puzzle pieces make more sense.

Then we went to sleep and woke up to another ordinary day. She had the flower shop and I had school.

And I needed to write a letter to Carol. She was freaking out. About Terrance. About Ernesto. And about a battle between two spiders.

Weird shit.

So I'd stopped off at Caffè Med to get a cup of coffee after my classes. I wasn't ready to go home and was avoiding the Panthers. Just for the day. I knew I should have been having that conversation with leadership, but frankly, I was scared, and the news from Los Angeles had me just as worried as the snake attack at HQ up here. Which, yeah, I dug it, leadership needed more info on that. But even after talking with Doreen, I still wasn't sure how to deal with it all.

How could I properly explain my sorcery and that snake attack when I still had no idea what the snake was doing here? Or where it had come from?

Or if the snake was even real?

Caffè Mediteranneum was a funky, busy place. The smell of cinnamon and ground coffee beans assaulted my nose as soon as I stepped beneath the blue-and-white striped awning and pulled open the heavy glass door.

"Hey, sister." I recognized the voice. One of the brothers who weren't in the Party, yet. All Army-jacketed, with feathers hanging from their ears, they hung around talking revolution but weren't quite ready for the discipline of the Party. At least, that's what Jimmy said.

"Care to sit yourself down?" His brown eyes did a quick scan down my body before returning to my face. Right.

"No thanks, man." I smiled tightly. "I've got some work to do."

"Right on, sister. Right on."

I chose a scratched-up wooden table near the windows. Good way to soak up some late-November sun.

It was cold outside, but warm in the café from the bodies, the sun on the huge panes of glass, and from the constant flow of steam from the big espresso machine, which had made the latte now sitting at my elbow.

Word was that the café latte was invented here. All I knew was that they didn't have them in LA, and I'd grown addicted to the foamy milk and espresso combination.

Never had espresso before moving here, either. I guess I never went to any Italian neighborhoods back home.

"You need to grow a spine, girl." My words stared back at me, blue ink on lilac paper. A gift from Cecelia before I left. A gift for writing letters to her.

But I was using it to write Carol this letter. She was struggling at the Mansion. Panicking with all the weird shit going down.

Laughter cut through the air from the back of the room. I looked toward the noise. Allen Ginsberg was holding court at a big table back there. Young men preened at him. A few white-chick poets sat around the edges, hanging on, never in the center like the men.

Carol was trying to convince me to come down to Los Angeles and help her. That so wasn't gonna happen. Carol Johansson needed to learn to stand on her own two feet. Besides, I wasn't about to go dealing with Terrance at this point. There was too much on my plate already.

We'd had one hurried phone conversation about it, where I got the particulars. Particulars I really needed to share with Doreen, but with everything else going on, I hadn't gotten to it.

Terrance writhing on the floor. Weird-ass spiders battling it out in a window. Ernesto chanting in the temple with who knew who else.

And Carol, avoiding her power so bad she was getting massive headaches, and thinking they were from something else. No way. Her skull was splitting open with power trying to move.

It was weird to me she couldn't see it. Or that Alvarez hadn't pointed it out.

Carol had stood up to Terrance, which was good, but to my mind, she still wasn't claiming her own power.

It wasn't so weird that she was avoiding herself. I got that it was scary. Not that I'd let on to her. Not now. But if I was being honest, I had to admit to all the things I was avoiding doing myself.

Like talking to Doreen.

Despite last night, avoiding talking to Doreen about magic was still as natural as tapping the waters of the bay. I could tell it hurt her, though she'd clearly been trying to reconnect. To the sorcery, and to me.

The scent of candles blown out in a hurry had greeted me more than once as I walked in the house after a Party meeting. And despite the fresh wards around her bedroom, I knew she'd been having troubling dreams. Magic dreams.

Mostly though, I hadn't been talking to Doreen because I didn't feel ready. She was gonna ask me to do more. And then I'd need to make the choice staring me in the face. The reason I wasn't at HQ right now. I could use my magic for the revolution, or turn tail and run back to the punk-ass Association.

Or the real choice, which felt like a stabbing in my belly. Use my power for the revolution or keep magic in some little compartment that I hid and never talked about.

With the Association, it was either dedicate your whole life to magic and the Association, or do your little bit at home and keep it quiet.

Either way, we weren't supposed to take the lid off the cauldron.

But like the Panthers carrying rifles to the capitol steps in Sacramento, I was coming to realize that magic needed to be carried out in the open, too. A lot more people had power than would ever know it. Like that girl from the bench on the quad, testing out her skills. How many other people never even bothered to try because they didn't know what was possible?

They didn't know that they weren't just crazy. That's what happened to most folks the Association or other groups didn't get to in time. They either actually went crazy, or they were so frightened of being seen that way, they locked everything down.

Funny, what was happening with Carol was almost the opposite. Here she'd been given this chance at the Mansion, gotten training, tutors, practiced magic every damn day…and was too timid to use her power properly.

Because of this, the Association itself was tamping her down. Instead of kicking her ass the way they should be, they encouraged her to think as small as she could.

Typical. Folks raised with wealth never thought folks raised without were worth much, until those people rose up shouting, or decided to snatch and grab directly from their hands.

I hoped that this crisis was going to be enough to shake things free. Carol was reaching the point where either she stepped into her real power, or she deflated completely. But what was inside her, singing in her bones, wasn't going to give up without a fight.

Thank the Powers for Mr. Alvarez. It seemed like he still saw who she was.

I turned back to the paper. *Carol, now's your chance. You have* got *to stand up for yourself. Use your magic, girl! That's what it's for. Don't let Terrance and Helen cramp your style.*

I chewed on the pen before putting it down and taking another sip of the warm milk and espresso.

Terrance and Helen. They were putting all of us in boxes. Carol. Doreen. Me.

Damn. I so didn't want to have to call them out. School, life, sex, magic, the Panthers...and being followed by that snake. It was all more than enough for a nineteen-year-old black girl, right?

The adults should damn well be taking care of themselves.

But they never were. They were making all kinds of messes we needed to clean up. I was starting to *get* that white kids' slogan, "Don't trust anyone over thirty." Because you couldn't trust them not to screw things up again.

Carol had to step up.

Doreen had to get her shit back together. Because magic workers never got a break, didn't matter how old or young we are.

She said she would try. Was ready to get back in the game.

And I had to step up my own game somehow. I wasn't sure where I'd get the extra hours in the day or night, but for sure something had to give.

Whoever was following me was gonna make sure of that if I didn't. And no way was I giving them the upper hand, dig?

I sighed and signed off on the letter, my name a blue scrawl at the bottom of the lavender page.

The brothers I'd seen on my way in raised a low fist at me as they swung toward the heavy glass doors. I raised my right fist off the table a few inches and smiled. Nice to be recognized as part of the movement.

Those brothers made me wonder, though. How it all was supposed to fit together. As I sipped at the creamy latte, I mused some more.

It seemed to me that things were changing everywhere. Black Power. Women's lib. Free Speech. The anti-war movement. Whatever the hell was going on with the Association.

There were fissures opening in the old order, everywhere. So what were our choices, really?

Fanon said, "Each generation must discover its mission, fulfill it or betray it, in relative opacity."

Things were getting less and less opaque, but it still wasn't totally clear. And likely never would be. But one thing was starting to make sense to me, and it tied in to that mission he was writing about. The mission of my generation was revolution.

But what did it look like? What did that mean? It meant one thing to the anti-war people. Something else to the Panthers. And the sorcerers would scoff at the very notion of it, despite the fact that the æthers were splitting apart and shit was clearly going down.

I finished my latte, folded up the lilac paper, and slipped it in a matching envelope. Time to get out of this café. Get moving again.

Here's what I was thinking: revolution had to mean as many kinds of freedom as we could take.

And taking freedom meant taking back our power.

All of it.

Chapter Twenty-Two
Jasmine

After that afternoon in the café, I did everything I could to keep to my decision. If I was taking back my power, it had to *look* like something. I had to increase my training.

That meant deeper magic practice, more conversations with Doreen, and my time at HQ in West Oakland needed more commitment, too.

I finally met with leadership.

"Why should we trust you?" Leroy said.

It was a small meeting. Just myself and Leroy, with Jerrold guarding the door. Jimmy was in the house, but wasn't allowed into the room for security purposes.

I understood that, but missed his presence nearby. Missed his gold-rimmed eyes and the particular earthy musk he carried on his skin.

Tarika had met with me for a few minutes before leaving on business of her own. I was enough of a threat that she needed to talk to me, but not important enough for her to stick around, I guess.

"You shouldn't," I replied.

I could tell that shocked Leroy.

"You have no idea yet what my magic can do. Until I prove something to you, you shouldn't trust me. You shouldn't trust any sorcerer."

"Show me," Leroy said.

Slowly, carefully, I drew on the ocean, and the moisture that hovered just above the waters of the bay. I called the fog that rolled in off the water during summer. I called the mist. I imagined rain.

Surrounding myself with a cape of gray and blue shadows, I could feel the moisture kissing at my cheeks.

There was a gasp. I smiled, staring at Leroy's face. Even Jerrold straightened up, guarding the door. I could see them both, and feel the other people in the house, but it was like I was looking at them through glass patterned with rain.

But they couldn't see me anymore.

A hand reached through the mist, groping, found my wrist, and grabbed.

I covered the meaty hand with my own and sent a jolt of blue-green fire into the fingers.

"Fuck, man!" Jerrold said, dropping my wrist.

"Enough!" Leroy's voice cut through the fog. I drew my power back into me, and let the mist disperse.

Jerrold was shaking his hand and Leroy was sweating.

"We want you working with security on this. We want to know everything you can do. And if you decide to use this against us..." Leroy's voice tapered off, but his intention was quite clear.

I would be in the kind of trouble I never wanted to see.

"Can you train others?" he asked.

"I don't know. I'm barely trained myself."

"Just stay close. We want you checking in."

Right. I was still an unknown quantity. And a sudden security risk.

But sitting in that room, I knew, a part of me was home.

I wanted to become one of the women who led, however I could. In my own way, I would learn to be like Kathleen, Ericka, Angela Davis....

They had something to offer me that the Association didn't. They had a magic all their own, one that Terrance had taught us to pay no mind. "Ordinary people? They have a place in society, of course, but they just don't have the same talents we do."

Maybe not, but they sure had something. I could smell it on them all. I could hear it. I could feel it.

I'd seen Huey on television, all soft voice and lilting Southern cadences. Even from prison, it felt like he rolled in on a wave. Clear. Thoughtful. Strong. His power was the power of earth and ocean. The man was locked behind bars, and I could still feel him in every meeting.

If there could ever be said that a patient revolutionary existed, it was Huey Newton.

Chairman Fred was the opposite. What came out of Fred was like the crackling electricity of the most powerful sorcery. Fred Hampton put thoughts together in a way I didn't know a person could. Theory walked the streets with him. Everything was *real*, not just words on a page.

These men made me feel like I could become real too.

And the women. Tarika, Barbara, Kathleen…so different, on down to the shade of their skin. I felt the way their energies worked to feed and fuel the revolution.

Angela Davis, not an official party member, was another, sharp as a diamond. Brilliant. So brilliant I wasn't sure how she was even able to put up with the ones who opposed her views.

I hadn't known this kind of power could exist outside of those of us who worked sorcery. The Association had insisted that our way was *the* way.

"You can go now, Jasmine," Leroy said, snapping me back to attention.

Right, he clearly had some thinking to do, and would need to check in with the rest of leadership. Jerrold let me out the door.

"Sorry, man," I said, gesturing at his hand.

"It's nothing," he replied, then the door latched behind me.

I can't deny that questioning everything I was raised with was hard. Sometimes it brought tears to my eyes and other times just filled me with a sense of anger and resolve.

My middle-class existence was losing its grip on me, but part of me still longed for it. I was repelled and drawn back in to comfort. The disciplines of study and community organizing were different than the disciplines of magic, but my training was holding me up like a raft in these strange waters.

I only hoped I would learn to swim in time, before I needed it desperately and risked my own drowning.

As I walked toward the kitchen, I heard Tanya and some others talking. Planning. What was happening with the safety escorts for seniors? And what did the clinic need? Neither of those were my projects.

But then my ears perked up and I paused. How was the breakfast program running? What were the numbers locally and nationwide?

Huh. Someone's voice was saying we were up to several thousand children fed five days a week across the country. The numbers had come back from Chicago: the tally was close to twenty-thousand children.

I slipped on through, not wanting to talk to anyone. Not right then. Stepping out onto the porch I glanced at the guards, who waved me on down. The cool air felt good on my face.

Twenty-thousand children. Every day. The implications of that staggered me. Those sorts of numbers meant that maybe, just maybe, we could do this far-out thing. We could fill hundreds of paper sacks every week for the neighborhood. We could run clinics. And the school.

Everyone from the elders to the babies seemed to be on board.

The Movement was happening. Huey was right. People needed to be educated through action, first, and that was exactly what the Party was doing. Showing people how socialism was done. McCarthy be damned.

What about me? What about Jimmy? What about the shadow hovering around, stalking my steps?

And what about whatever weird thing I felt around leadership?

I shook my head.

There would be time enough to ask and answer questions. But that time wasn't now. Now was the time to straighten up my spine and decide who I was going to be.

There was no time to be protecting fragile flowers when we needed to change the world.

It was all hands on deck, whether those hands were wielding magic, or wrapped around the grip of a gun.

CHAPTER TWENTY-THREE
CAROL

Ernesto led the way down the crowded sidewalk in East LA, bare biceps a brown complement to the pale blue short sleeved shirt he had donned that day. He never wore short sleeves inside the Mansion. And his arms were more muscled than those of a sorcerer who spent so much time in research should be.

The scent of frying pork skin was as much of an assault on Carol as the booming tuba and guitars streaming from apartments set above the shops that lined the street.

The Mansion may as well have been the surface of the moon, compared to this.

Barbershops. A tire store on the corner, garage bays open in the sun, men in coveralls rolling fat rubber across stained concrete. Scraggly palm trees reaching toward a pale blue sky.

Carol and Ernesto passed a shop that sold luggage, and one with bright piñatas hanging out front. They threaded past giant papier-mâché suns, donkeys, watermelons, and Mickey Mouse heads swinging from wires.

And there were the people on the streets. A lot of people. Men. Women. Children. Sauntering. Rushing. Holding hands. One couple argued up ahead, arms waving, faces close and tinged with red.

The sparkling bells of an ice cream cart called people to refreshment. A father was buying two fruit popsicles, one for himself and one for the little girl leaning in close to his hopsack-clad legs.

Carol made sure to keep close to Ernesto, almost touching his arm, just close enough to feel his warmth, despite wanting to clutch at his clothing like a child.

She didn't want anyone to move between them. Despite all Carol's years being friends with Jasmine, and being taught by Ernesto, walking through the barrio with her white, white skin and blond, blond hair still spooked her.

Carol would have been terrified to walk there on her own. She had to admit it. Who knew what they did to white girls around these parts? She'd heard all the stories about gang members and their initiation rites…killing. Raping. All to prove themselves. She didn't want to be one of those statistics.

Her cheeks grew hot. Flushing with shame and anger. Maybe the thoughts made her a racist. They probably did. But knowing that didn't make her fear and discomfort go away.

Boosting the shields around her mind, she just hoped Ernesto was too preoccupied to read her thoughts. Stupid chica blanca with her outlandish fears.

He probably knew it anyway.

Ernesto paused for a moment in front of a mercado piled high with fruits and vegetables. The combined scents of oranges and cilantro calmed her a little. Nothing bad could happen in front of a fruit stand, right?

"Start looking for a hand in a triangle," he said.

"Where?"

He swept his eyes up and down the brick walls of the open fruit stand, turning slowly to look at the shops next door.

Carol wasn't seeing anything but people, and the oranges, plantains, and assorted vegetables piled high. Something tugged at her solar plexus, and she turned to look across traffic to the opposite side of the street. There it was, next to a used-electronics store.

Painted on a weathered blue door was a yellow triangle surrounding an orange hand, the paint flaking with age.

"Mister A…Ernesto." Carol touched his elbow and motioned with her chin across the way.

"Ah. They've moved."

They'd moved. Even though the paint on the door was so old it was cracking. Even though it looked like something that had been there for fifty years.

"How long has it been since you've looked for it?"

"Six months."

Right. And it had just moved itself across the street, weathered sign and all. This was some crazy magic Carol had never even heard of before. And why hadn't she? The Association was supposed to keep track of everything.

"Let's go."

Within seconds, they were across the busy street and stepping through the door. Carol didn't even notice Ernesto knocking, but he must have. It seemed like the door had just opened as soon as he reached out an arm.

And then they were inside a cool, dark space, dotted with the flickering of candle flames. The space smelled of palo santo, the fragrant wood that came all the way from the Yucatan peninsula. It was one of the herbs and plants she'd had to study. Ernesto sometimes added it to spells.

He dipped his fingers into a small basin of water affixed to the wall near the door, and touched his forehead, belly, and both shoulders.

"Are you a Catholic?" she asked.

"Sshh," he breathed out.

Her eyes slowly adjusted to the dim light from the candles and filtering in through small windows near the tops of the turquoise-painted walls. The walls were covered with hammered pieces of tin in a variety of shapes. Hearts. Lungs. Legs. Whole torsos. Eyes. Brains. They glinted, waiting for the prayers they represented to be fulfilled.

A red wooden cross in the center of the wall was covered with more of the small pieces of tin.

"Milagros," Ernesto said, noticing her looking.

Miracles.

Jasmine talked about her mom, Cecelia, saying that every act of magic happened because something in the universe asking to be healed. Carol still wasn't sure what that meant, but knew that these hearts and lungs all represented people in pain, somewhere.

A jingling sound came from behind a woven red curtain strung across a doorway. A voice called out, "Ernesto, who have you brought to us today?"

Carol's body froze solid. The voice was terrifying. Ancient. She couldn't tell if it was male or female. Couldn't really even tell if it was human, except that it spoke English.

"I brought a young magician, Abuela."

A gnarled hand the color of manzanita pushed aside the woven curtain.

She must have been so tall when she was young, because even slightly stooped, the old woman was taller than Carol's five foot eight. Garbed in a black cotton dress, layers of silver jewelry gleaming in the dim light at her throat, fingers, and wrists, she was somehow luminous.

Beautiful. Sharp nosed, with high cheekbones and a jawline that was softer than it used to be, but still fully visible.

"A white girl, Ernesto?" She clucked her tongue against the roof of her mouth.

"She's been having visions, Abuela."

The woman looked at Carol with…eyes the color of citrine. Wow. Who *was* this woman? Carol could feel the power banked inside of the woman. No. Not banked. She wasn't fire. She was *contained.* This old woman was a tornado ready to blow the whole street down. How a person could control that much energy was beyond comprehension. Even at the Mansion, there wasn't a person like her.

She walked around the room as if she were ordinary. As if she didn't hold the power of lightning in her hands. Unruffled. As if she was… Carol had no way to describe her.

The magician was a bit like the old farm women in Minnesota. They could throw bales of hay around all day like it was nothing, and still bake blackberry pies in wood-fired ovens while stew bubbled on the stove.

Powerful. Simple. Ordinary.

Yet extraordinary all the same.

"She doesn't look like Air, Ernesto. Are you certain?"

Carol took two steps back, bumping into Mr. Alvarez's solid chest. He put his hands on her shoulders, and took a step sideways and back, keeping her in place while gaining some polite distance.

Right. Polite distance. As if Carol couldn't still feel his hands through her shirt.

The woman kept on coming, until she stood one scant foot away. It was all Carol could do to control her breathing so she wasn't huffing right into her face. Those citrine-green eyes locked on.

"She's Earth," Ernesto said, "but she's having visions all the same."

"Interesting." The old woman closed her eyes for a moment. Carol felt a probing around her edges, and then the sensation of a finger tapping at the center of her forehead. Carol's hands flew up, trying to cover the spot. It didn't help. She struggled to put up an extra layer of shielding. That did nothing. It was as though all her training was useless in front of this woman. This magic worker. This sorcerer.

Carol wanted to weep.

And then the woman breathed across her head and Carol's skull cracked open. Images streamed from her mind and her tongue formed shapes that babbled in a flow from tongue and lips. Carol's body started shaking from her bones all the way to the edges of her skin.

The pressure built and built until Carol screamed out the nonsense words, body quaking where she stood.

"Ah! Kee! La! Na! Kee! Ahna! Ahna! Ahna!"

She could barely feel Ernesto's hands gripping her shoulders, holding her upright.

The woman raised a hand then, tracing a line in front of Carol's body, up from Carol's navel to a foot above her head.

It all stopped then. With a mighty sigh, Carol's body collapsed against Mr. Alvarez. He wrapped his arms around her from behind, warm and true. She trembled there, too freaked out to feel self-conscious anymore.

"I see," the woman said. "You did well to bring her here. We need to know exactly what you saw, maga."

The woman turned with a swoop of dark skirts, heading back toward whatever was behind the red curtain.

"Collect yourselves and come into the back. I'll make some tea."

Chapter Twenty-Four
Doreen

If the damn phone cord had been any longer, Doreen would have paced the entire house. As it was, her feet tromped back and forth on the hardwood floor down the hallway, from the front door, past the living room and her bedroom, past the bathroom, to the kitchen.

Past the family photos and the picture of Dr. King. Pausing at the living room to gaze for a moment at the oil painting of a mountain lion in the California hills.

Then back again.

She hadn't even changed out of her shoes after work. Terrance had called the flower shop, and if there hadn't been customers in, asking about ordering centerpieces for their Thanksgiving parties, she would have shouted in his ear.

"This will have to wait," she'd hissed into the black phone. After he'd extracted a promise that she would call him from home, Doreen carefully placed the receiver back into the cradle before turning to the customers with a smile back on her face.

She was good at her job, damn it, and she was going to remain that way. No matter how big an idiot Terrance was.

And no matter how silky his voice sounded over the wire.

Damn his smooth-talking voice, anyway. He was doing it to manipulate her and she knew it.

Doreen's feet were starting to hurt. She was irritated that she hadn't changed into slippers when she got home. Clearly, the impulse to obey the head of the Association was still lodged inside. Despite the years away, and despite her anger.

So she'd called as soon as she'd dropped her bag in the living room. Stupid. She should have made him wait.

"Terrance, you must be out of your goddamned mind!" She yanked the cord and stepped around it, ready to pace the hall again.

The silkiness was all gone by now. He'd figured out she wasn't going to be persuaded by sex and charm today.

Charming white men were the cause of too much sickness in the world. They started wars, and traded slaves, ruined families, dammed up rivers, and poisoned soil. All in the name of progress. Of money. Of might is always right.

Masters of the damned universe.

Might was always *white*. That's the way it looked to Doreen, now that she'd woken up again.

But she was mighty, too. And the universe would crush them all into dust one day.

Terrance was squawking now. Talking off her ear about how he needed her to come down to the Mansion and take a seat on the board. Or if she wouldn't do that, could she please get her niece in order? There'd been rumblings about Jasmine and leadership was growing concerned.

"You know what concerns me, you devil? What concerns me is the lack of interest the *Association* is showing about what's going on right under your noses. You think this whole country isn't a powder keg? You think you can just ignore your responsibility…."

He was shouting back now. She shouldn't have called him a devil. Too late now. Satan was out of the bag. And Doreen half-believed it. Not really. But when she was this mad?

"Yes! Responsibility. You think you're just responsible to the sorcerers who line your pockets with silk and keep the Mansion running? You need to wake up, man. We took vows."

Doreen was at the end of the hall again. She yanked on the phone cord, whipping it behind her, and decided to pace into the kitchen. Might as well make some coffee. She wasn't going to be able to sleep tonight anyway.

And as soon as Jasmine came home, they were heading up to the dusty attic, gonna get some things in order. Start to plan.

"Those vows include service, Terrance. Did you forget that? You think we all should just be serving *you*? Is that what you think?"

Doreen could smell the cinnamon fire of magic burning at her skin. Damn fool was lucky she didn't blast him through the telephone.

Cradling the black receiver between her head and shoulder, she set the heavy rotary base on the Formica counter.

The coffee canister on the counter was empty. Reaching up into the cupboard, she only half listened to his fool words. She stretched up on her toes for a fresh can. Why in the world had she let Jasmine put it up so high?

Because usually in the morning, the time a sane person made coffee, Jasmine was around.

"No, you listen. There is nothing the Association has to offer me if you aren't willing to take a risk, Terrance. If all you'll do is cater to… No, I don't care what you did ten years ago. I know that was good work."

The ground coffee smelled so good it almost made her smile. Doreen measured it out and filled the percolator with water, then plugged it in.

She leaned against the counter, phone receiver still at her ear. Damn it. She was taking these shoes off. And she might as well sit down.

Something smacked into the kitchen window before she made it to the table. The scent of cordite and ozone filled the kitchen.

"Terrance, I have to call you back!" He was shouting, a tinny bellow, as she slammed the black receiver down, yanked open the kitchen door, and stuck her head around the edge, protecting her body, but needing to see.

A small, smoldering wreck burned in the flowers against the kitchen wall. Flames still burst from the bundle, licking at the wood siding. Doreen scanned the yard. She felt a presence just outside the fence. Waiting.

No time to run for water. Holding out her right hand, palm open toward the fire, she spread her fingers wide, and then curled them close, choking out the flames. They sputtered and died, smoke rising from the pile of ash, paper, wood…and bone?

There would be time to investigate that later. Right now, she had to find out who had sent the thing, while they were still close by.

Without exposing herself any more than she already was.

Drawing herself all the way back behind the kitchen door, she closed her eyes. Found her center. Slowed her breathing way down, until it was barely a whisper through her nostrils.

Her eyes fluttered, and she reached. And caught the cool, papery feel of scales. The scent of sawdust mixed with loam.

"Snake."

There was a snake at the edge of her garden, and she was not going to let it in. It wasn't the good kind of snake, the kind who would eat the rats that gnawed on phone wires and made nests in the attic.

This was the kind of snake that could squeeze the life from a kitten. Or sink its fangs into the ankles of a child.

The snake had finally tracked Jasmine to their home.

"All you serpents have wisdom," Doreen whispered, "But I think I don't like what you know."

Reaching deep into the earth, and all the way up into the winter sun, Doreen sent out a blast that cracked the edges of the property, electrifying her protections, igniting the wards she'd set so long ago.

She smelled scorched skin and smiled.

"I think we've taken care of you for now, mister."

Doreen shook off her hands, grabbed a box of salt, and walked out into the garden.

Time to deal with the present the old snake had left her.

CHAPTER TWENTY-FIVE
JASMINE

Doreen and I were in the little sitting room at the front of the house, watching the news. A painting of a mountain lion in dry hills watched over the room. Low bookcases flanked the wooden cabinet that encased the Philco television set. That cabinet TV set was ten years old if it was a day.

It looked a little bit like an old-fashioned radio, but with a screen. Doreen must've gotten it secondhand somewhere because I didn't recall it from her and Hector's house in LA.

I sprawled out, cup of tea warming my hands, legs slung over the arms of an overstuffed chintz-covered chair, no shoes on my feet.

Aunt Doreen was sitting upright on the loveseat as usual, her only concession to relaxation being that she'd pushed the stack of magazines aside and her feet were on the coffee table, in light blue crocheted slippers.

She was looking better than she had. Less tired. And she had a sleek new haircut that followed the nice shape of her head, coming to curled wisps around her face. It shaved a few years off her, too. Doreen said Patrice had dragged her to the beauty parlor. I was glad.

Doreen needed more fun in her life.

My parents' house didn't have a television. My dad and I went to the library once a week to pick up a stack of reading materials, and mother wanted me practicing magic instead of, as she said, "rotting your brain." Novels were all right, but television was strictly out, despite my flagging popularity at school.

Doreen watched the news in black and white every night. The flickering images of horror coming back from Viet Nam embedded themselves in my eyes and brain. Occasional news items pertained to the Panthers, including the one clip of Huey I wished I could have watched again and again. Mostly, the news showed images of black men in berets with rifles on their backs. Some of them, I knew.

Hook in hand, glasses perched on her nose, and a ball of soft purple acrylic yarn at her side, Doreen was crocheting another pair of slippers for me.

How she could calmly crochet when a weird, magic snake bomb was still smoldering in a tin bucket at the bottom of the garden, I didn't know. Granted, we'd covered it in salt, and Doreen had warded the shit out of it, but still…I was feeling jumpy.

Too jumpy to leave Doreen for tonight's meeting, no matter what was on the agenda. No matter how much I was supposed to be showing up so they could see how trustworthy I was.

I wanted to be dealing with the thing in the bucket, but Doreen said we had to do the attic temple up. Deal with it right.

"It'll keep for now," she said. And she was too tired to clear the attic for ritual right then.

So here we were, watching TV news.

Then a pasty white, bulbous face filled the screen, leaning over a desk, mouth forming words my ears couldn't hear over the buzzing that started in my head. This was the man my parents, a few of their friends—and half the white folks in Los Angeles, it seemed—talked about with mouths twisted up like they were eating lemons.

J. Edgar Hoover. Something about him was wrong. It was as though, through the pale shades of black and white, I could feel an emanation off his bleached-out skin. It wasn't exactly magic I was sensing, but…

"Aunt Doreen? You notice anything about him?"

She pushed her reading glasses down her nose and looked at the TV. "Hoover? He's kind of pasty and portly and looks a little mean. But he always looks that way."

Doreen turned her head to me then, inquiring.

"No. Not that," I said. "Something...there's something... It isn't magic, but look just behind him. Look over his shoulders. Those weird threads."

Doreen actually set the crocheting aside at that point, slipped her feet back to the faded, rose-patterned carpet, and leaned in toward the television. I could feel her settle into her belly and open up her Sight. When she did that, it felt like the lightest of feather touches near the hairline at my temples. I sipped my tea and waited.

She drew a strong, whistling breath through her teeth. "I think you're right, Jasmine girl. There's something emanating from that nasty man. Like puppet strings."

A commercial interrupted her examination with a loud blast of horns and a smiling, vapid white woman with smooth hair holding up a box of laundry soap. I swung up from the chair and flipped the dial to off. The television hissed and crackled as the screen irised itself down to darkness.

Doreen had a hand to her lips, pondering.

"These times we live in, girl, they are something big. Something strange." Leaving her ball of purple yarn and half a crocheted slipper on the couch, she rose and shook out her hands. "We're going to the kitchen. I need a cup of tea myself."

She shuffled down the hallway. "Or maybe a small glass of wine."

I followed her, shoulders tense with what I thought I'd seen, not able to make any sense of it. If Aunt Doreen wanted a glass of wine, it couldn't be good. I don't think I had ever seen the woman take a drink more than once or twice a year at parties when I was a child. And I hadn't seen her drink alcohol at all since I moved north.

My socks slipped a little on the wood floor in the hall. By the time I entered the kitchen, Doreen was already in the pantry, rummaging. She came out with a bottle of red Italian wine. The kind with the bulbous base and raffia wrapping. Chianti.

"Get out that salami, girl, and see if we have a block of cheese. If I'm going to have a glass of this, I need some food."

There was a thick chunk of yellow cheddar next to half a hard salami in the fridge. While I got the cutting board and knife, Aunt Doreen poured the wine into small water glasses. I raised an eyebrow at her and she tsked.

"You're old enough to have a glass of wine, girl. I haven't let the government into my kitchen yet, and I'm not about to begin. Sit down."

The wine tasted slightly of cherries and was just a little acidic at the base. I decided I liked this one. And the salty salami was just right.

When I was out with folks, beer was our drink of choice, not that I drank often or much. It affected the magic, decreasing my power. Huh. Now that I thought of it, no sorcerer I had ever encountered drank more than a beer or occasional cocktail, if they even drank at all. My parents didn't keep alcohol in the house, only buying some special for an occasional party.

I'd have to ask Doreen about that.

She sipped at her glass, occasionally cutting off a piece of cheddar or salami. I knew better than to interrupt a sorcerer while she was thinking, and rolled another sip of wine across my tongue.

I could see why people liked drinking wine. If it didn't mess with my head, maybe I would be one of those regular drinkers. As it was though, I just couldn't see it.

Finally, Aunt Doreen set down her glass and spoke again. "There is definitely something wrong with that man, but I'm damned if I know exactly what it is. And if those were some kind of puppet strings, which direction were they going?"

She looked at me and asked, "What do *you* think?"

I stammered a little bit, caught off guard.

"Me? All I know is I saw something strange." I searched my mind for the right words, casting back to what first alerted me that there was something less than usual. Something wrong.

"I didn't see the strings you're talking about. It seemed like something was around him. Something dark," I continued. "I don't want to say it wasn't *human*, but I just don't know what it was."

Doreen was still watching me. Intent. She seemed to have forgotten all about the salami and cheese, and the half full glass near her hand on the red Formica table.

I took a breath. And a slow drink of the wine. Stalling for more time, I sawed off another piece of salami and cheese, the taste of cheddar and salty meat mingling on my tongue. Damn. Doreen was still waiting.

"Okay. It seemed like…like something was *cloaking* him. Like some creature had wrapped itself around him like a robe, you dig? I don't know, does that sound crazy?"

Doreen paused for a moment, then answered, "I'm sorry to say, Jasmine girl, that doesn't sound crazy at all. It's interesting that we picked up on different images, though."

She picked up her glass of wine and took another drink.

"I'm starting to think you are right about the Association. It needs to get off its high horse and do something. *I* need to do something."

"Do you think you're ready?"

Doreen waved her hand at that, like she was swatting away a fly. "Enough of that. All the Powers are telling me it's time to get back to my work. I've known it since before you showed up on my doorstep. I could feel it coming with you, all the way up the coast."

I didn't know how such a thing was possible. My magic didn't reach that far. Not yet. But here we were, her words hanging between us in the air.

We sat there in that kitchen, under the hanging light, at the red Formica table, drinking Chianti and eating cheese. We sat there for another hour, but neither of us spoke again that night.

But I was wondering what the connection was between the white man on the news and the spell covered in salt in Doreen's backyard.

Chapter Twenty-Six
Jasmine

Doreen and I both dove back into magic like our lives depended on it. Later, we would figure out they did.

The Panthers wanted to know exactly what I could do for them.... I had to keep saying, "I don't know," and go home to practice more.

They didn't much like that.

I put in extra time on breakfasts and at the pantry to make up for their disappointment.

Doreen and I packed more salt around the spell. It finally stopped smoking, though it still stank. Doreen hadn't been able to put a trace on it. We were hoping to get more information once we had a better working space. One that wasn't in the house itself.

We worked all the next day clearing out the attic space above the small bungalow.

By the following evening, a good chunk of floor space was open and boxes were stacked neatly along the edges of the slope-ceilinged room. Doreen didn't have too much stuff herself. I could see that most of the boxes were things shipped up by Cecelia, my mother, postmarked around ten years ago.

Turned out that they were magical supplies.

We set up at a long table, with two wooden folding chairs, under the bare bulb in the center of the room.

"Have to get a shade for that," Doreen muttered. We would, if we were to be spending any significant amount of time up here. The light was harsh to work by, white-yellow glow bouncing from the Douglas fir planks beneath us to the exposed redwood beams above.

The whole room smelled of old wood and cardboard. Not a bad smell, but not exactly what I thought of when I thought about magic.

I had a feeling we'd be changing the scent of things pretty soon.

So far, we had been opening up the cartons, box by box, sorting through to see what might be useful, and what were old ingredients, long past their use-by date, crumbling away in velvet pouches or paper sacks.

One thing that stuck out was an amazing quartz crystal ball. I mean, this was no clear glass party orb, this was the real deal, with fissures and milky places marring the gorgeous clarity.

"That was your grandmother's," she said, jerking her chin toward the sphere as I polished it with a piece of old T-shirt in my lap. "She was the best sorcerer I ever met. As a matter of fact, she was the best sorcerer of her whole generation."

Doreen went back to rummaging through the carton at her feet, pulling things from the cardboard and unwrapping them on the table. Tarot cards. A wooden pendulum, and then a brass one of a smaller size. A round sheet of onyx glass…and another batch of crumbling, dried-out incense that smelled of frankincense and dried roses.

She continued, "She trained a lot of people, your grandmother. Men, women. Black. White. Korean. Mexican. Even folks that weren't sorcerers. Everyone came to her."

"Was it hard for you and mom, being the daughters of someone like her? Or was it cool?"

Doreen smiled at that. "A little bit of both, I think. Momma was a powerhouse. We were all a little bit in awe of her, I think. But we loved her, too. She had a kindness to her heart." Doreen paused a moment, musing. "That kindness was the true proof of her power."

I set the gleaming quartz sphere on the wooden base I'd found wrapped next to it in the box. As soon as it left my hands, I felt a little sad. Like I wanted to cradle it and gaze into it for the rest of my life. Strange. I'd never had that reaction to a magical object before.

"You like that one because it's tied to the power of ocean. Momma took it down to the ocean the first full moon after she received it as a gift. Took it down and bathed it in the waters every full moon for a full six months before she ever looked inside it. Said it gave her true dreams and told her what was in every person's heart."

I needed to think about that. It felt important, like there was a secret hidden in Doreen's words, and Momma Beatrice's too. But I couldn't process them yet. The sphere, much as I longed to touch it, would need to wait.

"Doreen, what did you mean that kindness was the proof of Grandma's power?"

She kept thumbing through a stack of papers from one of the cartons, a variety of shapes and sizes. Some of the papers were clearly handmade, set with flowers and herbs; others looked like parchment. These were mixed in with old, lined pages that looked ripped out from someone's school notebook.

"Well, magic, you see," Doreen said, not looking up from the papers, "is all about resonance. I'm sure Cecelia passed that along to you."

Mother had. It was one of the earliest things she tried to teach me. I got it in principle, and could feel when my magic grabbed ahold of that connection.

Doreen continued. "If a person is open to other people, and animals, plants, stars, anything, really, that person has a stronger tie to the resonance of everything. An angry person is closed. A hateful person might generate a certain kind of power that is useful in its way, but that person's magic will always be limited by their need to force the æthers through their anger."

I could feel my brow furrowing at that. "I don't get what you're after, Aunt Doreen. I can't figure out what you're trying to tell me here."

She sighed and looked up at me. "It's so simple, once you get it, but I recall feeling just as confused as you do, once upon a time."

Setting the stack of papers aside, she reached for another carton and began dragging out more wrapped parcels, placing them on my side of the card table. I reached for one, feeling the smooth surface of the newsprint under my fingers.

I'd need some cocoa butter before bed. All this paper and cardboard was drying out my hands.

"So imagine this: when two people are best friends, or when they fall in love, don't they have more resonance with one another than two people who barely know each other? Or who fight all the time?"

"Yes," I replied, unwrapping a five-inch-tall statue of an Egyptian figure. A lion-headed woman sitting on a throne. She had an orb over her head, and small, upright breasts beneath her tunic. My mother had a statue very similar to this one.

Sekhmet. Goddess of medicine and war. Goddess of women's flow of blood. Really, anything to do with blood was in her realm. Cecelia called on Sekhmet's magic to help women with all kinds of troubles. I wondered what Doreen used her for.

"Okay. So you see how resonance works. You learned that when your powers first came on. But now tell me which pair of people generate more power, the ones who barely know one another or the two who fight all the time?"

A glimmer of understanding rose up inside me. "I think I get it now. The fighting people generate more power than those who don't really care. So a sorcerer can raise power and channel it that way. But the anger and fighting also limits their ability to work in other areas, or with other flows of magic?"

"Yes. That's basically it," Doreen said. "So your grandmother's kindness helped her magic because she was more open to the magic everywhere. She didn't close off her heart and mind to those around her. As a consequence, everything around her helped feed into her power."

Doreen sneezed, then tossed a bundle of old herbs into the small metal trash can she'd made me carry up the stairs.

"I'm not saying Momma was always *nice*, mind you. But she was kind. It's good for sorcerers to know the difference."

There was a pile of papers at my feet from the unwrapping of the past two hours, and three statues on the table—Sekhmet, Isis, and Osiris. I bet the rest of their family was still wrapped up in the box, but I all of a sudden felt tired. I couldn't take in anymore.

And I had a meeting to get to.

"Doreen? Do you mind if we call it a night here? I want to think some more on what you've said,"

She gave me a look, like she wasn't one hundred percent fooled by me, but nodded her head.

"You go on, Jasmine girl. You do what you need to do. Just make sure you don't go too far away."

Doreen's words felt like a warning and a blessing, all combined. Part of me was sure I'd understand in time. The rest of me just wanted to head off to West Oakland. And Jimmy.

Chapter Twenty-Seven
Doreen

It was chilly and gray, already dark outside. Winter was coming on fast and Doreen wished she'd buttoned up her coat before locking the front door of the shop.

Her navy coat was flapping as she wrestled with the gate that always seemed to roll back just fine in the mornings and stick like hell when it was time to close.

"Come *on*!" Doreen gave a huge yank, the metal grinding at her hands, and almost fell as the gate decided to let go of its grip and slam closed.

"Damn," she muttered, forcing the padlock through the two holes in either side, securing the front of the shop from thieves.

Not that anyone wanted to steal flowers, but some folks were always in the market for petty cash.

She heard a car stop at the sidewalk and turned as a black man in a dark suit circled the car and opened the passenger door.

Helen stepped out, all white-skinned and gleaming under the yellow streetlight that bounced off a tasteful green skirt-suit and practical heeled pumps.

Practical heeled for someone who didn't stand on her feet all day. Doreen was aware of her own lace-up shoes and the dark support stockings covering her legs as if she were an old lady.

Well. Some people worked for a living.

Helen sure was beautiful though, chestnut-brown hair swept back into a chignon, highlighting sharp cheekbones. And her magic tasted like licorice.

Doreen could almost smell it now, weaving through the scents of gathering gray clouds, the oil slicks, old piss, and newspapers.

Damn it. Doreen couldn't afford to think of Helen that way. Couldn't afford to think of anyone right now, let alone the possible enemy.

"Doreen."

Helen moved toward her on the filthy sidewalk Doreen had just swept clean that morning.

Then there were Helen's lips, cool, first on one cheek, then the other. And the scent of talcum on her skin.

And just a hint of licorice.

Damn it all to hell.

"What are you doing here?"

Doreen didn't even say her name. Throwing the shop keys into her handbag, she snapped it closed. "Terrance send you?"

"I'm not here to fight, Doreen. I just wanted to have dinner. To talk."

"Hah! You mean to tell me you flew all the way up here to have dinner?"

Helen's jaws clenched at that. Good.

"Terrance doesn't know I'm here. Please. Will you get in the car?"

Okay. That was interesting news.

"All right. But we have to do the night drop at the bank."

Doreen eased into the town car's leather seats, told the driver which bank she needed, and looked at Helen, who hadn't stopped staring at her the whole time.

"So, talk," Doreen said.

"You've changed. I thought I felt something all the way down south, but now that I'm next to you, I can see that it's true."

Doreen looked out the tinted window at the barber shop, the record store, the boarded-up former bakery. This was her world, not the woman sitting next to her.

"I'm doing magic again." Doreen faced Helen, looking into those light brown eyes. "But that doesn't mean I owe the Association anything."

The car shushed to a stop at the bank, and Doreen looked around for the handle to crank the window down.

Helen quietly said, "John."

The window whirred and slid down, easy as you please. Of course.

As soon as the money bag clunked into the night drop, the window rose again.

"What kind of food are you in the mood for?"

"Helen. Really. I don't care."

"John? Chez Panisse, please." She turned back to Doreen and smiled. "I made a reservation, just in case."

Doreen groaned. The fancy place in Berkeley had just opened. If Helen was paying, that was fine.

"We need you, Doreen." Helen's pale hand slid across the dark leather to touch Doreen's arm. She could feel Helen's magic reaching for her, cool like ice. Doreen's fire responded, rising to meet the spot Helen's fingers rested.

Doreen didn't want this. Didn't want any of it. The Association could be damned, for all she cared right then.

But her magic thought differently.

Stifling a groan, Doreen moved Helen's hand off her arm.

"Helen, did you know a sixteen-year-old boy was just killed by police here? Did you know they are bashing students heads in? Do you watch the news at all in that fancy house on Mulholland Drive? Have you ever even been to Watts?"

Helen's lips thinned. "The Association is in trouble."

Well, that stopped Doreen colder than the glacier gathered at the base of Helen's spine.

A shot cracked Helen's window, showering her pretty green suit in cubes of glass. Doreen slammed her down to the seat, ducking their heads as close to the floor as possible. Glass scratched at her hands and cheeks. She fought to slow her breathing down.

The car stopped then, and started rocking. Tilting her head, Doreen could see bodies pressed against the windows. The front door opened and the driver was dragged out.

Doreen gave a quick thanks to whoever was keeping the men on Helen's side busy rocking the car instead of reaching in and throttling them.

Time to stop this.

"You okay?" she asked Helen.

"Fine. Yes."

"I'm getting out to stop this. You stay in here if that feels better. Your white skin might not make these boys too happy."

"Just give me a minute to catch my breath."

The rocking jostled Doreen against Helen. She could hear the driver's voice shouting.

How was she going to open the door?

Doreen pushed the fire up into her fingertips and lightly touched the metal casing the window on her side of the car.

"I'm going to light up all the metal, so stay on the leather."

"Wait! I can help you."

Helen put her hand on Doreen's back. She could feel the ice enter her field, boosting her fire.

"Fire and ice," Helen said. "My people say they once created the world."

"Let's see if they can bust us out of this."

Taking a big breath, Doreen let the two forces twine themselves together and then pushed them through her fingers. Licorice and cinnamon. Glacier and flame. The metal groaned and then sparked.

"Shit, man!" The shouting outside the car changed and the rocking stopped as men yelped and shoved each other, trying to get away from the car.

Doreen just hoped John the driver was still okay.

Tamping the energies down, she could smell singed cloth and skin. Not hers. The men outside.

"I'm going out."

Shoving the cleared door open, small cubes of glass falling from her lap, Doreen was greeted by shocked and angry faces. All men. All different shades of brown.

"Watchu doing, sister?" one of them called. "They kidnapping you?"

Doreen spread her hands out, fingers flexed. The men all took another step back. The driver was on the ground, panting. There was blood on his face and his pants were torn.

"John, do you need help?"

He pushed at the tarmac, hissing with pain, and struggled into a sitting position. "I'll be fine."

Good man.

Then Doreen smelled something else. A strange undercurrent that didn't belong on a street in downtown Oakland.

Damn it.

It was snake.

Scanning the men all the way around the car, she couldn't…

"I would stay put, if I were you," Doreen called over her shoulder. One of the men froze. He had decided to use her turned back to creep closer.

No one ever counted on a sorcerer's heightened senses.

"This really isn't your fight," she said.

And then she saw him, a slight man in a black suit, tie knotted at his neck, pale skin and crisp white shirt gleaming under the yellow streetlight. He stood bold as you please in front of the gas station half a block away, hands in his trouser pockets like he didn't even need to protect himself from anything.

The sun was so far west it was almost night, but the man wore dark glasses on his almost incandescent pale face.

Then that white man smiled.

Oh yes. He was a snake all right. Doreen could feel the papery scale sense of him slithering across the road.

She put a command into her voice. "You men had best be on your way. There's nothing for you here."

The driver was standing by now. Helen had wisely stayed in the car. If she hadn't, all bets would have been off.

Doreen gave a little shove on the edges of the raggedy circle of men. "C'mon man. Let's go."

One of the men looked at Doreen as he turned to go. "You best tell your rich white friends that Oakland don't need them around."

"I'll do that."

When she looked back toward the gas station, the man in the black suit was gone, and the streetlight in front of the gas station was dark.

Chapter Twenty-Eight
Carol

There was a big storeroom behind the red shop curtain, and Carol wasn't exactly sure how she'd gotten there.

Ernesto set a thick-sided brown mug in front of her. Its steam smelled like sage and honey. When she wrapped her icy cold hands around it, he said, "Careful! That's very hot."

"I'm just so cold."

The woman rummaged in a low chest at the back of the room, set under a bank of high windows with mottled privacy glass. She came back with a purple blanket, woven with stripes of green and cream, and draped it around Carol's shoulders.

It was warm enough outside—autumn in Southern California—but Carol was cold down to the core, still queasy from the visions, though the shaking was slowing down at least.

The woman wanted to know what Carol had seen.

What she had seen were volcanoes erupting from beneath the city streets. Stars melting in the sky.

What Carol had seen was her own death. She had felt the bullets enter, smacking muscle, fat, and bone, jerking her body up and back as puffs of smoke exited the wounds.

Carol had felt herself falling. Falling into water that closed over her head. Falling into oceans filled with massive humpback whales, barnacles covering their flesh. Falling from the light into a place blue-green with shadows.

Falling and falling and falling until she fell through a hole carved into the center of the universe. The pressure building until it just...stopped.

And she saw two spiders there, weaving silk. Two spiders making webs.

"Two spiders," she murmured into the cup of fragrant tea, clutching at the heavy ceramic cup even though it was still almost too hot to hold.

It was all Carol could do to stop her teeth from chattering.

"Drink that tea, maga mia. Get the warmth inside," the woman said.

Carol blew across the fragrant brew, trying to cool it enough to take a sip. It burned a little as it hit her tongue, but the woman was right, the warmth felt good going down. And the honey was delicious.

Ernesto sat on a spindly wooden chair across the round walnut table. It was barely big enough for three people, really a table for two, tucked back in a tiny kitchen area in the middle of the big storage room.

Carol's eyes scanned the floor-to-ceiling metal office shelves, barely taking in the boxes and jars until they stopped at a quart jar stuffed with what looked like pale seed pods.

The woman—Carol still didn't know her name, and it didn't feel right to call someone she'd barely even met "abuela"—noticed.

Carol doubted the woman missed anything. Ever.

"Those are the seeds from the mountain laurel. They remind us that even things filled with poison bring beauty to the world."

The woman rose and took the jar down from the shelf. Bracing the jar, she unscrewed the lid and shook a few of the pale, pink-tinged white seeds into her hand. They were shaped somewhat like small plums with tapering ends.

She handed the jar to Ernesto, who screwed the lid back on and returned it to the shelf.

"See," the woman said, cracking open one of the pods. The seeds inside were bright, bloodred. "These seeds are poison to eat. But the laurel tree is a beauty, creating purple flowers in the spring. Its leaves cure many illnesses of the skin, cooling heat and irritation."

Those green eyes speared Carol once again. "So you see, not all poisonous things are bad. Everything in life is a mix of many things."

She set the pods on the dark wood and looked over Carol's head. Carol's scalp tingled in response. The woman wasn't looking past her; she was looking *at* Carol with some sort of elsewhere sight.

Ernesto was still working with Carol on that, even though she should have mastered it by now. He said the sight was always hardest for Earth magicians. Earth sorcerers who shouldn't be cracking their skulls with visions.

The woman must have approved of what she saw because she nodded her sharp chin.

"Tell me about the spiders."

Casting back to the visions made Carol's stomach lurch, and she took another sip of tea, trying to calm it down. And buying a few seconds more of time.

Clearing what felt like a seed-pod-sized wad of phlegm from her throat, she sipped some more before letting out a sigh and gathering her thoughts to speak.

"One was a sickly kind of white. Not really white, but so pale it almost looked white. It was huge. Bloated looking. They were both huge…"

Carol looked down into the mug where the pale tea softly rippled from the shaking of her hands. As if she could use it as a scrying bowl, and call the images back through the green-tinged water.

"The other spider was darker. A bit smaller. Brown. They were both spinning silk as fast as they could, and weaving webs. But they weren't walking around, or, you know, rappelling, making webs the way real spiders do. It was weird."

She continued, "They sat in the middle of their webs and cast the silk out from their bodies, sending it as far as they could, making shapes in the air. Like they could do it with the tips of their legs. Or with their minds."

The woman had her head in her hands, as though by just listening, she could see. She probably could.

"It felt like they were in competition. And like they weren't the only ones doing this weaving. I got the sense that they were part of some kind spider network."

Ernesto grimaced at the inadvertent pun.

Carol grinned at that. It felt good to smile, even at something so dumb. "Sorry about that. I couldn't think of a better word."

"No," the woman said, "network is just the right word. We know these spiders. We have seen them. The brown spider seems to be a friend."

She reached out a hand to cover one of Carol's and leaned in close.

"The white spider? It is spreading poison without beauty. The bigger and fatter it gets, and the more its webs grow, the less beauty it contains. Entiendes?"

"Do I understand? I'm not sure. I mean, I can feel it. I can sense what you mean. But I can't really make my brain understand it."

"That is okay, maga. You can understand in your skin for now. That is the best way for you Earth sorcerers to learn things anyway."

"Can you…" Carol paused, and changed what she had been about to say. "Can you tell me your name?"

"Ah! Yes. Of course. My name is Rosalia and you have my permission to call me that. I am the head of a group of people who have no leader." She smiled. "We are called Las Manos by those who need to know."

The Hands. The hands of magic? The helping hands? The hands of the ancestors or the Gods?

"All those things," Rosalia replied, even though Carol hadn't said a thing. Shit. She'd have to guard her mind, if Ernesto brought them back again.

"Can you teach me what I need to know, Rosalia?"

The woman threw back her head and laughed at that, smacking her hands on the walnut table and jostling the tea.

"You need a lot, maga mia. And this one"—she gestured with her head to Ernesto—"he's a pretty good teacher for you still. But yes, yes. I see there are more things you need to know."

All of a sudden, Rosalia was perfectly still. "I will teach you what you need to know about these visions. And you will tell Las Manos all you see."

Rosalia held out her right hand.

"Do we have a deal?"

Fear struck Carol's chest then, as she stared into those green eyes. Breaking the gaze, Carol glanced down at the seed pods. Poison. And beauty. Spiders weaving their webs.

She looked to Ernesto and saw that he kept his own face empty. The shields on his mind were impenetrable.

Carol had to make this decision on her own.

Was she about to eat poison? Or was she being offered a chance to grow something good?

All of a sudden, she felt the full weight of her eighteen years.

This must be what it would be like from now on. She would have to make more and more decisions without knowing whether or not they were the right ones.

Throwing off the purple blanket and shoving the tea mug away with a scrape, she looked into Rosalia's green eyes again.

And held out her right hand.

Chapter Twenty-Nine
Jasmine

The meeting room was packed and I was starting to feel closed in. Trapped.

That thing had followed me to HQ again, I was sure of it. I'd gotten permission from leadership to set some wards around the property. I hoped they would hold against whatever it was that had attacked here and at home.

Meanwhile, I thought I'd feel safer in the house, surrounded by my comrades, but I just felt closed in.

The old office chair creaked beneath my thighs as I shifted, trying to find a comfortable position without the whole thing collapsing beneath me. I swear, you'd think I was one of the more lush sisters, the way the chair was groaning and complaining every time I moved.

Cigarette smoke was thick in the air, yellowing the white walls and curling the edges of the political posters everywhere. I'd taught myself to breathe through my nose, despite the sting. At least the air got filtered a little bit that way.

I hadn't quite gotten used to it yet. My parents never smoked, and didn't allow their friends to light up in the house.

It was a Wednesday evening and I was at a meeting of the Liberation School. Jimmy was up front, quoting Chairman Mao. I'd read the

Little Red Book, of course. We all had. But I far preferred the words of that righteous brother, Marx. Marx made sense to me. His words felt grounded in human experience, despite his idealism.

There was something about Mao I didn't quite trust, and I couldn't tell you why. So I kept my mouth shut and tried to listen. But my mind kept wandering.

Carol had called, wanting to talk some more about her visions, and meeting some powerful old hechicera in East LA.

So we had a white spider. A brown spider. And now a snake. I couldn't see how it all fit together. If it did.

"Our point of departure is to serve the people whole-heartedly and never for a moment divorce ourselves from the masses."

I struggled to pay attention to Mao's words and what Jimmy was saying about them, but I really couldn't focus all too well.

It should have been Huey leading the meeting. Despite huge organizing pushes to get him free, and crowds still out in the streets, he was still in prison, accused of killing a cop. We all knew that wasn't true. Too much evidence to the contrary. The case had finally gotten international attention. That was something, I guessed.

Landing in Oakland and the first place I went was the courthouse surrounded by Panthers? The threads of destiny had tugged me here.

Synchronicity is always magic, Mr. Alvarez taught us. But what about these spiders and snakes? In all the magic Carol and I had been taught, the fact that people could use insects and animals to get at us? I didn't recall it ever being mentioned.

We learned everything there was to know about working with the elements, but no one ever stopped to tell us to pay attention to ladybugs, or cockroaches, or eels. I mean, I was supposed to be aware of ocean creatures, but that was just because my affinity was for water.

Never did I make the connection that there might be other reasons to pay attention.

Was the Association censoring magic? All this made me wonder what else we hadn't learned. I shook my head.

Tanya gave me a look across the smoky room. I must've been scowling, too. Shooting her a quick smile, I shook my head again to let her know, "not about this meeting."

Except, I had some questions about all this now, too. How was Huey still alive? By all accounts, the stomach wound he took in the crossfire should have killed him.

My suspicions regarding that were deep. But what exactly…?

"Political power grows out of the barrel of a gun." Jimmy was quoting Mao again.

How had Huey even gotten caught? None of the truly powerful Panther leaders seemed to get pulled in. You'd think the police would want to capture leadership, but here they all were. Tarika and Barbara were free. And now, in Chicago, Fred was free. In Los Angeles, Angela, Ericka, Geronimo Pratt, and the others were free.

How was this occurring?

Who the hell were these people, and where had they come from?

And what else didn't I know?

Jimmy was pacing in the front of the room, lithe and sexy in flared jeans and a tight green, ribbed turtleneck sweater. He was talking about Bobby Seale now.

Another Panther captured.

Bobby was in prison in Chicago. They shackled him to a chair in the courtroom. Gagging him. Can you imagine? A judge gagging someone in the courtroom, and chaining them to a metal chair?

"They used steel chains on our brother. And the pigs had to gag his mouth to silence him. They were so afraid of the power of his voice. They *knew* Bobby's voice was the voice of the people!"

Jimmy sent a shiver down my back. The cold lodged in my belly.

There was something…tapping at the back of my skull. Something I was supposed to be paying attention to, that I hadn't gotten yet.

Shifting on the cushions of my chair in the back of the room, I felt the weave scratching at the bare backs of my arms. I'd have to remember to wear long sleeves to Liberation School in the future.

But I had wanted to look nice for Jimmy. So I wore a frilly, short sleeved blouse.

A low grumbling cut under Jimmy's words, and a strong scent underscored the acrid cigarette smoke. I swear, if they could, some of the brothers would've been pacing the room by now.

"When we gonna bust some heads?" Carlos growled.

"When we gonna bust Huey outta jail?" another voice replied.

Jimmy paused, arms crossed over his slender chest. "We have to plan the revolution. You know the sisters and the rest of the committee are working..."

Leroy stood up, a towering mass of muscle, sideburns newly clipped into shape. "With all respect, man, you been teaching Mao tonight. And Mao Zedong himself says"—Leroy cleared his throat—"'If you want to know the taste of a pear, you must change the pear by eating it yourself. If you want to know the theory and methods of revolution, you must take part in revolution. All genuine knowledge originates in direct experience.'"

"We *are* learning theory here tonight, man," Jimmy replied. "And what do you think our patrols are, and the Breakfast for Children Program, the school, the clinic? What do you think they are? They look like revolution to me, brother!"

Leroy held up a hand. "We need more action, brother. Two of our strongest cats in jail, man. How you think that looks to the people we're trying to organize? How you think that looks to the Man?"

I was staring at Leroy. Did I see a glimmer of something around his skin?

The musky scent increased in the room.

Despite the cold in my belly, sweat broke out on my face, mixing with the cigarette smoke. My skin began to sting. It was all too much.

Scrambling for my fringed bag, I grabbed my coat and began to shove my way out of the room.

"I'm sorry. Excuse me. I don't feel well."

Whether the tightening of my throat and my stomach meant I was excited or afraid, I couldn't say.

I just knew I needed air.

Chapter Thirty
Jasmine

When I stumbled out the front, brocade coat in my hands, a guard turned his head from the foot of the steps.

"You should stay on the porch awhile." He held his rifle in both hands, across his chest. Not aiming, but ready to shoot.

I looked down the walkway, past the black wrought iron fence, into the play of light and shadow that was always night in Oakland.

The other guard, skinny Jerrold again, stood in front of a black town car arguing with someone who was blocked from my view.

What the hell was that fancy-ass car doing in this part of town?

The car had barely made it to a stop front of the house before the guards stopped it. I could see a shape through the blasted-out passenger window, a pale movement behind the remaining chunks of glass.

"What's happening?" I asked.

"Just stay put, please."

A whiff of cinnamon caught at my nose and I recognized the second voice.

"Aunt Doreen?"

"Jasmine!" Her voice carried, strong above the noises from the house behind me and the street just past the drive.

"Tell this man who I am!"

I started toward her, pausing two steps down. "It's my aunt."

The guard nodded and let me through.

My boots crunched on the walk and a gust of wind hit me. So cold. I dragged my coat on as I walked. Yep. That was definitely a white woman in the car. Shit. It looked like Helen. What the hell?

"Jerrold, meet my Aunt Doreen." Jerrold kept his .22 in his right hand, but I could see his shoulders relax.

"I tried to tell him that, but he wouldn't let us through."

Jerrold spoke then. "You come barreling up to HQ in a fancy car with a shot-out window and we're going to be cautious, ma'am."

That was an understatement. Frankly, Doreen and Helen were lucky they weren't both on the ground.

"Hey man." The door slammed. I turned and saw two other men had come out to the porch from the house. "We got to get to SF to put out the paper tonight."

I wanted to touch Jerrold's shoulder to reassure him, but knew better than to ever touch a guard. Shoulders relaxed or not, the cat was still pretty keyed up.

"Aunt Doreen, what's happening?" *And why is Helen here in that damn fancy car?* I wanted to ask.

"Jasmine." The cinnamon scent was coming off her in waves, and I could feel the magic popping off her skin. The crackling iceberg smell of Helen's was quieter, but still present. What was going on?

Doreen continued. "We just got shot at. And it has something to do with the present that was dropped at the house."

My own magic surged, and my brain struggled to snap the information into place.

Jerrold stiffened up again. "What exactly do you mean, ma'am?" he asked, voice a quiet knife that, frankly, freaked me out a bit.

"And did you lead someone here?" he said.

I practically felt Jerrold's hand gripping the gun as he spoke. Spit filled my mouth and I tasted the steel from my molars.

Steadying myself, I spoke. "Jerrold. It's not as if folks don't know where all the Panther offices are. There's no secret who we are. That's part of the point."

"Don't lecture me on the Panthers, sister." He raised his gun slightly.

"And don't raise your gun to a sister." Jimmy. I'd been so focused on Jerrold and Doreen, I hadn't recognized his footsteps on the stairs, figuring it was just the other guard or one of the men heading to the San Francisco office.

Jerrold and Jimmy faced off, the light from the porch and the streetlight highlighting that, though they were both thin and muscular, with tightly packed Afros, they couldn't be more different.

Jerrold's face had a cruelty that I hadn't quite noticed before. There was a twist to his mouth and a harshness in his eyes. He couldn't help his pockmarked skin, but harsh eyes were something a man cultivated. My daddy taught me that. Jimmy, even steeled for confrontation, just looked beautiful to me.

"Stand down, man," Jimmy said. "These women aren't a threat to you."

"It's on your head, man, if these bitches bring a fight to our door. This one already brought some weird shit." Jerrold jerked his chin my way.

Cinnamon met ocean, met ice. I could feel Doreen and Helen feeding me their magic. I mashed it all together in a ball, keeping my hands down below my waist, hoping the men wouldn't notice anything. Ready.

"Let it go, man," Jimmy gently pushed Jerrold's gun down, gaze locked on him. "Why don't you take a break?"

"Nah." Jerrold spit on the ground at Jimmy's feet. "I'm on my shift, man. I don't walk away."

"Come back on up the porch, man. Give the cat some space." It was the other guard, whose name I didn't know.

Jerrold glared at Jimmy, nodded, and walked away, boot heels striking the steps like hammers on an anvil.

Some teen boys from the neighborhood had gathered on the sidewalk by this time, and old neighbors were standing on their porches or peering through curtains, checking out the fancy car.

"Can we get outta here, man?" said one of the other men.

"Go," said Jerrold, taking up his post in front of the door again.

The two men loped down the steps, smacking the black town car with their hands before running across the street to a patched-up blue Impala.

The heavy doors slammed and the engine rolled over.

"What is going on, Doreen?" I asked.

Jimmy talked over me. "It isn't the best idea for you to be here, ma'am."

Doreen's jaw set. "Would the two of you be quiet? I need to speak!"

She lowered her voice then. "Jimmy, I don't know what all my girl here tells you, but we got a nasty surprise delivered to our house this week. And our window got shot out tonight, as you can see."

Doreen looked straight at me then. "What I'm trying to tell you is that the two things are related. I saw him tonight."

"Saw who?" Jimmy and I both said.

Doreen huffed at that.

"And why is Helen here?"

"The snake. The snake is here. And the snake means us all harm. This is more than just us, Jasmine girl. This is about the whole situation. And we've got some thinking to do."

"But Helen..."

"Helen is here to help us. She managed to convince me, and I aim to let her convince you, too."

Helen ducked her head so we could see her face, which was pinched with fear. I'd never even known she could be afraid.

But then, I bet she'd never been shot at before.

"You too, young man. If you want to know," Doreen said.

Jimmy shifted on his feet, back and forth. Looked at me. Then back at Doreen.

"I do, ma'am. But not right now. I still have work to do here tonight."

I didn't blame him. I didn't want to know right then either.

But it seemed I had no choice.

Chapter Thirty-One
Doreen

By the time the three women got back to the house, Jasmine was terrified and Doreen was spitting mad. Helen retreated into herself, biding her time.

They trooped into the kitchen, Jasmine flinging that big fringed bag of hers onto the table, even though she knew Doreen hated it. Doreen kept her lips closed, went to the sink and ran the water until it was cool. She needed a drink.

"Helen, would you like a glass of water?"

"No thank you," she murmured, sitting down on one of the red padded chairs that matched the Formica kitchen table as if she was at a white-cloth-covered table at Chez Panisse.

There was no fancy dinner on the schedule anymore. And Doreen still had no idea why Helen was even there.

Doreen had no desire to do this thing. To confront the conversation that had been brewing like a storm for weeks, battering at the windows of her tidy home.

Doreen stood there on the white linoleum floor, hands crossed over her breasts, smelling her own cinnamon scent swirling up off her skin.

Her heart pounded and the taste of salt filled her mouth. Jasmine. That ocean magic of hers.

In that moment, Doreen didn't want any of it. She and Jasmine stared at one another, straight into the eyes, and Doreen found she was growing sick of the middle-class morals of the Association. Helen, as far as she knew, was still in the middle of it.

"How did you know where to find me?" Jasmine finally said.

Doreen snorted. "You think I don't know where you are? You think I don't see the pamphlets stuffed into that giant purse of yours?"

She slammed her glass of water on the table. "You think I didn't notice the giant holes in that story you told me last night? One of us is a fool here, girl, and it isn't me."

"There's a war going on in this country, in case you haven't noticed," Jasmine said.

Ooh. Doreen's fingers started twitching at that. She moved them from across her chest to down by her sides. Easier to strike from that position.

"Doreen," Helen said.

Doreen ignored her.

"Don't you be talking to me about war, girl. Do you think I don't know what goes on outside my door? You think I don't watch the news, or hear the talking in the streets? You think my magic doesn't feel it every time someone else gets shot down? You think I'm not connected to this place, after all these years?"

"You gave up your magic. How exactly are you connected like that, Aunt Doreen? And if you're that hooked in, what the *hell* you doing to help these people?"

"Don't you...!"

"What good's our magic for, Doreen? It didn't save Uncle Hector and it isn't saving the rest of our people, either."

Jasmine's shoulders were hunching up like she was itching to be gone. Well, that was just too bad.

"And you." Doreen turned to Helen. "What are you doing up here? Come to spy on us? Lay down the law?"

Helen didn't rise to the bait, but her lips pursed at that. So far she was staying silent, which was smart, but was starting to piss Doreen off all the same.

They were both making her angry.

Any minute now, she was going to scorch her own damn kitchen.

"You're both hypocrites!" Jasmine shouted. "You don't even care!"

"Come on, girl, you twelve years old? Let's both calm down." Doreen sighed.

Seeing Jasmine's youth come out like that flipped a switch inside Doreen. She calmed right down, and felt Helen relax in response. Helen must have been waiting for that. Waiting to see how much control Doreen still had.

Well.

She could do better than just calming down. Slowly, from her belly out to beyond her hands, Doreen started building magic. She made it thick, strong, moving out layer by layer. In between each layer, she set an intention. On top of that, she set new protections. On top of those, she layered pure power, the heart of the fire.

Jasmine gasped and grew still. Helen's glacial ice built around her, too, until the whole kitchen was filled with the power of ice and fire.

Then it stopped. Doreen beckoned Jasmine to the center of the room. She stood, shaking, and positioned herself directly between the two sorcerers.

"Jasmine." Doreen looked right at her. "I want you to feel this. And I want you to match us."

"Why?"

"Because you need to know what kind of power you have. And the three of us need to go to the attic in a moment and take care of what needs doing."

"Doreen…"

"It's either that, or we call it quits. You want help with your revolution? You start that here. You start now. You start with my magic, and Helen's."

Confusion warred with the anger on Jasmine's face.

"You aren't the only one keeping her own counsel around this house," Doreen said.

"Terrance wants me back at the Mansion. I've been fighting him. The damn fools at the Association are stuck back in I don't even know what time. White people foolishness. You, too, Helen. Though if you're here, maybe you're starting to think the same as me. I just don't know yet."

Doreen spared Helen a glance. She was completely steady on her feet, like a rock. Matching Doreen's magic, but still not saying a word. Not giving anything away.

"What..." Jasmine said.

Doreen spoke to Helen again. "You all've been thinking you can stay out of what's happening. Terrance thinks it doesn't affect him any. The fool is wrong."

Helen cleared her throat. "That *is* why I'm here. I need more information, and I need it directly. I think the Association is in trouble."

"Wait a minute." Jasmine laid her hand on Doreen's arm. "You'd take on Terrance, Aunt Doreen? For the Panthers? For me?"

"Jasmine, don't you see?" Doreen said. "This is so much bigger than the Panthers. It's bigger than the Association. It's bigger than all of us."

"I don't think doing magic for the Panthers is such a good idea..." Helen protested.

"*Nothing* is a good idea right now!" Doreen shouted. "Something is coming. That spell we still have to deal with in the back of this yard, those shots fired through your window? That was all just a taste of it. I *felt* it. There's snakes out there. And spiders in the Mansion. And that nasty man Hoover. And the Association is cracking at the seams."

"Hoover?" Helen said.

Doreen grew so cold when those words left her own mouth, as if she'd been plunged into the center of the Arctic Sea. The magic faltered.

"I didn't think..." Jasmine said.

"No. You didn't. And you shouldn't have to. The Association should be run by *adults* who take care of things. Instead, Terrance is a mewling child, stubborn as all get-out. Not listening to anything but his ego."

A huge cracking sound came from the back of the house, right outside Jasmine's bedroom. The scent of ozone slammed through the kitchen.

Jasmine ran for the kitchen door, Doreen right behind her. Helen grabbed at Jasmine's arm.

"Hold up, girl! Don't be foolish."

That stopped her in her tracks.

Helen dropped Jasmine's arm. "We need to assess whether the threat is still there."

"Okay. What do we do?" Jasmine asked, face grown two shades paler around her eyes.

Doreen slipped a palm into both women's hands, sent a thread of magic out, linking them all. Fire. Ocean. Ice.

She cast her attention outward, weaving the three forces as it went. Showing Jasmine how to braid the elements together.

Taking a bigger breath, Doreen deepened into the flow. If she could surround herself with this feeling forever, she would have. It felt that good.

Wrenching herself from the feeling of the magic, Doreen allowed her senses to see, taste, and touch what was in the backyard.

There it was, just on the edges.

Nothing.

She cursed softly, and broke the link. The tide washed out of Jasmine, and Helen withdrew, leaving Doreen empty, with the memory that something fine could happen in the world. That magic was more than she had ever thought it could be without Hector.

And that she had missed it terribly.

"Guess we don't have to deal with that nasty spell anymore, girl," Doreen said.

Opening the back door, the three women stepped out into the evening air. Sure enough, where the salt-covered spell had been was a blackened crater, about the size of a bowling ball.

Doreen sniffed at the air. "The snake came back for it, it seems."

She pulled the kitchen door shut behind them, and scooped up a handful of dirt from the crater.

"We're heading to the attic now. I need to see if we can track this thing at all. Helen, you're going to have to help us."

Chapter Thirty-Two
Carol

Carol was in the Mansion lab room, trying to work.

The long wood table was strewn with feathers, shells, a dish of water, a stick of Palo Santo, and matches. A chunk of gold glowed softly in the light from the tall windows along the eastern edge of the room.

Ernesto was at one of the tall work benches under the windows, Bunsen burners aflame beneath two alembics.

Gods only knew what he was working on, but an acrid smell belched out occasionally, drifting Carol's way. His battered leather-bound journal was weighted open with two black glass discs, and he kept glancing between the notebook and the fat-bellied glass retorts.

The Mansion was boiling. Not from physical heat—it was in the low 70s outside—but from all the magic, both active and suppressed.

Mostly though, it was the emotions. Tempers were crashing, though a non-magical visitor to the Mansion might not notice any difference in the atmosphere. Perhaps they'd pick up on some subtle tensions, but the Mansion was quiet and lovely as always.

Since the visions started, Carol needed to re-learn shielding. The stuff she'd started on during her first week from Minnesota, at thirteen years old. The stuff they taught to five-year-olds. She had to re-learn it all, and despite being an Earth sorcerer, she had to learn it from an Air perspective.

Rosalia's orders. And Carol had the strong sense that when Rosalia gave someone a task, they complied without question or complaint. Always. Leaders of leaderless bands get in that position because they've proven their power and authority in countless ways. So you might as well listen.

At least, that was what the whole thing looked like. When Carol asked Ernesto about it, he shrugged and said, "She knows her stuff. Of course I listen."

Besides which, it was pretty clear the hechicera could decimate anyone with a single lift of her hand.

Ernesto had been working with Carol on the shielding since that first visit to what turned out to be Rosalia's botanica, work room, and all-around meeting place in East LA.

Carol was to return to her every other week for expanded lessons, but Rosalia trusted Ernesto to walk Carol through setting up proper inner wards to protect against dreams and random prophecies...all the things an Earth sorcerer shouldn't be troubled with.

But Carol was. And she was practicing shielding double-time that particular Tuesday afternoon because Terrance was more angry than she'd ever expected he could get.

The crystal wine glasses were practically humming on their shelves when she walked past the dining room.

The oil paintings hanging in the long hallways were all very slightly askew. The gardener had been told to not mow the lawn because the sound was irritating Terrance further. Carol had seen the man in his floppy hat quietly trimming the box hedges and camellias with big green clippers before she'd come down to start working.

The whole Mansion was supposed to keep quiet. To not disturb Terrance's mood.

No one had asked Terrance to not irritate everyone else.

The pressure in Carol's head was intense, like two hands squeezing the edges of her skull.

It was all Jasmine's fault. Jasmine's and Doreen's. Carol knew this because Jasmine had told her, and because Terrance had been questioning

Carol about Jasmine, asking oblique questions at first, and then shifting to more pointed queries that almost bordered on rude.

Two days ago, Helen had actually told him he needed to back down. She'd said it quietly, of course, and with perfect politeness, but Carol could feel the edge in her voice. Terrance felt it too, and Carol didn't doubt the words had been delivered with a small shove at his energy fields, reminding him that, though Helen *was* only second in command, Terrance did need to listen to her counsel.

His mouth had gone tight, but the spark in his blue eyes calmed down a bit. "I'm sorry, Carol, I didn't mean to push you. We just need as much information as you can offer us."

Right. And Carol was going to offer as little information as she could. At least until the Association dragged themselves into the twentieth century and started acting like they should. Like real sorcerers. Who actually helped people, not just the spirits of the dead. Not just the beings on the astral planes.

People with meat sheathing their bones.

Carol had been worried about Jasmine at first, at her increased anger. But the more she listened, the more she knew Jasmine was right. AMAS had to refocus itself and start working in the world again.

Terrance's term hadn't been a good one, in that regard. Oh, he'd needed to get warring magical factions together, and that was good. But now that they were all working more or less with one another, wasn't it time to give back to everyone who supported the Association?

Including the people who supported the Association by simply living and breathing in the cities where Association members were? Who cleaned their houses, and delivered their food?

Carol had asked Terrance that, during that previous conversation. It was part of what made him so damned angry.

"You've been listening to Jasmine too much! We are not to reveal ourselves directly to the world. You know that. You were taught that!"

When he said that, Carol rooted her feet more deeply, sinking into the thick blue carpet, reaching through the bottom of the Mansion to the soil beneath.

"I was taught that, but I *don't* know it, because I'm not sure I agree. Magic workers have always helped their people."

"Yes!" he bit out. "But not out on the streets in open battle! Do you realize what they're asking the Association to do? Open warfare! With the police!"

She kept drawing on earth, though the pressure from his anger grew on her skin. Carol felt a headache coming on, like sharp fissures opening behind her eyes.

"What are they planning? You have to tell us, you ungrateful…"

It was at that point that Helen stepped between them, voice like ice.

"You will calm yourself now. You will calm yourself, and you will apologize to Carol."

"I will not!"

"You will. And you will do so now."

The pressure eased up, though Carol could only imagine the pressure around Terrance was increasing.

Holy shit. She never thought she would see Terrance challenged directly.

"Miss Johansson, I'm not myself. Please excuse me. We'll continue this conversation later."

That was two days ago. They hadn't talked since, and things in the Mansion were only getting worse.

Carol had been dreaming of spiders. Every night they came to her, spinning and spinning. She woke up with red welts on her arms and legs.

Ernesto had the housekeeper send someone in to vacuum every corner of Carol's bedroom. Carol even took everything out of the closet to make sure there were no little white cotton nests or strings of webs inside.

There was nothing.

"Just because we can't see something, doesn't mean it isn't there, Carol. What are the spiders telling you?" Ernesto had asked.

So she was working on that, along with shielding. She could feel the messages tickling at the edges of her brain but she couldn't bring them home.

Carol was starting to wonder if she weren't going crazy. If they all weren't. Ernesto. Mr. Sterling. Even Jasmine. What was Jasmine thinking of, anyway? Hanging with those terrorists. And Ernesto was still hiding those radical newspapers that spoke against the United States. Traitor.

"Carol? What are you doing?"

She snapped back into the room on a shuddering breath that hurt her lungs. Ernesto shoved a handkerchief at her nose.

"Tilt your head back, maga."

That made it worse. She fought him off, grabbing the white handkerchief out of his brown hands.

"What are *you* doing?"

"Look," he said.

The handkerchief was stained red with blood, but that wasn't what Ernesto was pointing at.

He was pointing at Carol's notebook, where'd she'd been drawing the same sigil. Over and over. Scratched large and small in overlapping glyphs.

"What is that?"

She stared at the black marks pressed deep into the paper.

"I don't know."

The marks made no sense at all. Except that she knew them. Like she'd seen them before.

"Ernesto. I don't know."

Or like something from her dreams had drawn them through her hand.

Chapter Thirty-Three
Spiders and Snakes

The Master was humming in the darkness, words mixed with a strange, whistling toning that buzzed behind his fat, moist lips.

The sound caused the hairs on Samuels' arms to stand on end under his dark suit. Hoover was always spooky, but he was growing stranger with every passing week. His pasty white face was slick with sweat that dripped down his cheeks and hovered from the tip of his bulbous nose.

Stains blossomed under the armpits of his white robe. The dark stains would turn to yellow half circles, and need to be bleached pure white again. Samuels pitied the ones who had to clean the stinking things.

The Master hunched over a pile of papers in the center circle of a vaulted room deep beneath Headquarters, crouching like the bloated spider that he was. In a room of polished granite, candles lined gleaming black shelves set up against each wall of the underground cube.

A circle was inscribed onto the floor, rough gray patches hewn from the sleek black. The candlelight didn't quite reach it and, this night, at least, the Master had insisted that there be no candles in the center of the room.

The room was dark enough that Samuels' eyes were finally, fully comfortable. All of the training and recalibration caused him to wince even at normal levels of light. It had grown easier to just wear the regulation dark glasses all the time.

Except in here, which looked almost normal to Samuels, and must have been lit up like day to Hoover.

The Master. The Puppeteer. The Magister. The one they all turned to for direction, and forced their bowels to stillness in front of, when his dark gaze turned on them with the slightest questioning.

He could still their hearts with a thought. They all knew it. At least that was how it felt.

Samuels was never certain how much power the Master actually had, and how much was embellishment and emotional control. Both forms of power, if you thought about it.

Samuels had his own ways to control. There was no mistaking that his training was not at the level of the Master's, but it was equally clear that Samuels far outstripped his cohort. It was the only reason he was in charge.

Sometimes Samuels thought it was the only thing keeping him alive. He stroked the snake ring with his thumb, then stilled his hands again.

The Master looked like a strange fat toad crouching in a nightdress.

Except this toad was filled with the sort of power that struck terror into people's hearts and minds. Politicians quailed at his name, and a visit from one of his operatives was enough to make powerful men run to the toilet with stabbing pains gripping their guts.

Samuels resisted the urge to tamp a handkerchief on his upper lip. Any movement might disturb the Master, and once disturbed, there was no telling what he would do.

Samuels was already in trouble. Things weren't going well with the plant. Not yet, at any rate. Samuels had his concerns that the man had gone native, sympathizing with that charismatic young man who was the leader of the rebel group in Chicago. The upstarts. The Black Panther Party.

Domestic terrorists, they were calling them. But really, they were a foreign power on American soil. Brought there unwillingly on stinking ships across the Middle Passage years before, but foreign all the same.

Fred Hampton had his own power, and a type of magic Samuels hadn't yet quite placed. He had his suspicions, of course, but nothing yet that could be confirmed. Samuels just hoped the plant they'd placed within the group would man up soon. Give them some real information. Stop dancing around it all.

Shit. He really hoped the man hadn't gone native. Hoped that picking out his afro hadn't damaged his brain somehow.

Samuels grimaced at the thought, knowing it was the thought of a lesser man. The trained magician didn't think such things. He kept an even keel. He looked at the world objectively, without the petty judgments of other men.

That way the magician always judged true.

Truth was, Samuels was worried and it was affecting his own brain patterns, making it more and more difficult to sink in to the deep meditations that kept his magic steady and his mind strong.

Something was going wrong and he didn't know what it was. Along with the Chicago plant dragging his feet, strange things were afoot in Oakland and Los Angeles. The whole thing stank of magic.

And the Master was interfering with it somehow, undermining Samuel's work? Or setting traps of his own?

Samuels kept quiet about his fears. It wouldn't do to let on to the Master. Fear was always punished, and uncertainty about something as important as the Chicago plant?

It would be Samuels' own spinal cord drawn out from base of his skull until it snapped. It would be his own entrails spilled out onto this floor, and read like sheep's intestines on the dark of the moon.

Burning asafetida ground its stink up Samuels' nose, making it almost impossible not to sneeze. He invoked all his training and willed his body to cease. Be still. He rocked his feet a little inside the black polished shoes, trying to regain a sense of his own grounding, his connection to the earth beneath this fortress outside Washington DC.

His connection to the serpent encircling the tree.

The Master was keening now. "In Time! In Tiiime. Elevate our Lives!"

Gave Samuels the cold spooky. He hated this stuff. Hated it with a passion. More than anything. More than the rats in the walls of his childhood apartment. More than being tortured by the kids down the street, taunted, and beaten bloody in the empty building at the end of their block.

He hated it more than killing someone. That, he'd forced himself to get used to. There wasn't any getting used to this.

It hadn't always been this way. He'd thought the magic would save him, once upon a time. It gave him a sense of his own power. Made him feel safe.

Not anymore.

Not with Hoover turning into some gibbering idiot, rocking back and forth on a polished granite floor.

Not with the shit that was about to go down.

Samuels tested the walls on the inside of his skull. The barriers were still in place.

That was close. It wouldn't do to let the Master know Samuels was concerned. Let alone show the worry and contempt that grew more and more difficult to hold at bay.

The Master's keening grew louder. The papers in the middle of the circle began to flutter. Samuels could feel the shifting air on his own face. The room should have been still. Even though it was the wrong phase of the moon, the Master was raising power.

"Come, Oh Intelligence! Now in Time..."

"Come, Oh Intelligence..."

Samuels ground his heels into the granite slabs, sweat popping all across his back.

He willed himself to stay.

Chapter Thirty-Four
Jasmine

I was running late, like I had been all day long.

I needed two showers that morning, after one of my magical experiments backfired badly. Aunt Doreen was in a snit. I'd have to do a lot of extra cleaning to get her temper even again.

She was also mad about the ritual we'd done with Helen. Trying to get information from the tainted garden dirt had led us nowhere.

"Okay, girl. Ward the space," Doreen had said that night. "Then I'm going to put some of this dirt in my mouth and we're going to look into this crystal ball."

Even with Helen helping, it was hard to see what good the ritual had done. All Doreen saw after putting the nasty earth in her mouth were snakes, spiders, and some weird, glowing sigils that we couldn't understand.

I did remind Doreen that the spiders must mean that Carol's visions and the snake spell were connected. There was that, at least.

Doreen about bit my head off when I mentioned it. "What good are these damn half-visions and muddy messages? We need a way to *act*!"

Helen had tried to talk to her, but at that point, nothing was calming Doreen down.

So I left her to it, slamming through the kitchen and her bedroom, preparing who the hell knew what.

Heading to a place regularly patrolled by police felt safer than Doreen's tidy little house.

The tension hit me as soon as I stepped off the bus two blocks away from HQ.

Oakland's streets were wet from last night's rain so the air should have felt fresh. Clean. Instead the air pressed on my face like Los Angeles smog. But it wasn't the air. It was something else.

Walking past the liquor store and the barbershop, I turned the corner onto a residential street, where the neat little house stood. Two stories of white wood behind black wrought iron, with a big sign out front announcing that I was at the Black Panther Party Headquarters.

Something was wrong. Very wrong. I was about to reach for my magic, but then realized it didn't feel like there was an immediate threat.

There was a buzzing at the base of my skull and the taste of iron on my tongue. Adrenaline and anger.

Someone had kicked the hornet's nest.

As I reached the chipped black fence surrounding the small yard, I saw that there were two guards on duty again instead of one and that neither was sitting down. Black painted steps led from the cracked walkway to the narrow porch. The comrades stood tall in calf-length black leather coats, berets tilted right and left on their heads. Their shotguns hung at their sides instead of on their backs.

I paused and took a breath. The guards didn't move, so I went on up the walkway. When I got to the bottom step, the brother on the left stopped me.

Usually I didn't get questioned anymore. All the comrades knew my face if not my name. I wondered if Doreen and Helen showing up in the shot-up car had changed things.

The guard unclipped a walkie-talkie and spoke into it, voice rumbling. "It's Jasmine. She clear?"

There was a long pause. Cold was seeping up from the driveway through the thin leather soles of my brown boots. Inspired by Kathleen, I'd started switching up my cords with dresses and boots more often, thinking of Jimmy's eyes on me, making me feel like I was the most beautiful thing in the world.

As I stood there starting to shiver in the brocade coat that was plenty warm enough for Los Angeles, but not quite enough for a Bay Area December, I felt foolish, and every bit of nineteen. Like I'd been caught playing while serious shit was going down.

Bay Rum. One of the guards must have been wearing it. It was my dad's scent. For the first time since coming here, I wondered if I should go home.

The Panthers had never made me feel that way before. I'd arrived at a good time, people said. A time of transition. Little Bobby Hutton's death had galvanized a lot of locals. The food and education programs were going full force. There was more to *do* and it was easier to feel a part of things. Like we all mattered, not just the muscle.

That's what people had told me. And that was how I had felt until this moment.

A car rumbled by on the street, the lead of its exhaust hitting the back of my throat, making my stomach clench. I was a little queasy.

This morning's magic felt far away.

The walkie-talkie crackled. I heard a man's voice through the static: "She's clear."

The guard on the right waved me up and opened the door. I climbed the black steps like I was heading into the lair of a dangerous animal. It wouldn't be too much longer before I found out just how true that was.

Inside, the air was thick with cigarettes, anger, and some fear. There was something else there, too, that I couldn't quite place. It bothered me, because it felt like I *should* know what it was.

Shrugging out of my coat, I hung it on the already overburdened rack by the front door. I slipped my fringed purse back over my shoulder.

Clumps of people huddled in the living room and kitchen, and I could hear voices arguing down the narrow hallway toward the back of the house.

I saw Tanya, my comrade from children's breakfast. She was sitting, the edges of her pressed hair frizzing slightly around her face, shell-shocked, in a straight-backed kitchen chair, arms crossed over her breasts, barely breathing. Her forehead was sweaty and the front of her cream work blouse looked damp.

Tucking my skirt around my legs, I crouched next to her.

"What happened?"

She turned to me, face blank, and blinked. I could almost see her brain turning over, assimilating the information that I was someone she knew, and that I had just spoken.

"It's Fred."

There was only one Fred. Chairman Fred Hampton Jr. Our poet. Our philosopher. Our leader. Head of the Chicago Panthers.

"What happened?" I repeated.

"You better ask Jimmy or Tarika. I don't have that kind of clearance."

I nodded, though I wanted to shake Tanya. I stood up from the crouch and smoothed my skirt back down over my thighs. I knew Tarika would already be in that meeting in the back of the house, one of the few women in the room.

I needed to find Jimmy.

The energy of the room was so thick it was getting hard for me to breathe. It wasn't just the cigarettes. I'd gotten used to those. People were excited and freaked out. A weird pressure knocked up against my chest.

Something big had happened. Jimmy crossed the living room, about to go down the hall. I knew if I didn't catch him before he got to the shouting voices, I wouldn't catch him at all.

I scurried onto the old carpet runner and down the wood-paneled hall past the stairs leading to the second floor.

"Jimmy!"

He paused and turned.

"Jasmine." His face softened, then closed up again. "I need to get back to the meeting."

"Can you just tell me what's going on?"

He stared at me for a minute in the orangey light of that hall. Such an ordinary hallway in such an ordinary house.

He reached some sort of decision and came back toward me, close enough that I could smell that combination of earthy leather, musk, and cigarettes that caused a tingling along my fingertips and a rush of warmth somewhere else.

"The CPD busted in Fred's door this morning when he was asleep. Likely some feds there, too. Shot up the whole apartment. Shot up him and Deborah."

A rush of heat ran up my skin.

"He's dead? Fred is dead?"

Jimmy looked startled.

"No. Fred's just fine. Him and Deborah both. Left a lot of dead cops."

The heat turned to cold. I grabbed the newel post at the bottom of the stairs.

"Jasmine, you okay? You gonna faint?"

Jimmy put an arm around my shaking shoulders and eased me around the railing to the bottom step of the stairs. I wished I had my coat.

"Put your head between your knees."

I tried to do what he said, but my tight skirt made it hard to comply. Jimmy made an impatient sound in the back of his throat and hiked my skirt up higher, gently pressing on my back until I was staring at the squared-off toes of my boots.

"Breathe slow."

His hand felt good on the small of my back, but I…my mind couldn't. It kept starting and stopping. Trying to make sense.

"Fred isn't dead?"

"No. He and Deborah are in hiding somewhere. We're trying to figure out what to do." He cleared his throat. "But I've probably told you too much already."

Standing up from his crouch, he patted my shoulder. I sat back up. Slowly.

"I've got to get to the meeting, Jasmine. Stick around if you can. There might be more information later."

I felt a kiss on the top of my head, then heard his feet shushing down the carpet. The voices near the back got louder. The door clicked, and they became less distinct again.

What could it mean? Chicago police shot up the whole apartment when Chairman Fred was *sleeping* and he hadn't died? And some cops were dead?

The magic was starting to itch under my skin. I had to get out.

I was no longer sure if I was equipped for revolution.

Feeding people? Education? The health clinic? All that stuff was great. The guns? Well, my parents would disagree, but I was willing to put up with the party line that as long as cops were killing us, we had the right to self-defense.

But something else was going on here, and I was starting to suspect I knew what it was.

I'd been a fool to not notice it before.

Chapter Thirty-Five
Jasmine

I walked all the way back to my aunt's house, boots pinching the last mile. By the time I got back to the small blue house, the concrete was wearing a hole in the right boot and I could feel blisters forming on my heels. Limping up the front steps, I fished in my giant fringed purse for my keys. Before I could get at them, the door opened. Aunt Doreen stood there in her neat blue dress, worried eyes flashing.

"Jasmine?"

"Give me a minute, please, Doreen. Something has happened, but I…just give me a minute."

I could feel Doreen's impatience as I went to my room to change. The smell of cinnamon wafted through my door, and heard her crashing around the kitchen.

Limping into the kitchen, Band-Aids on my blisters, I folded myself into one of the red, high-backed chairs at the matching Formica table in the middle of the kitchen.

The same kitchen whose deep zinc sink I had scrubbed just that morning. A lifetime ago. The red-and-white striped curtains were open over the window above the sink, looking out onto a lemon tree.

I was back in my green bell-bottoms, topped by a Black Power T-shirt.

Aunt Doreen had made coffee while I changed. She set a china cup of it in front of me, along with a white sugar bowl and some cream.

The spoon clinked against the cup as I stirred. Doreen could be patient when she needed to be. But I knew I would have to speak eventually.

"I have something to tell you. About the Panthers..."

She snorted at that. The least refined sound I'd ever heard her emit.

She stood and brought back the percolator. Topped up our cups with the watery brew. Doreen's coffee might have been weaker than I drank it these days, but it was smooth. Tasted good.

"Trouble. I knew those Panthers were going to bring more trouble to our door, despite what I've been telling Terrance. So talk to me, girl."

Her eyes no longer looked worried, like when she'd greeted me at the door. Doreen was back to being shrewd.

"This is a breach of security for me to say..."

"Just tell me, girl. Quit stalling."

I took a breath, chest tight under my thin cotton T-shirt. I could feel the magic again. It didn't seem like it was all mine, but I pushed that thought away.

"The head of the Chicago Panthers..." I realized I wasn't even sure how to explain this. Took another sip of coffee. Fussed with the sugar bowl.

I tried again. "This morning, the cops—and maybe the feds—raided Fred Hampton's apartment in Chicago. They shot the whole place up."

Aunt Doreen's lips grew thin and tight. She held a napkin up to them, as though it was a dam holding back a river.

"Thing is, Fred and Deborah got away. And some cops are dead." I looked out the window, stomach cramping up again. Cramping with the knowledge that I hadn't spoken yet, not even inside my head.

"I think something is going on. Something magical. But it isn't any magic I've ever really felt. Not since I was nine or ten. And I can barely remember what that was, only that I've felt this thing before. A long time ago."

Doreen slid a work-worn hand across the red Formica. The tips of her fingers were cracking. It didn't matter how much Queen Helene's she rubbed into them at night. I asked her once if they hurt her. She said she didn't think about it much.

I slid my hand to meet hers, my smooth brown fingers touching her cracked, dark ones.

"I knew this day was coming," she said. "That I'd have to tell you about it. Your mother should have told you already, but I guess... Maybe she was waiting for me."

Somehow, I knew what she was going to tell me. I didn't want to hear it, wanted to shove the words she was about to say so far back down her throat nothing could pry them loose. But I longed to hear the words just the same. I needed to know.

"That was your Uncle Hector you felt, Jasmine. He died when you were nine."

The tiny wisps of curl at the nape of my neck stood straight up, I swear.

"That's when you gave up your magic." My voice was small, soft, squeezing its way out of my tight throat. That was the thing I knew, that my little girl eyes had seen, and my little heart had felt.

That was the thing she still wasn't quite telling me. And that I didn't want to hear.

"That's because I couldn't save him. He'd been out wandering in the hills out Laurel Canyon way. When I still lived with your uncle in Los Angeles, near your mom and dad."

"And me."

She continued as though she hadn't heard me. Took her hand from mine.

"Someone must have called them in. They came after him with rifles instead of a tranquilizer gun. I could feel him running across the rocks. He was throwing images into my head. But he'd taken the car to get to the hills and I couldn't get your parents on the phone."

She put the napkin to her mouth again and squeezed her eyes closed. Cleared her throat.

"So. I had no way to get to him. Not fast enough. They shot him ten times. I tried sending magic to protect him, but he was too far away. He kept moving after the first shot. Even after the third. They chased him for another half mile before he fell on nine. They finished him with ten shots. That's when I lost track of him."

I reached back across the table and clutched her hand.

"By the time your parents got to me, I think I'd gone a little crazy. I had started a fire in the barbecue grill out in back of our bungalow and was throwing all my magic tools and books into it. Doused it all with lighter fluid. By the time they broke into the house and got out to the yard, everything was in flames."

The cinnamon scent was stronger, tinged with something else. Something stronger. More potent.

"Aunt Doreen. I'm so sorry."

She looked up at me, tears in her eyes. I hated to intrude on her grief this way, but I had to know.

"I don't understand though." Even though I did. I hadn't heard it yet. So maybe it just wasn't true. "You said he was running in the hills. You said tranquilizer gun…"

"Your grandfather was a mountain lion, Jasmine. My Hector was a beautiful, golden lion of a man."

Chapter Thirty-Six
Doreen

Well. It all came out after that. Women in the maternal line tended to be magicians. Jasmine knew that part. It also turned out that a lot of them fell in love with The People. That's what the animal people called themselves. Funny. It was like every form of human thought they were the chosen ones.

"I had no damn idea," Jasmine said.

Doreen tsked a bit at her language, but let it slide.

"Well, your mother left it to me to tell you when I thought the time was right." Doreen stared into the sheen of milk fat on her cooling coffee. "I just never thought I'd need to tell you because of this."

"Because of the Black Panthers," Jasmine said.

Jasmine was pissed off, it was clear. And rightfully so. But Doreen was a little angry herself. Angry that Jasmine had been closer to danger than she knew.

Angry at herself for not figuring this out sooner. If it hadn't taken Doreen this long to crawl up out of the burrow she'd dug for herself, she might have noticed sooner.

Prolonged grief was a selfish thing.

And all this was literally right under her nose. Jasmine coming home from "studying" with that fringed leather bag of hers stuffed with pamphlets and fliers she was trying to hide.

Smelling of musk underneath the scent of ocean.

Messing around with a bunch of black men and women calling themselves Panthers.

Doreen shook her head. It had been so obvious, and she had missed it.

"Why the hell wouldn't my mother tell me this herself?" Jasmine asked.

"She thought you weren't ready yet, girl. You needed to grow into your magic more and were having enough trouble adjusting to that."

Jasmine's face was tight. Her long fingers tapped at the coffee cup that she'd already emptied and her afro had lost its perfect arc, devolving into choppy segments where she'd tugged at it in frustration.

"I've smelled it on you, you know. But I didn't quite register what it could mean," Doreen said.

Jasmine's eyes snapped wide at that. "What do you mean by that? What smell?"

"Come on, girl. Musk. Big cat."

Just like Hector used to smell. That must have been what was bringing on her dreams. The scent of cat had entered the house, smuggled in on radical pamphlets and political theory.

"How stupid could I possibly be?" Jasmine said.

"You aren't stupid, girl. If anyone should have figured it out, it was me. How were you supposed to know?"

All the information had been right there.

Doreen had been too preoccupied. Too busy trying to figure out how to work magic again. Too wrapped up in seeing Hector in her dreams.

Doreen got up and poured more coffee from the percolator. Seeing the lemon cake she'd made just that morning, she plunked it on the Formica table with a cake knife and two plates.

"May as well let the body enjoy itself while the mind and heart work themselves out."

Jasmine cut them both thick slices of the yellow cake, cracking through the white glaze frosting with the wedged knife.

"Who said that?" Jasmine said.

"Your grandma. Beatrice. The one who left us the crystal ball. Too bad you never knew her. Her power was really something. But I've told you that before."

"Was she stronger than Terrance or Helen?"

Doreen snorted at that. "Huh. Terrance and Helen couldn't hold a candle to Momma. She should've been in charge of the whole Association. Didn't want to be, she said. But I always wondered."

"You think they kept her from it?"

Doreen chewed the spongy cake, just the right combination of tart and sweet.

"I think she knew it would've been too big a fight to get what was rightfully hers."

"Where is Helen, anyway?" Jasmine asked.

Doreen sighed, a bite of cake halfway to her mouth. She set the fork back down.

"She's still in her fancy hotel, but she's heading home tomorrow morning. We met for lunch today. Things aren't good at the Mansion. But I'm still not sure what we'll end up doing. She isn't quite ready to go up against Terrance, worried as she is."

"Are you?" Jasmine asked.

The accusation in her voice grated. Doreen waved a hand and picked up her fork again.

"We're talking about you, girl. And those Panthers. Does anyone in leadership carry a gun?"

"No. No one carries guns except the muscle."

"And does leadership always travel with muscle?"

Jasmine sat stock still at that. Then shook her head.

"Damn," she said. "Why didn't I ever *see* that? They make sure the rest of us have protection, but leadership doesn't seem to."

Doreen shoved her plate away, excitement tightening her belly.

"Don't you see what this means, girl?"

Jasmine's fork clattered to the table.

"Fred Hampton must have killed those police with his own claws."

Chapter Thirty-Seven
Carol

The streets of East LA still terrified her, but Carol was determined to become less dependent on Ernesto.

So, two buses and an hour and a half later, she was back on the crowded streets, trying not to look as if she were clutching the green leather purse to her side. Trying to walk with her head up instead of scurrying. Fighting down the bile rising from her throat into her mouth.

Trying to not to think about the black marks scribbled in the notebook, so heavy inside that purse. Trying not to think about the fact that something had been inserting thoughts into her head, twisting her own fears into something dark and nasty.

Trying not to think about the fact that it was already growing dark out, and the streets looked completely different from the sunny afternoons when Ernesto had brought her there.

Stupid. Stupid. Stupid. When she'd set out from the Mansion, it had been sunny still. She just hadn't thought about the fact that by the time the bus dropped her at her destination, autumn dark would have filled the sky.

Carol was in so far over her head, it wasn't funny. Ernesto knew she was scared, even though she'd been trying to bluff her way past it. That episode with the nosebleed and the weird glyphs made it pretty obvious.

Jasmine told Carol to stand up for herself. Ernesto was trying to teach her to do the same, in his own way. But the magic felt as if it were cracking her apart.

Carol's head ached constantly from the visions and the sheer weirdness of it all.

A person would think Carol would've been trained for all this. But they'd think wrong. Her life at the Mansion had always been lived in Jasmine's shadow. Not Jasmine's fault, really. She was just so good at everything, and so confident. She just knew how to take up space.

But Carol was trying. Here she was, back on the sidewalk, walking past the tire store and piñatas, looking for the blue door with the painted hand. But this time, yellow street lights cast a weird glow over everything, and men stood in clumps on corners, making kissing noises as she passed.

She tried to walk even taller, like Jasmine had taught her when Carol had first arrived from Minnesota. She had dragged along after Jasmine's sheer bravado through the Los Angeles streets, days that Jasmine could slip Cecelia's tether.

There never seemed to be much space left over for Carol. It wasn't that Jasmine was self-centered. Well, maybe a little bit. But Jasmine just figured it was up to everyone to barrel their way through, as if it came easy to them the way it came easy to her.

It wasn't easy. Nothing was easy.

And having a late-puberty magical awakening, as though Carol was getting her period at age eighteen? It felt like moose crap. A big stinking pile of it.

There was the door, just like last time. That was a relief, at least. Carol wasn't sure how often it moved. Ernesto didn't seem to know either.

"Rosalia has a different magic. She does what she wants with it."

"Including defying the laws of physics?" Carol had asked.

"Even that," Ernesto said.

Here was the blue door. Carol put out a hesitating hand. She hadn't seen it the first visit, but the few times since, she'd noticed a slight force field over the wood. Her knuckles buzzed as they approached the door.

Taking a breath, Carol knocked. Then tried the knob. Like it had every single time, the door opened.

She exhaled with relief.

Then about jumped out of her skin.

"Rosalia!"

The hechicera was standing inches from the door when Carol turned to shut it, though she could swear Rosalia hadn't been there before.

She was looking through Carol. Making her head feel even worse than before. Clenching her teeth, Carol stood there, purse straps digging at her shoulder, the weight of the sigils in that journal dragging the whole thing down.

Then Rosalia's gaze withdrew.

"This isn't good, maga." Rosalia turned and walked through the botanica, toward the heavy burgundy curtain leading to the back room. "Come. We will have tea, and pan dulce from this morning."

Carol followed through the burgundy velvet. Rosalia was already putting the kettle on. These magic people seemed to drink a lot of tea. Weird.

Rosalia brought a hand-thrown blue plate with flowers in a ring around the edge and gestured for the white paper bag on the counter.

Carol handed her the crinkling bag.

"Sit down, maga. You don't look so good."

Carol did just that, suddenly grateful for the hard wooden chair. The bus ride, the walk, the glyphs, the headaches and visions, it was all too much.

Rosalia's silver rings flashed as her hands rustled in and out of a white paper bag. She stacked rounds of pink and yellow bread onto the plate.

A pot joined two tea mugs on the table.

"Lavender?" Carol asked.

"For your head," Rosalia said.

Carol just nodded. Of course Rosalia knew. She rubbed her temples as Rosalia poured the fragrant brew.

Rosalia. A person like her should have a proper title. She likely did. Carol was also unlikely to ever be in a position to know that.

Sometimes, names were secret. Other times, the position that one held was closely guarded. If ever there came a time Carol needed to know, someone would tell her.

She hoped that day would never come. Carol couldn't handle what was being thrown at her as it was.

"Drink your tea, maga. It will help your head, and calm you down."

There was barely any flavor to it, but the scent wreathed around her temples. Rosalia was right: it helped.

"And here." She plopped a pink round of bread with a hatched grid on the top onto a small plate. "Eat something. A little sugar and flour will do you good."

Rosalia chose a pale yellow round for herself, poured another mug of tea, and gave Carol that look again. Carol wanted to fall into that look, and it also made her want to run away. Rosalia could protect Carol, if she chose to, but Rosalia also knew way more about her than Carol ever wanted anyone to know.

"So. What do you need to tell me, that you made the trip here all by yourself?"

Carol heard the door to the shop open.

"Señora?" a man's voice came through the curtain.

"Excuse me, maga."

Rosalia rose, smoothing her skirts, and left her to her tea.

What was Carol going to tell her? Rosalia was right. She came here because…those damn glyphs had scared her half to death.

Carol heard Rosalia's voice rising and falling, asking questions, and the man answering in Spanish. The sound of jars and drawers opening. Scraping. Then the sharp scent of clove oil.

And then… "Maga Carolina, come here please."

Carol bumped back from the table, jostling the mugs and slopping some of the tea water onto the small table.

Peering out from behind the curtain into the front of the shop, she saw Rosalia behind the counter, facing a man in a crisp blue shirt and black slacks. A few acne scars covered his otherwise handsome face. Thick black hair swept back from his face, shining with hair oil.

On the wooden counter was a large jar, a small vial of oil, a red candle, a skein of silk, and a white piece of paper with black markings on it.

"Carolina, is this what you have seen?"

Carol's breath caught in her chest as she moved closer.

On the paper was the glyph marring her notebook.

The one she'd drawn over, and over, until blood ran down her face.

She felt the man's hands clutching at her arms as she went down.

Chapter Thirty-Eight
Jasmine

After Doreen's revelation, I needed to get out. To see Jimmy. To get some reassurance that even though shit was weird, I still had a place in the world.

I was tired of running. From my magic. From what I now saw was my responsibility. From the truth about who exactly the cats in the leather coats and berets were, and what that might mean for my future, and the future of us all.

So when Jimmy called and said they were heading out dancing, I said yes and changed my clothes.

The groove was deep at the Beacon. Skin glistened under the red and purple lights. Sly and the Family Stone blasted through the air, wanting to take us higher.

It was high in the jam-packed room, all right. Men and women in their best: silky dresses, halter tops, tight bell bottoms, fringed vests, 'fros picked out as big as they would go. Everyone was grooving to the music, cheap bourbon, and each other.

Leaning on the tiny table shoved up against a black wall, I looked out at the dance floor, drinking tart red wine. Every time I took a sip from the small water glass, my tongue curled a little. Jimmy had downed a shot of Jack and was sipping on some kind of pale beer.

We'd been heading to Sweet Jimmie's, which was owned by Huey's uncle, but the cats *my* Jimmy was rolling with that night—Leroy and Jerrold and some other men I barely knew—decided they'd had enough of the blues for awhile. They wanted something a little funkier, so we switched direction and headed to the Beacon.

Wherever we went was all right by me. I just needed one night's escape before dealing with the mess we were all in the middle of.

And when you rolled with the Panthers, people weren't too particular about checking a person's identification at the door.

I was getting the impression that they weren't much checking IDs at all, if you were wearing a miniskirt and green eye shadow. The giant of a bouncer, brown leather coat straining at his shoulders, waved both Tanya and I in without even the pretense of checking.

The music shifted. Marvin Gaye. Grapevine.

Jimmy slid his body around mine. "Ready to dance?"

I could smell his musk. It went right to my crotch.

Abandoning my wine on the table, I grabbed his hand and moved out toward the floor.

He was staring at my face, gold-tinged eyes looking into my own plain brown. Everything in my body reached for him, though I pretended it wasn't happening. I just kept dancing, staring into his eyes, as our bodies moved closer and further, closer and further, twining and releasing.

I drew my mouth close to his ear. "Jimmy, I know."

He pulled back, startled. "What?"

I pulled him back in. "I know you're a real panther."

His shoulders grew tense under my hands, and he exhaled a long breath.

Then he leaned all the way in and put his lips on mine.

God, it was like I was falling into him. One of his hands gripped the base of my neck, my dangling hoops brushing at his wrist; the other touched my waist, just his fingertips, as though if he touched any more of me he wouldn't be able to stop.

I wouldn't be able to stop.

A loud pop came from the back of the room and the scent of cordite mixed with the smell of bourbon, beer, and bodies. Someone screamed and a bunch of people hit the floor around us. I pulled Jimmy down, though he resisted for a moment.

"What the fuck is happening?" a man crouched next to me spat out.

As Jimmy and I hunched and ran toward the front door, I reached out with my senses. Nothing. Shit. Something was blocking me.

All of a sudden, everyone was running and pushing with us toward the door.

We reached the heavy padded black door and shoved it open right before bodies started slamming into us, spilling us out into the streets. Police sirens were coming fast.

"Jimmy," I said, pitching my voice just for his ears. "Someone's working magic here, but I can't tell who."

"Fuck. Nothing?"

"Nothing."

The rest of the crew we'd arrived with were on the sidewalk now, guns out. How they'd gotten those past the bouncer, I wasn't sure.

"Jasmine," Jimmy said, "can you do anything to help?"

Could I do anything…

Could I do anything?

My brain was racing while every cell in me reached out for the bay. Ocean water poured through my veins, pooling in my palms, ready for me to use the energy to…do what?

A jumble of confusion clicked through me. Doreen's face. The scent of fear in the club. The sound of sirens coming. My mother. The Association. Carol. Jimmy. Tarika.

"Give me backup!"

"Hey!" Jimmy's voice cut through the panicked clamor. "Brothers!"

Three Panthers, fully strapped, ran over.

"We need cover!" Jimmy said.

"For what, man?"

"Just trust me. Jasmine's working on something."

"We gotta go, man! The pigs almost here!"

"Just give me a minute!" I snapped out, then dropped into myself. Down beneath the maelstrom. Seeking...yes. There it was. The pool of stillness at my core. I breathed into that. Deep, belly breaths.

I knew just what to do.

Weaving the magic within me, I grabbed it all, the energy in the bodies around me, the energy of the police cars, who were almost on top of us by now, I swear, the energy of the sidewalks themselves, all the energy accrued in the nightclub from every dance and every kiss, from every joint smoked and whiskey downed.

From the gunshots and from the bullets that had never left their chambers.

"Duck!" I shouted, and felt every body drop toward the ground. I threw out a solid wall around the block, radiating diversion, diffusion, safety, normalcy.

And heard the sirens dopplering away.

Holding the shields steady, I turned toward the nightclub.

Then I spoke.

"I know who's being used. It isn't his fault, but he needs to be contained."

"What?" said Leroy.

"Who is it, Jasmine?"

"Jerrold."

Jerrold. Who'd been around longer than me. A man who was never going to rise too far in the ranks, but whom they trusted enough to play guard.

"Fuck you, bitch, Jerrold's no snitch."

"Leroy, don't speak to a sister like that. Ever," Jimmy said. "Jasmine?"

It took me a second to realize exactly what he was asking me. Right. They needed proof.

"Check his gun. I guarantee you its been fired."

Reaching out again, I sought beyond the barriers of my mind, beyond the cordon I'd set up around the block. The cops had headed elsewhere, as though that was where they'd been going all along.

I sighed, and pulled what was mine back into me, releasing the rest to the wind that started blowing through the scraggly trees holding their ground on the sidewalks.

There was a tickle on my right hand. I looked down.

A small white spider was crawling toward my wrist. I stared at it for a moment.

"Jasmine, you okay?" Jimmy's breath was sweet on my face.

I shook the spider off my hand and stepped on it with the tip of my sandal. Felt a slight clenching in my gut.

"I'm fine. We should get these people out of here and tell the rest of the Party what the hell is going on."

Jimmy looked at me for a moment, face and body completely still, like he was about to say something. Then he nodded once and turned to the other Panthers.

"Let's go. If you aren't injured, walk on out. But don't go alone. If you need an escort, raise your hand."

Jimmy turned to me for a moment. "I'll be right back," he said, then loped off to help the brothers who were tending to the people who'd been injured in the crush.

I stood there on the sidewalk, watching people help each other to their feet, walking in small groups, some east, some west.

Jerrold. Casting my mind back, over every interaction, I tried to see. Was there anything there? A sign? Something?

I couldn't see it. I looked down the treeless block, lit with yellow light and shadows.

Just like I couldn't see how the hell a small white spider had gotten to me through the mayhem at the club.

Chapter Thirty-Nine
Jasmine

Three days later, I got off the bus in West Oakland with Aunt Doreen in tow.

We stepped off the rear of the bus, me in sturdy black lace-up boots under my green bell-bottom cords, Doreen in sensible black walking shoes.

My brocade coat had been replaced by boot-length leather from a Telegraph Avenue thrift store, and my hair was tucked beneath a black beret. I was a member of the Party and wasn't going to pretend otherwise anymore.

And the Party itself was going to have to deal with that.

Doreen's usual neat dress was hidden beneath a black coat and a blue scarf covered her hair. A black patent leather bag was tucked in her left arm. She was a seething mass of magical power beneath a thin veneer of middle-aged respectability.

The barber shop was just opening, the proprietor shaking out the welcome mat before setting it in front of his door. It smelled like someone had broken a bottle of brandy in front of the shuttered-up liquor store next to it. As we rounded the corner, walking up the block to the white house, I braced myself.

There was no way to tell what the reception would be, or what might have changed since last time I was at HQ.

Our purses were loaded with spells and small objects Doreen called "magic bombs."

Our own magic coursed strong along our skin. Not trying to mask it anymore, Doreen reeked of spice and fire.

I smelled like the whole damn ocean that lined the coast.

The white, ramshackle Victorian with black steps looked quiet on the outside, though two guards were still on point, one with a rifle and walkie-talkie, the other with a snub nose, black 9mm.

I knew more about guns now than I ever wanted to before. I also knew there would be other guards in back.

As we approached them, I called out up the steps, "You remember my Aunt Doreen. We've come to offer help."

"Stop there." The guard with the 9mm motioned.

They stopped us at around ten feet from the steps, and the one with the rifle got on the walkie-talkie.

The other guard looked us up and down. Not checking us out as women, but as possible threats. He was a big guy, black leather jacket straining at his shoulders, beret barely fitting his head. I'd seen him many times and knew he recognized me. "What kind of help?" he said.

The scrutiny made sense to me. They'd never seen Doreen before; I had accused one of their own of being a possible plant; and I'm sure a lot had gone down since that night at the Beacon.

"Some help you really need."

After about five minutes, Jimmy bounced down the stairs. He looked both excited and tired.

"Hey Jasmine. Where you been, girl?" He looked at Doreen. "Ma'am."

"You remember my Aunt Doreen? We've come to offer help and need to speak to leadership."

"That might be difficult. There's so much shit going on."

Jimmy's face flushed a little darker and he turned to Doreen, rocking forward and back on his boots. "Sorry ma'am. I don't mean offense, but everyone's on deck right now."

"That is just fine, son. If you think I've never heard cursing in my forty-three years, you would be mistaken."

I looked at Doreen and she nodded sharply.

"Hold out your hand," I said to Jimmy.

"What?" He looked genuinely confused, and his usual earthy musk smell grew stronger, making me want to lean into his shoulders. Get it under control, girl.

The walkie-talkie squawked on the steps, and Jimmy's head jerked toward the perch. "Jasmine, I got a lot to do."

Doreen cleared her throat. "Young man, I'm afraid this is necessary. Please listen to my niece."

Planting my boots in that dirt-and-gravel driveway, I stood tall, staring him down. "Hold out your hand."

He did.

I could feel an ocean gathering, streaming up from my boots into my belly. Then up to my heart, down my arms, and…

Into my hands.

A blue ball of electricity shot from my right hand, landing in the middle of Jimmy's palm. He gave a small yelp of surprise and jumped back half a foot before looking up at me, brown eyes flashing gold before he got them back under control.

Flashing gold like a panther in the wild. How had I not…no time for that now. We were in a state of emergency.

Jimmy was shaking his hand and both guards had hands on their guns. Ready to blast me.

"Shit girl! What the hell *was* that?"

I raised my voice, just a little, to carry over the low sounds of morning traffic. "That was magic. Remember that? Well, it's not just defensive. Your guards have guns? Doreen and I are weapons of protection and minor assault."

Doreen spoke, voice soft as warm butter. "We have a whole collection of spells inside our bags. What you men might call an arsenal."

"Doreen is even more powerful than I am. She is to be treated with respect," I said.

I adjusted my fringed purse over my shoulder.

"And we need to meet with leadership. Now."

Jimmy nodded and turned, said something low to the guards. They let us through.

We met all day.

Women ferried in sandwiches, coffee, and more cigarettes. I was rubbing my eyes with weariness and from the smoke by the time evening rolled around. Doreen still looked as neat and put together as when we had left home. I had to learn some of that magic, for sure.

Fred Hampton and his girlfriend, Deborah—who was pregnant, can you imagine?—were still on the run. All the chapters were organizing, figuring out what to do, waiting for the cops to come busting in every minute of every day. Guards were on rotation both inside and out. People were scared, but excited.

And there was a new moon in three days. Apparently, new moons did something to shifters. More shit I hadn't known. I'd never even noticed there were no meetings on those nights.

Leadership agreed, tentatively, to our plan. They would need to see some tests, more than the little parlor tricks of sending them balls of electricity or fire. The important thing wasn't the Party. They were with us on that.

The important thing was that every neighborhood in every city that was under Panther protection could use our help.

We would start with Oakland, but needed to prep the rest.

As soon as we left HQ, with an armed escort and a big burgundy Buick to drive us home, we knew what the plan was.

Aunt Doreen was calling my parents first. Then they would contact every magician in every city where the Party was organized, Association be damned.

And I would start preparing the local people to defend themselves. By any means necessary might not have to include bloodshed on their ends.

We were setting them up with magic.

Chapter Forty
Carol

The Mansion was silent, still. The air thick with magic. Terrance's scent was everywhere. It was only eight thirty, but the encroaching dark of winter made it feel much later.

Ernesto had picked Carol up from the botanica—Rosalia had insisted after Carol almost fainted again. So embarrassing. He'd told Carol that Terrance had another episode while she was gone.

They'd barely made it through the front door when a pale-faced Helen approached them, practically ringing her hands.

"Terrance needs to see you both. Right now."

Ernesto put a reassuring hand on Carol's shoulder. They followed Helen down the hall to Terrance's office.

He was sitting in one of the chairs grouped near the gas fireplace instead of at his desk.

Instead of his usual sharp suit, Terrance had on slacks, leather slippers, and a blue cashmere sweater. And he had a heavy cut tumbler of amber liquid in his hands. Carol had never seen him so casual, or with alcohol in his hands.

"Please, sit." He gestured the three of them to the other chairs. "Pour yourselves whisky, or soda if you like."

A cabinet was open in the far wall. Carol saw more crystal tumblers, two cut glass decanters, and a soda syphon. She'd never seen that cabinet open before. Things must be bad.

"You are still in frequent contact with Jasmine Jones, yes?"

Oh shit. She should have figured. Another one of these conversations. Carol locked that thought well away, as quickly as she could. Debilitated or not, Terrance could likely still read her like a book.

"Yes sir. I am."

Terrance was quiet. Waiting.

She'd learned enough from Jasmine's tutelage to keep her mouth shut and sip the soda water Helen handed her. Carol felt a sudden wish for a joint.

Jasmine always said, *Unless it's a conversation you're controlling, only answer the questions you've been asked.*

Finally, Terrance spoke again, voice strained. "Will you tell me what your conversations have been about?"

Carol shifted in her seat. Risked a glance at Ernesto, who sat, legs crossed in dark blue jeans, calmly sipping at the whisky in his own glass.

He just tilted his head at her, as if to say, "Your call."

Great. Carol suddenly felt angry. All the fear she'd been feeling, and the wrung-out-washrag state of her body, mind, and soul made her just not care anymore.

She was tired of protocol and systems. She had no clue what was better yet, but knew it wasn't this.

"I think you know what we've been talking about, sir. We've been discussing the recalcitrance of the Association to step up and help Doreen and Jasmine in fighting the forces of evil in Northern California."

Recalcitrance. Carol rolled that word around her mouth. Jasmine would be proud. And bringing Doreen into it, too, even though Carol knew Jasmine hadn't told her a thing. Doreen meant leverage.

That was another thing Jasmine had taught Carol; Ernesto, too: "Use the enemy's power against them, whenever you can."

Terrance cleared his throat at that. "Recalcitrance," he repeated. One point for Carol.

He swirled the whisky, staring at the heavy glass.

"I wouldn't put it that way, young lady."

Carol held her tongue, fighting the flush of fear along her spine.

"The Association only interferes in the case of magical attack or magical need. You should have been taught that in your first year here."

He stood at that, crossing the room to pick up a smoky crystal obelisk from a shelf behind his desk. Glancing down the side, toward the tip, he nodded, and put it down again.

"Isn't that correct?" he asked.

"Yes, it is. And I think if the Association examined the case more closely, they would find that a magical need exists."

There is even suspicion of a magical attack, she wanted to say. *And spiders, which you know about. And sigils. And snakes. And a whole bunch of other weird stuff going on.*

But there wasn't solid proof yet.

At least, not that Jasmine had told her.

"What do you think the Association should do?"

Carol looked up to meet his sapphire eyes. "I think we should give Jasmine and Doreen anything they are asking for. The situation sounds very dire, sir. All you have to do is look at the newspaper and read between the lines. Something is going on up there. Something bad. I think it may be country-wide."

Terrance's face screwed up as if he were in pain. He clutched at his temples and sagged against the desk. Helen was up in an instant, and at his side.

"Sit down," she said, guiding him into the cushioned chair behind his desk. Ernesto and Carol rose, but Helen waved at them to stay back.

Crouching next to Terrance, Helen felt the pulse in his wrists. "Are you having another attack?" she asked.

"Get everyone into the Temple," Terrance croaked out. "Now."

Chapter Forty-One
Jasmine

We trained every day, with anyone who was willing. Some weren't, and retreated behind locked doors with as much food stock-piled as they could afford.

We could smell pots of beans and greens cooking throughout the neighborhood. Doreen and I made spells as fast as we could at night and I showed people how to deploy them during the day.

Doreen's friend Patrice finally asked her why she kept canceling dinner dates. Once Doreen told her, Patrice offered to drive us and the spells wherever we needed to go when she got off work.

Thanksgiving came and went with barely any notice. And school? I just stopped going, even though it would bite me in the ass later. There just wasn't time for anything but the revolution we were preparing for.

Drake became my right-hand man, corralling the young people in particular, but he was good with just about anyone, child to adult. On that first fearful encounter on the sidewalk, with his split-open fore-head, he saw how magic could work, and it impressed him.

Drake took to learning the simple spells with us as quickly as he could. He didn't have much talent, but what he did have was a big help. Without him, things would have been a hell of a lot harder.

Drake made a bridge between the folks who were head-blind, with no magic whatsoever, and the more common folks who had some shine but just never gave it much mind before. People trusted him. They were still a little afraid of Doreen and me.

We trained and practiced. We spent nights up in the attic, prepping spells, and went out the streets day after day, Doreen spending the bare minimum at the flower shop, despite it being a busy time, what with the holidays and all. She would have up and quit, if we didn't still need food and heat.

And then the rain came back. Doreen wasn't sure how far her Fire spells would telegraph in the hands of a non-magical person during the middle of a rainstorm. We were working on it.

Luckily, my Water spells should have more traction than before. They were always going to be strong enough because of the proximity of the ocean and the bay, but any extra water in the atmosphere should give them a boost.

We hoped that would balance things out, and set to pairing up the fire holders with the people who had my spells.

And then word came down.

Cops were massing, paddy wagons, night sticks, and riot gear, ready to come in.

We were set to gather. Everyone knew where the standoff would be, ready or not: DeFremery Park.

The park in West Oakland that the neighborhood folks now called Little Bobby Hutton Park, was a fitting place for battle. The huge old gray Victorian mansion with white gingerbread trim was a place the community had met for years. Generations of children had played under the oaks. It was a place worth fighting for.

Everyone who could come, did come, walking down the streets in clumps, carrying handmade weapons, toting bags of pre-loaded spells.

Everyone between sixteen-year-olds whose parents couldn't keep them away, to fed up sixty-five-year-olds.

The war had been happening in these streets for years, but on the terms of the ones with the badges and the prisons and the courts.

This battle? It was ours. We were setting the stage.

CHAPTER FORTY-TWO
CAROL

They'd gotten two men to carry Terrance up the stairs. He couldn't quite make it on his own.

Ernesto threw open the doors to the Temple room. The men staggered past, and laid Terrance out on the edges of a giant hexagon with a pentagram inscribed in the center. The symbols were inlayed onto the wooden floors, mahogany meeting walnut meeting oak.

Concentric circles bounded the large symbols, each layer inset with ancient languages. Carol recognized Theban and Hebrew, with the Alchemical symbols traced around the outside edge. There were other alphabets she didn't comprehend.

Ernesto set up a small brazier at the very heart of the pentagram and got charcoal burning in the copper dish.

Helen threw Carol a white robe. As the other sorcerers filed into the room, Carol saw that they were all wearing white robes, too. As though it mattered.

"Pick your battles," Ernesto murmured in her ear.

Carol nodded and pulled the white linen over her head. Who knew? Maybe it would even make a difference.

Carol could feel the energy building already. She had no idea what Jasmine and Doreen were doing up north, but she could feel that something was brewing all the same. Carol knotted a white cord around her waist.

"Ernesto, do you know what you're doing?" she asked.

He shook his head. "No. But I know we have to do something. We're going to try to contact that white spider. Smoke it out."

"And Terrance?" she asked.

Helen stepped over at that, face flushed, hair mussed up from pulling her own robe over her head. "I'll take care of Terrance," she said, mouth tight. "You two concentrate on the rest."

Well. Okay then.

"Can you draw the sigil again, maga?" Ernesto asked. "We're going to need it tonight if we're going to catch this thing."

She nodded, grabbed a sheet of clean white paper, a pot of black ink, and a magic-laced metal-nibbed pen.

Chanting rose around them, filling the room with sound, giving it texture Carol could feel on her skin. The smoke from the burning charcoal was acrid. Someone threw frankincense on the brazier.

Two of the sorcerers began weaving a web of light and shadows, enclosing them in a sphere of threads. At the top center of the dome, Carol saw a spider flickering in and out of view. A brown spider. The one they thought was their friend.

She knew the white spider was just on the other side. She could feel its tiny feet prodding at her scalp, tickling behind her ears.

It wanted in.

And the sigil would make that possible.

And she couldn't let it.

She started to draw, scratching out the black lines onto the white, white paper. She drew until the design was clean and clear.

The chanting increased. Louder and louder. The brown spider wove and spun, spun and wove. Carol could feel its white counterpart matching it on the other side, thread for thread.

"Throw it on the charcoal, maga!" Ernesto shouted.

Carol stopped, perfectly still inside the swirl of magic and sound. And she knew then, she knew what needed to happen.

She took the ink-stained metal pen and stabbed it at her hand. A single drop of blood hit the sigil, marring the perfect design. She mashed her hand onto the paper, panting, heaving, sweating.

"Take that, you fucker!" she said. And threw the paper on the fire. Her head exploded and she began to scream. Terrance screamed with her, their voices raw with terror, and anger, and shame.

Carol felt Ernesto grab the power of it all in his two sorcerous hands and shove it up through the center of the great domed web.

The sphere cracked with a boom and the spiders, brown and white, disappeared.

Then the room went dark.

CHAPTER FORTY-THREE
DOREEN

Never in her forty something years had Doreen expected this to happen. And yet it was.

She was preparing for the sort of battle that sorcerers only talked about as legend. She was preparing for the sort of battle that might have kept Hector alive.

Her fingers were sore from crafting spell bags. Letting magic move through her was second nature again. It felt good. Her limbs and joints were loose from the cinnamon fire. She felt younger than she had since the sheriffs stole her youth away as they chopped off her beloved's head.

But sewing up packets? That hurt the fingers after a while. Thank goodness that boy Drake Jasmine had enlisted finally suggested they just tie the cloths together with twine.

Doreen had balked at first. Spellwork needed to be done a specific way, every step clear and clean.

Jasmine had smirked at that. "This is the people's magic, Aunt Doreen. The revolution won't be won by even stitches."

It went against everything Doreen had been taught about traditional spellcraft, but in the end she had agreed. The little spell bombs went much quicker after that. The spells weren't supposed to last, anyway.

They'd gotten others to help at that point. People in the neighborhoods could put the ingredients together with instruction, and Doreen or Jasmine could zap them all en masse.

A magical assembly line. Terrance would choke.

Doreen, though? It turned out she was made for this.

For the first time in years, she felt fully alive.

Chapter Forty-Four
Jasmine

DeFremery Park ran two city blocks by three city blocks, with a playground in the middle, and a vast gray and white Victorian mansion on one edge, built by the rich white man who first owned the plot of land.

The scent of rain-wet grass filled me up as much as the sight of all the people gathering.

Night was coming fast.

Doreen, the non-shifting Black Panthers, and I got the ersatz spell casters set up near the edges of the muddy grass, circling the whole park.

The neighborhood people looked like cannon fodder, but were our special surprise. If it didn't work, we might all be dead.

If we didn't try, most of these people would end up touched by death anyway. Most already had been. That's why they were out here.

The muscle and their shotguns came next, in a broad ring behind the people loaded with our spells. They included the Brown Berets and handful of folks from Yellow Peril. At the heart of the park was leadership. The Animal People. Shifters. The *actual* Panthers.

I looked to Doreen, tension crawling in my belly and sorcery crawling up my skin. She looked unperturbed.

Squeezing my hand, she said, "We've done our best, Jasmine. The rest is up to the magic, the Panthers, the people here, and whatever destiny needs to unfold. Me? I'm praying to the Powers now."

There was a low rumbling of motorcycles a few blocks away to the west. This was joined by another sound. Sirens undercut by something else. It took me a minute to figure it out and then it clicked. It was the sound of hundreds of boots, marching toward the park.

"Spellcasters, stand firm. Remain calm!" I boosted my voice with small magic so it carried across the park.

The shifters were taking off their clothing. The rain had stopped and we were just about at sunset. Tonight was the dark moon, the most powerful time for The People to change. We were taking full advantage, not waiting for the cops to instigate this time.

Action. Not reaction.

We needed every advantage we could get.

Then a voice came over a bullhorn from the center of the park. A powerful voice I didn't recognize. "Comrades! This is our hour!"

I turned.

Standing proudly on a small metal merry-go-round in the center of the park was a tall man with his hair shaped into a wedge, thick sideburns hugging his face. Someone else was holding the bullhorn mic to his mouth because the man's hands weren't quite human anymore.

He was naked from the waist up, khaki soldier's pants starting to strain around his thighs. I could see black fur forming on his belly. His chest was still smooth, but climbing up his arms from massive paws, the shining black fur had almost reached his shoulders.

"We are here tonight to fight! We're going to fight racism not with racism, but we're going to fight with solidarity!"

I didn't know that voice, which was growing deeper by the minute as he changed, but I knew that face. I knew those words. It was Chairman Fred.

I closed my eyes for a moment and said a prayer to a deity I didn't even know I believed in.

The sirens were getting closer.

Fred spoke over them, almost shouting, "We are here to fight for one another! We are here for our freedom and the liberation of our children! Stand strong. Be proud."

Then he raised that massive paw into the air.

"I want to hear you say it with me: I am a revolutionary!"

Every person in the park responded. Clenched fists answered him, punching at the sky. Throats opened and roared. "I am a revolutionary!"

"All power to the people!" he shouted.

"All power to the people!" we shouted back.

Tears streamed down my face. I drew strength from that water.

Cops in riot helmets, holding body shields and truncheons, came streaming from the side streets and began massing in formation, circling the park.

The police cars, blue and red lights flashing, screeched to a halt and slammed open their doors. The motorcycles roared in, forming a phalanx between the foot police and the cars.

Doreen raised her arms to the sky. I did the same.

Boosting my voice again, I shouted, "Comrades! Plant your feet! Raise your arms!"

They did. The whole beautiful mass of them, circling that patch of grass in the middle the ghetto they called home.

"NOW!"

And a lattice of blue and red formed a sparkling, humming sphere around the park. The police looked around in confusion, not breaking rank, but not sure what to do.

Someone must have given a command, because the front rows of cops dropped to their knees and the line behind them began firing.

Our beautiful, shimmering shield of magic held, bullets flaring at the edges of it before tinging to concrete below.

The cops kept firing.

Doreen and I pulled up all our magic. It was flowing through me like a mighty wave. I'd never felt anything like it. It was as though a tidal wave had risen in my skin and poured itself from my hands, my mouth, my eyes.

We fed that shining latticework.

They kept firing.

Sparks were flying off the edges of the sphere as steel met magic. We fed the sphere. Our people all stood firm.

The police kept firing. Until they didn't anymore.

"Comrades! Don't drop it!" I shouted.

I could feel the shifters moving behind us, smelled the musk over the damp grass and spent bullets. One of the Panther soldiers shouted, "Hold your fire! Do. Not. Fire!"

"Ready, Doreen?" I didn't want to turn my head. Feeding the sphere was taking all my focus.

"Yes," I heard her say, and a red fireball flew through the sphere, hitting a police car and engulfing it in flame.

Then Chairman Fred's voice rang loud and clear.

"You dare to struggle, you dare to win! You pigs gotta know, we have the people on our side. And our people have magic and power you cannot even imagine yet. We will win justice for our people."

I could dimly see some of the police running toward each other, while others stood stock still.

Fred spoke again. "We have no doubt that you will be back with tanks and helicopters. With machine guns and napalm. But we want you to know this: we will face you with every single thing we have. And there are more of us. We are everywhere. We are your worst nightmare and we will win justice for our people. No matter how long it takes."

Doreen turned, raised up her arms again, and shot another blazing orange-and-red ball toward the opposite end of the park. This one took out two motorcycles.

Fred spoke again. "I suggest you put down your guns and leave. These panthers here like the taste of fresh meat, and being Marxists trying to feed our people, we haven't had as much meat as we like these days."

There was silence in the park, except the crackling of the magic and the occasional squawking from a police radio.

Full dark was moments away. I could feel the ebbing tide of the ocean and had to hold on to the sorcery with every inch of me. Despite the cold evening, at some point in the middle of all of this, I had started to sweat.

"Doreen, I think I'm losing it."

"I'm coming back in."

The red-and-blue latticework of light grew brighter then. I let out a breath I didn't even know I had been holding. With her magic supporting mine, I could hold on for a while.

"Jasmine, look."

I looked past the shining sphere again and saw something I never thought I would see in my life.

The police were, group by group, section by section, marching away. Cars started up, and motorcycles revved.

Twenty minutes later, it was just the people in the park, and the quietly flaming remains of a cop car and the motorcycles. The shifters were pacing, rubbing up against each other's fur, butting each other's heads.

Chairman Fred had changed fully back into a man, dressed in khaki trousers and a white T-shirt stained by mud and rain. Lit by the red and blue of our sphere, he climbed back on the small merry-go-round. This time he held the bullhorn in his own left hand.

"Power anywhere where there's people. Power anywhere where there's people! Listen here!" The bullhorn crackled.

"We ain't gonna fight no reactionary pigs who run up and down the street being reactionary; we're gonna organize and dedicate ourselves to revolutionary political power and teach ourselves the specific needs of resisting the power structure, arm ourselves, and we're gonna fight reactionary pigs with international proletarian revolution. That's what it has to be. The people have to have the power: it belongs to the people."

I let out a heavy breath. Yes. The power belongs to the people.

Then Fred raised his right fist into the air.

"All power to the people!" he shouted.

"All power to the people!" every voice shouted back.

Then, strand by strand, Doreen and I took down the sphere. People hugged each other. Cheered and cried. Some fell down weeping to their knees on the muddy grass.

The war wasn't over yet. But this one battle, we had won.

CHAPTER FORTY-FIVE
JASMINE

Tears ran down my face. My body felt good, strong, but every emotion was crowding up behind my eyes. I just let them flow, clogging up my nose and leaking from my eyes.

There was really nothing else I could do. I was grateful. Sad. Overwhelmed. In love. Furious. Spent.

This was my life, and these were my people.

No one wanted to leave the park. I couldn't blame them. Someone played trumpet on the little metal merry-go-round and someone else must have run home to get a drum because the rat-tat-tatting of sticks on a skin joined the rise and fall of brass.

The people who had been hiding behind closed doors poured out and streamed into the park. Bringing food to share. Cheap bottles of wine. Pitchers of water and thermoses of hot chocolate were passed around and shared.

Taking a shuddering breath, I caught the low-slung, dark shapes of some of the cats who hadn't changed back yet. They were letting people touch their fur and press their foreheads to their massive faces.

One of the panthers padded toward me, a sleek and slender cat, coming across the wet grass, mud splashed up on the black fur. Its eyes were rimmed in gold.

Jimmy.

I rubbed the back of my hand across my face and searched my coat pockets for a handkerchief. Soft cloth met my fingers, thank the Powers. Still staring at the panther, I blew my nose. This panther would just have to get used to it.

Sometimes Jasmine Jones was going to be messy, it seemed. I just wish Doreen had told me using big magic was going to affect my emotions this way.

The panther was gorgeous, sleek, muscular, and black as the far side of midnight.

I would recognize him anywhere, I realized. The panther stared at me as it came, with those gold-rimmed eyes. Everyone just moved out of his way, as though he were parting the sea. Easy. No fuss.

As though the people in this neighborhood had been around panthers their whole lives. As though magic was something that just happened.

And maybe, just maybe, as though a sorcerer could be an ordinary thing. Just standing in the park, overwhelmed and crying, part of the neighborhood.

As the panther drew closer, I could see how large it was. I nodded. It was just around Jimmy-sized. Its shoulder came up to my waist and it looked to be around six feet long. It smelled like earth and musk.

I held out my hands. "Jimmy."

Jimmy laid his massive head inside my palms and closed those gold-rimmed eyes. We stood together like that for awhile. Just breathing. His fur soft on my skin.

The park, the night, the celebrating people, it was all there, and yet it wasn't. There was all of that, but there was just me and Jimmy, too.

Falling to my knees on the wet grass, I put my arms around his neck and sighed. His shoulders holding me up, I felt his back legs sink onto the grass. I cuddled closer.

For the first time in a long while, I realized, I felt safe. At home.

"Is that Jimmy?"

I looked up. Doreen, Drake, and Patrice were standing there. Drake was eating a cookie, looking tired and satisfied. Doreen and Patrice... were holding hands.

"Yes," I said.

"He gonna change back?" Drake asked.

I looked into the gold-rimmed eyes. "You gonna change back, Jimmy?" The big head slowly moved, side to side.

"Not yet, I guess."

I felt like I should stand and join Doreen and the rest, but my body kept me firmly glued to Jimmy's side.

It was the place I belonged.

Chapter Forty-Six
Carol

It was early December, and the short walk from the car through the streets of East Los Angeles had brought Carol and Ernesto past many decorated windows. A lot of the shops had shrines set up out front with statues of Our Lady of Guadalupe.

"Ernesto, what's with all the shrines today?"

He flicked a cigarette into the gutter. Events had driven him back to smoking, though he insisted it was only temporary. That he would stop again at the new year.

"La Virgin's feast day is coming up in another week. The people here, they don't forget how she has helped them. For thousands of years, she has stood by the side of the poor."

That didn't make sense to Carol. They ducked into a fragrant panadería to pick up the pan dulce Rosalia liked so much. Carol had come to like the sweet bread herself.

As they stood in line, waiting for the children in front of them to pick out their particular flavors, Carol turned to Ernesto.

"But the Spanish only brought Catholicism here in what, the 1500s?"

"Give me a minute, maga. It's our turn. You want the pink ones?"

"Yellow," she replied.

Back on the street, white bakery bag in hand, he finally answered her.

"La Virgin isn't only Mary here, maga. She's also much older than that. She is the Earth Mother, Tonantzin, and we are her children."

They walked in silence for awhile, past the twinkling lights, the piles of vegetables and sandals, the tire store. Almost every place had a small shrine, or at least an image of La Virgin.

As they approached the weathered wooden door, Ernesto turned to Carol, giving her a serious look from behind his round tortoise-shell glasses.

"She helps the oppressed people. And someday, those people are going to call on her name and rise up. It has been foretold."

She didn't even know what to say to that, so she just followed Ernesto's back into the shop.

Then they were through the door, and there was Rosalia, arms outstretched.

"I am so glad to see you!" she said, throwing her arms open to Ernesto first, which gave Carol's eyes a chance to adjust to the candles and filtered window light.

Sure enough, a large statue of the Virgin of Guadalupe held a pride of place on the long counter, roses at her feet, candles flickering in jars around her, a conch shell resting on its side.

The scent of copal resin rose from an abalone shell, drifting smoky patterns back and forth in front of the statue.

Carol left Rosalia and Ernesto together, and walked toward La Virgin. It was as if Carol had never seen her before, even though she must have, in all the years of living in Los Angeles.

"Maga! Come say hello!" And then Carol was swept into Rosalia's velvet and silver embrace.

Rosalia set a plate of the sweetened breads on the counter and got Ernesto and Carol perched on stools at the long counter, sorting through beads and seeds.

Rosalia bustled around the botanica, green velvet skirt swirling around her ankles, silver necklaces rattling together on the front of her black blouse.

"There is so much to be done, mijo," she said to Ernesto as she ground herbs and resins together in a giant black mortar with a stone pestle, elbow crooked up to the ceiling as she mashed the herbs down.

"I knew you would be busy, abuela, but we needed to see you."

She tilted the mixed herbs into small drawstring packets of cloth.

"Put one shell in each, maga," she said to Carol, looking over her work. Rosalia paused then, and leaned next to Ernesto, placing a hand on his shoulder.

"I felt the change, mijo. It is good you came today. Las Manos will be wanting a full report, from both of you, but for today? It is good to just be together."

Ernesto sighed, some of the tension he'd been carrying exiting his body. Carol actually felt it leave, and felt her own body relax.

But something still bothered her. She needed to ask. She shoved some fragrant herbs into one of the small packets, and grabbed a smooth cowrie shell from the pile on the counter.

"Ernesto, the thing I don't understand is, why did Terrance collapse like that? I thought he would be so powerful, being a Quintessence…"

Ernesto grew still beside her, but it was Rosalia who shook her head and moved her green eyes from Carol's face back to the painted face of the Virgin.

"Maga. You don't know yet. You see us, and think the magic flows with ease. That there is some key you don't have in your hand yet, but that as soon as you get it, the magic will become easy."

Walking over to the statue, Rosalia pinched some copal between her fingers and dropped it, nugget by nugget, onto the charcoal in the abalone shell, sending wafts of smoke up again.

Her back still turned, she bowed to the statue and continued speaking, as though Mary, or Tonantzin, was the one she was speaking to.

"Magic always has a cost, maga. The more magic we have, the higher the price we must pay."

Carol nodded to Rosalia's back. "I guess that makes sense. But I don't really get it yet."

Ernesto gave a small bark of laughter. "You'll get it, Carol. The magic always teaches us consequences, sooner or later."

Right. The headaches. The jittery feet. It must all be the magic assimilating, or Carol resisting.

She'd figure it out if she survived. If any of them survived.

Well, they had survived this battle at least, and that was a good thing.

Rosalia turned then, and smiled, as though she was reading Carol's thoughts. That woman read everything. But Carol realized it didn't bother her. It made her feel safe, somehow.

"We always survive, maga. Even if they kill us, we survive." She held out her hands, gesturing for them both to come toward the altar.

"Make an offering to the Virgin. She'll protect us. And it is always a good thing to give the Powers thanks."

CHAPTER FORTY-SEVEN
DOREEN

Doreen rolled over and looked at the woman beside her. What a surprise. Patrice. Her face was limned in the light coming through the white curtains of Doreen's bedroom window. Her hair was sticking up in ways that would horrify Patrice should anyone else catch sight of it. It made Doreen smile.

She knew exactly how her friend's hair had gotten that way.

And Doreen wanted to do it again.

The magic was fully awake inside of her now, rising with its cinnamon smell on her skin. When magic woke up, it brought everything else roaring to the surface.

For Water sorcerers, it was often emotions. For Earth, it was the body.

For Fire sorcerers like Doreen? It was the electrical charge of energy that wanted to connect her with something, anything. Art. Music. People on the streets. But really, for Doreen, it had always been the electricity of sex. That was part of what she'd had with Hector.

After she and Jasmine had taken down the sphere last night, and she'd seen Patrice hurrying across the grass toward her, it was all she could do to not sink onto the grass and mud with her right there.

As it was, Patrice had grabbed ahold of Doreen and just held her. Doreen pressed herself as closely to Patrice as they could get, breathing her in. Feeling the electricity that hummed between their bodies.

And they had kissed. One simple, little kiss. It sparked on Doreen's lips like the world would catch on fire.

After that, Doreen wouldn't let Patrice go. They held hands as they went to check on the others. Jasmine was in no condition to see to anyone herself. Doreen felt responsible for all the people who had joined them in the park.

Luckily, the casualties were few. Some singed hands, and dehydration, and one old man had passed out cold. Mostly though, people were smiling. Exhilarated. In awe.

Doreen smiled at the memory. This was what the Association should be doing. Protecting whole cities, not just their little pockets and enclaves. Sharing the magic. Teaching the people. Not hoarding it all for themselves.

She stretched her arms, wriggling her naked body against the sheets. Oh, it was so good to feel good. Alive. Awake.

"Good morning," Patrice said quietly beside her. "Or is it already afternoon?"

Doreen looked at her friend. Those deep set eyes. The brown lips, denuded of their usual bright lipstick. She looked beautiful.

"It's late morning," Doreen said, holding out an arm. Patrice scooched over, and laid her head in the crook of Doreen's shoulder. The weight of it felt good. Patrice smelled good, too. Warm skin, cocoa butter, Aqua Net, and sex.

"You want some coffee?"

"Only if I don't have to leave this bed to get it."

Doreen smiled.

"I'll get up and make some in a minute." She kissed the top of Patrice's head and relaxed back onto her pillow.

"You going to teach me some more magic?" Patrice murmured.

"Last night wasn't enough?" Doreen laughed.

Patrice laughed, too, and raised her head up until she was staring in Doreen's eyes.

"I don't want it to ever be enough." The women kissed.

"Now I really want that coffee."

Nothing would make Doreen happier than to get her some.

Chapter Forty-Eight
Jasmine

I wasn't that girl anymore. The one who arrived on the bus, wondering about her magic. Wondering about her life.

The suburbs were still in me, but they felt so far away.

I was a city creature now. A creature of magic. A sorcerer. A woman.

And this woman was angry.

It made me understand why Doreen had crumbled for awhile and needed to rebuild herself, almost from the ground up. This anger wasn't a pleasant thing to bear. While I could taste it in my mouth as a type of righteousness, there was more bitter to it than the sweet I used to carry, just months ago.

One thing I'd learned, though, was that sweetness could mask poison. And every black person in America was being slowly, surely killed, whether they tasted the bitter or the sweet.

I didn't like being this way, but I couldn't not be it any more than Uncle Hector could have avoided changing into a tawny California mountain lion. Or my mother, Cecelia, could shake the magic from her hands. We just were these things.

Maybe someday my magic would uncouple itself from my anger, but I couldn't feel how. Couldn't see it.

Oh, I could picture my future self with a baby at my hip and another with small arms hugging my knees. I could picture the man who would be standing at my side, helping me, loving me, fighting with and for me.

But even that was all for the revolution. There was no image of peace in my life, even with the bright sparks of happiness.

I had left the peace in Crenshaw, the minute I stepped onto the Greyhound bus.

It was a lie, anyway.

I would learn how to live the truth, from now on, even if it killed me.

My name is Jasmine Jones. I'm a proud member of the Black Panther Party.

Chapter Forty-Nine
Spiders and Snakes

The Master rocked on the floor of his office in his sweat-stained white shirt and dark pants. He'd long ago taken off his shoes and socks, and his suit coat was abandoned on a chair.

The men guarding the doors, faces impassive, pretended not to notice, like they always did.

Samuels waited, leaning up against a wall, wondering if he would ever get further instruction, or if it was time to take things into his own hands.

The Master was tracing something on the floor with one of his fat white fingers. A sigil Samuels couldn't quite make out. He traced it over and over and over.

"Come, Oh Intelligence..."

A distant booming sound crackled through room, a slice of ozone through the air, followed by the scent of frankincense and smoke.

The Master's head snapped sideways with a gasp, as though he'd been slapped. Samuels rushed forward, but the Master held up a hand to ward him off.

A thin white line of spittle traced a pathway down the Master's chin.

Then he looked up, staring at Samuels with eyes that focused very far away. Someplace outside that room, in a realm Samuels couldn't even begin to see.

"Bring me my vitamin shot," the Master said.

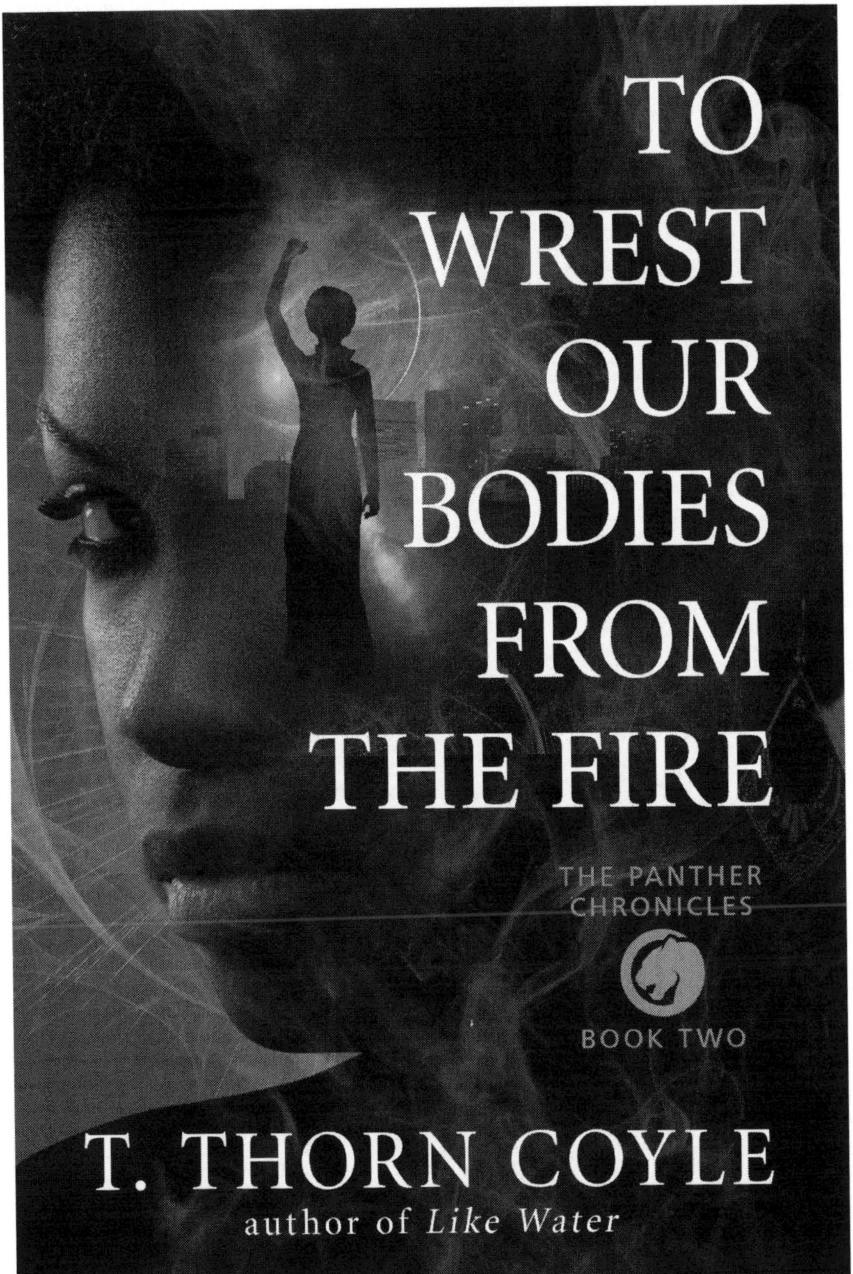

Turn the page to read a sample
of the next novel in the Panther Chronicles,
To Wrest Our Bodies From the Fire.

Chapter One
Jasmine

The magic pricked at my fingertips, ready to burst out and drown someone's ass. Any minute now.

My bare feet were practically wearing a hole into the flowered rug on the floor of my small white bedroom off Aunt Doreen's kitchen. I paced, black rotary phone dangling from my right hand, receiver held up to my ear with my left.

There wasn't much room for the pacing. From my door, to the single bed with its white chenille spread and pile of paisley and denim pillows, past the student desk under the window reflecting morning dark beneath its sheer white curtains.

Che Guevara looked down at me from the wall, alongside an op art poster of a gorgeous woman, whose perfectly round natural was framed by flower mandalas. Black is Beautiful, the poster read. She gazed at me from beneath the orange and yellow flowers framing her head.

I sighed. May all the Powers damn Terrance Sterling, head of the Association of Magical Arts and Sorcery, whose clipped voice was now lecturing in my ear.

Heat rose off my skin like boiling water, despite the chill of an Oakland, California, December morning. That was the sorcery, rising on my anger, wanting out. I was figuring out one of the perils of being a

Water Sorcerer was that the more my powers increased, the more they played with my emotions.

I needed air.

I set the heavy black phone down on the desk, Terrance's voice still squawking in my ear. At 6:30 on a rainy Monday morning, the little desk lamp cast a pool of light over the books and desk, forming a golden puddle that spilled over on the roses hooked into the rug.

Leaning across the narrow, white-painted wood desk, I cracked the window open, letting in the fresh scent of rain tinged with the brackish water of the bay. Rain pattered onto the glass. There was the added note of biscuits baking coming in from under the door.

That would be Aunt Doreen, baking away her fury. My stomach growled at the warm, yeasty smell of the biscuits, and the percolating coffee. I hadn't really eaten for a couple of days. Too tense to keep much down.

"You have to…"

Damn. Terrance never did like to let anyone talk. Especially a member of "the younger generation" as he called it. Younger generation my ass. He was going to listen.

"Terrance…" The man was still going.

"No. You have to listen!" I yelled. "I don't care how much more magical experience you have! You and the rest of your cronies up on your fine hill in that fine mansion don't know anything about what is going on in your own backyard!"

The streets of Los Angeles felt like they had been on fire for three years. But the white folks with money seemed to neither know, nor care.

"No. It can't 'wait until later in the day.' You think I'm happy to be up this early, hearing that folks are getting shot to hell down there?"

A particularly large crash sounded from the kitchen. Aunt Doreen must be picking up on my frustration through the door. Either that, or I said that last bit much louder than I thought.

Really, listening to Terrance go on and on about our responsibility to one another, and to the magic, and for the good of the Association itself, and how we couldn't get involved in politics because we remembered what happened last time....

I was pretty much ready to send a strong magical zap down the phone wires and into his ear. This cat was so full of crap. My middle class upbringing be damned.

Bourgeois folks never noticed much until something exploded across the newspaper headlines as they sipped fresh squeezed orange juice from tiny curved glasses. They would tsk and turn the page as they dipped their toast into the runny yolk of a perfectly cooked egg.

I wasn't far from that, growing up. My parents tried to shelter me from the realities of the world outside our white-picket–fenced neighborhood. Yes, I got the talk about avoiding being alone with white men, and always walking home from school with a friend.

And I knew my father sometimes had trouble getting jobs, and my mother had things she just never told me about.

But it still wasn't the reality I saw people living with every day since the Panthers had woken me up. It was all around me here in Oakland, and now that I could see it, it was down in Watts and the parts of South Central my family just never much made it into.

The sorcery was still rising on my skin, and the scent of ocean grew stronger. So was the taste of cinnamon...Aunt Doreen again. That was the scent of her Fire. She was all up in here with me, inside my energy field, closer than usual. We only got that intertwined when something had us both upset at the same time. Usually we kept better walls around our magic. Took care to not spill over. Control the bleed.

But this was big. The cops were in the middle of raiding the LA Panther's HQ as we spoke. I'd woken instantly, on the first ring of the phone in the kitchen, knowing it meant trouble because I'd smelled the gunpowder in my dreams.

Aunt Doreen had met me in the kitchen when I was still on the phone with my boyfriend, Jimmy, who was calling from Oakland HQ with the news from Los Angeles.

We had argued about who should call Terrance Sterling and alert the Association that there was a magical need.

"He'll listen to you, Doreen. You're in his age group while I'm still considered wet behind the ears."

"But I'm more likely to kill that man," she said, full lips pressing almost straight into a line. "You better make the call. If you can't convince him, I'll get on the phone and wup his behind."

So here I was, with the long phone cord snaking under my bedroom door, shut to try to muffle the increased banging from the kitchen. I was trying to convince a wealthy white man whose life had been too comfortable for too many years that people were in immediate danger a forty-minute drive from his fancy home.

Trying to convince a man who had spent too many years exercising the arts of magical diplomacy. Keeping the peace among once-hating factions who had finally agreed to work together.

"We can't be sure who is right in this situation, Jasmine. And you know the Association doesn't involve itself in these sorts of disputes." His voice grated my spine like tin on a chalkboard.

Yeah. That was Terrance all right. Mister "I once was a powerful sorcerer, but now I find it best to not get involved." A honky with too much money and power who never did a damn thing with either.

I was sick of that. It was time to force his hand.

We didn't need diplomacy; we needed folks angry enough to throw some magic up between the tear gas and the bullets in order to save some people's lives.

It was time to bring the Association into this thing my friends in the Party were calling a war.

And it wasn't going to happen through Terrance Sterling.

"Goodbye, Terrance." I cut the call short.

I looked at the pile of books and my notes from last night. Damn. I should have been working on a paper this morning instead of dealing with crisis. I also had a statistics test to study for.

It was the last week of classes and I couldn't care less.

"Welcome to the real world, Jasmine Jones," I said. The real world where cops shot at my friends, my boyfriend was an actual shape-shifting panther, and there was out–and-out war in the streets.

I needed my sorcery. Listening to the rain, and smelling the distant bay, I began to breathe water into my pores and exhale it out again. The power of it built inside my belly and rose until it cascaded down my arms and toward my hands.

To become a badass sorcerer, I needed to be free.

To be free, I needed this connection to the Element that had marked me at my birth.

To be a badass sorcerer, I couldn't let Terrance and his hang-ups hang me up. That cat was too beholden to the Man. For every little thing.

The whole Association of Magical Arts and Sorcery were hip deep in the muck of the oppressors. Even though the Association always insisted we didn't work in politics, no one in America got that much money from keeping their hands clean.

Well, the Association was just going to have to deal with Jasmine Jones.

Author's Note & Bibliography

This series came about because for many years I've wondered what racial justice in the United States would look like if Fred Hampton had not been brutally assassinated by the FBI and Chicago PD, and if J. Edgar Hoover's COINTELPRO had not purposefully decimated so many groups and coalitions working toward equity, autonomy, and justice.

With encouragement from others, what started off as a 10,000 word short story turned into a four book series.

Am I the right person to tell this tale of sorcery, shape-shifters, and the Black Panther Party? There are likely far better candidates for the task, but the story pushed its way through me nonetheless, for better or worse.

There's a lot of history in this alt-history fantasy. 1968–69 was a time in which so much happened, it is almost impossible to keep track of events. The infiltration, assassinations, psychological warfare, disruption, and attacks on anti-war and civil rights groups by the FBI was far worse and more comprehensive than I could even being to include in these novels. Many of these tactics continue into contemporary times.

I chose only a few key events to highlight in the story, and concentrated on Oakland and Los Angeles, though events were going down in cities across the U.S.

When possible, I used the words of Panther organizers like Fred Hampton and Huey Newton. I also tried to remain respectful of the

Panthers still living and doing good work in the world. That is why so many key historical players are barely mentioned, or appear as very minor characters. I didn't want to put words in their mouths. That is not my place. Many of them have told their stories, and you can find a few in the books below. There is a wealth of information not included here.

If you are interested in more actual history, here is a resource list to get you started:

Film

- *Black Power Mix Tape*
- *1971*
- *The Black Panthers: Vanguard of the Revolution* (this film is controversial among some of the remaining Panthers)

Books

- *The Fire Next Time*, James Baldwin (not about the Panthers in particular, but a great background that frankly, everyone should read)
- *To Live and Die for the People*, Huey P. Newton
- *Revolutionary Suicide*, Huey P. Newton
- *The Nine Lives of a Black Panther*, Wayne Pharr
- *A Taste of Power*, Elaine Brown
- *Seize the Time*, Bobby Seale
- *The Ten Point Program of the Black Panther Party*, https://web.stanford.edu/group/blackpanthers/history.shtml
- *Assata: An Autobiography*, Assata Shakur (Panther history after the time period of this series)
- *J. Edgar Hoover: A Graphic Biography*, Rick Geary
- *Chicano Movement for Beginners*, Maceo Montoya
- *Youth, Identity, Power: The Chicano Movement*, Carlos Muñoz, Jr.

And of course, the repercussions from this time roll forward.

Some Additional Key Resources

- *The New Jim Crow*, Michelle Alexander
- *The 13th Movie*, Ava DuVernay
- *From #BlackLivesMatter to Black Liberation*, Keeanga-Yamahtta Taylor

Many of the Black Panther Party continue to do public work in the world.

- Fred Hampton and Deborah Johnson/Akua Njeri's son founded the Prisoners of Conscience Committee: http://chairmanfredjr.blogspot.com/
- Elaine Brown is an activist and author. http://www.elainebrown.org/
- Ericka Huggins is an activist, speaker, and spiritual teacher. http://www.erickahuggins.com/Home.html
- Bobby Seale is an educator, author, and activist. http://www.bobbyseale.com/
- Angela Davis is a professor, author, and active in the prison abolitionist movement: http://www.speakoutnow.org/speaker/davis-angela
- Tarika Lewis is a violinist, artist, activist, and art teacher: https://en.wikipedia.org/wiki/Joan_Tarika_Lewis

Acknowlegements

Every published book requires both an author working alone, and a host of friends and community.

Thank you and love to Robert and Jonathan, for helping me build a home all these years.

Thanks to first readers Leslie Claire Walker, Thealandrah Davis, and Luna Pantera. Thanks also to Al Osorio for the occasional consultation on the series! These would be lesser books without all of you.

Thank you to Dayle Dermatis, editor extraordinaire.

Thank you to Carl of Extended Imagery for the gorgeous covers.

Thanks to my first and third Saturday writing cohort. It's great working with you.

Thanks to Kris Rusch, who told me this wasn't just a short story, but a novel series.

Most of all: thanks to all of the activists and justice organizations who do the work day in and day out. May your lives and work be blessed.

About the Author

T. Thorn Coyle writes books, drinks tea, and agitates for justice.

She is the author of the Panther Chronicles series, the novel *Like Water*, two story collections, and multiple spirituality books including *Sigil Magic for Writers, Artists & Other Creatives* and *Evolutionary Witchcraft*. Thorn's work also appears in many anthologies, magazines, and collections. She has taught people all over the world.

An interloper to the Pacific Northwest, Thorn joyfully stalks city streets, writes in cafes, and talks to crows, squirrels, and trees. Sometimes she gets arrested.

Want to learn more?

Follow Thorn on Twitter and Facebook
Sign up for her monthly newsletter at her ThornCoyle.com
Read advance copies of essays and stories via Patreon